I0689148

The Lights Went Out In Dixie

Joel Cobbs

www.jncobbs.com

Copyright © 2016 by Joel Cobbs

All rights reserved. No part of this publication may be reproduced or transmitted in any form or by any means, electronic or mechanical, including photocopy, recording, or any information storage and retrieval system now know or to be invented without permission in writing from the publisher, except for a reviewer who wishes to quote brief passages in connection with a review written for inclusion in a magazine, newspaper, or broadcast.

This is a work of fiction. Names, characters, places, and incidents either are the products of the author's imagination or are used fictitiously. Any resemblance to actual persons, living or dead, businesses, companies, events, or locales is entirely coincidental.

Cover design by Callie Cobbs

For Callie, with all my love.

For the 238 Alabamians whose lights never came back on.

WEDNESDAY, APRIL 27

Ryan Peterson

The opening drums of "Move Along" by The All-American Rejects pierced the air. Since he first heard the song years ago, Ryan made it his alarm for waking up. He hated the song. It was repetitive and made Ryan cringe. What better song to guarantee he got up in the morning? He reached for his phone and pressed the screen. His phone had no snooze so he had to get up now.

He looked at his phone. Five missed messages. His Twitter addiction fed his unlimited text message plan with numerous tweets from famous people he was unlikely to meet. Most mornings he woke up with more. He sat up and rubbed his eyes. He needed to get moving.

The Petersons had been adding onto their house for some time now. Ryan wanted some privacy and decided to move into the incomplete addition. It had running water and an extension cord running from the powered part of the house to his room. The floors were still plywood, the ceiling insulation, and the walls bare. The wiring was visible and made a strange path that intertwined along the rooms. He could see clearly from one side of the house to the other, even a little down the stairs.

The sun wasn't out yet. He put his feet on the wood floor. Every morning he feared he would end up with splinters in his feet. He'd walked on it for some time now and it hadn't happened, but that didn't mean it wouldn't. He looked at the message Hannah sent while he was asleep.

"Hello. Finally going to bed. Goodnight."

He smiled. They'd known each other for years and only started dating four weeks earlier. He selected the notification.

"Good morning. Glad you made it to bed," he replied. He set the phone down and walked into the makeshift bathroom. He had some clothes and towels in there with him to make it easier to get ready. He started to set his glasses down and stopped to look outside. The sky was overcast and he could see signs of rain. Tomorrow was his birthday. He'd be 22. He didn't have any big plans. He would take off work and enjoy his nice long weekend. He put his glasses in their case.

The rush of the hot water felt good. April in Alabama was like a warning. It wasn't the thick, muggy summer heat, but it wasn't the cool, crisp feeling of spring either. Ryan had trouble with cold and would gladly take the hotter time of the year.

It's Wednesday, he thought. Study Day on campus. Finals start tomorrow, meaning he could put in some extra hours today and go straight home. He only had three classes and wasn't worried about them. Two finals were papers and one was Music Appreciation. He had an A in the class and didn't really need the final, but decided it couldn't hurt. The teacher dropped the lowest exam grade so he might as well take it.

The thought of the exam was unpleasant. He was a terrible test-taker. He went through many tutors and none helped. He could study for hours and when he looked at the papers, it all went away. He washed the thoughts from his hair and reached for his toothbrush.

He brushed his teeth in the shower. It seemed crazy to some. His girlfriend always gave him a hard time about it. She thought it was strange. They had so many conversations about it.

"That's crazy," she would say. "Nobody does that."

"Plenty of people do."

"Like who?" she would ask.

"Not for me to say," he would respond. He rinsed his mouth out, put his toothbrush and toothpaste back in their slots and turned off the water. The cool air caught him off guard. Normally that side of the house was hot, but not now. He heard his phone go off as he stepped out of the shower. It was most likely Hannah. She didn't usually get up this early, but she had several classes to study for. She was a perfectionist when it came to school.

He got dressed and walked over to his phone. He smiled.

<u>Hannah Leon</u>

Hannah rolled over and let out a sigh. She didn't want to be awake. It was too early and her bed was so comfy. She closed her eyes and thought back to the dreams she had the night before. She remembered something about Santa. Santa needed her help because the reindeer had pneumonia and couldn't fly. So she needed to invent rocket boots for the elves so Santa could stay home and take care of the reindeer. She chuckled. Her dreams never made sense but always entertained her. She rolled over to her nightstand and looked at her phone. She saw the message from Ryan and smiled.

"Good morning to you too," she replied. She missed him.

She rubbed her eyes as she thought about him. She didn't like being up this early, but it had to be done. Most morning she wouldn't be up for another few hours, but not today. She thought about all the studying she needed to do. It was going to be a long day. Her phone buzzed.

"How did you sleep?" it said. She smiled.

"Not nearly long enough. You?"

"Can't complain. You up and going yet?" She smiled. The night before she'd asked him to check on her and make sure she was up.

"Working on it. I'm not a real person yet. Can't rush these things," she replied. She pushed the sheets back and stayed there for a minute. Tomorrow was Ryan's birthday. Their first birthday as a couple. She wanted to be with him or drive up there to surprise him, but it didn't look like that would happen. Both had finals and weren't going to be able to make it. She wanted to be with him to wish him a happy birthday.

Birthdays, holidays, and the like were important to Hannah. She wanted to take the time to spend it together and enjoy their time together. She enjoyed the spoiling of someone because it was their special day.

Ryan wasn't used to that. It wasn't his way. His family always took care of him on his birthday, but Ryan wasn't a fan of the attention. He preferred to just relax and have his day to himself where he didn't have to do anything he didn't want to.

Which is usually what he did. Last year he'd gone out with a few friends and celebrated his birthday playing pool. He and Hannah weren't as close then as they were now so she only knew about it from what he'd told her.

She sent him a reply and tossed her phone on the bed.

The Spencers

BEEP! BEEP! BEEP! The alarm blared through the darkness. Jon turned the alarm off and got out of bed. He rubbed the sleep from his eyes and patted the bed.

"Tracy?" he whispered. "Tracy, are you coming?" His wife shuffled around in the bed but didn't respond. He chuckled and walked to the bathroom. He kept listening to see if Tracy would join him, but the sound of her CPAP machine going was the answer he needed. He put on his jogging outfit and tied his shoes. He walked down the hall to check on the girls.

Lisa and Laura were both sound asleep in their rooms. They were 16 and 14 and both drove him crazy. He never realized girls had so much to be worried about in life. Boys, looks, other girls. Drama, drama, drama. He felt the pressure just by listening to them talk about their days. He got downstairs and started stretching. He hadn't heard anything about rainy weather this morning. The windows facing the backyard showed the sun on its way up. It was still early, which is how he liked to do this. He deactivated the alarm and stepped into the garage.

The morning was cool and overcast, which Jon preferred. Running in the mornings helped him think about his upcoming day. He looked in both directions, a habit he couldn't explain or break, then began running. He started timing his breathing with each step he took. It helped him get in the groove of running and made it easier for him to focus. The rhythm of his feet beating the pavement provided a strange sense of comfort. He paced himself, taking two short breaths in and one long breath out.

He'd begged Tracy to start running with him or at least power walking. He wouldn't mind power walking if they were doing it together. Sometimes she would agree to do it, but when it came time to get up, she couldn't do it. He smiled at the thought of it. She was definitely not a morning person. She waited until the last minute she could to get out of bed. It'd been several years into their marriage before him getting out of bed didn't wake her. Now it didn't faze her.

He reached the end of his street, circled around, and started back. He was sweating heavily now. He noticed it was unusually cool this morning though he didn't know why. He figured they had some rain due at the end of the week or something like that. Right now there weren't many clouds out so he wasn't expecting any that day.

Wednesday! he thought. *Gotta get those orders in and make sure the shipments go to the right building this time.* Sometimes deliveries had trouble with the address, but if he remembered to give them instructions, it was usually taken care of. He reached his driveway again and started walking. He felt invigorated and ready to tackle the day. He walked inside and turned the coffee on. Tracy wanted one of those Keurig machines, but Jon just couldn't give up the taste of regular coffee. It didn't seem right to him to take away from the joy he received from brewed coffee. Then again, he was a notorious stick in the mud and didn't like to change.

He went upstairs to shower and get ready. Tracy was still asleep, though now she'd moved to the middle of the bed. He smiled and went to shower and get ready for his day.

<u>Sharon Rogers</u>

For the last nine years, Sharon had taken care of Colleen Boone. They went to church together for many years. Colleen had worked with Sharon in the nursery for a long time. They would rock the babies and feed them and keep them content until their parents returned. Many times, new parents would feel skeptical of leaving their children there, but Colleen's kind, little-old-lady smile would put them at ease. Sharon primarily did the caring while Colleen took care of the parents and the rocking. Soon, Sharon noticed Colleen showing up less and less. Sharon worried something happened and wanted to check on her. The directory gave her an address and she went to visit her. She'd taken care of her ever since.

Colleen was an elderly lady with diabetes. Her voice was strained, worn from years of singing, and her skin seemed transparent due to the many veins that appeared. Her arms and legs were weathered. Her hair almost all gone. She couldn't take care of it like she wanted and, no matter what Sharon did, it continued to fall out.

Sharon put the milk into the grocery buggy. She was getting groceries for Colleen and this was for breakfast. The woman demanded the same thing for breakfast every day: oatmeal squares. The cereal was made by Quaker Oats. It was somewhat expensive, but Colleen insisted on having it. One bowl, seven days a week. Her only issue with the milk involved the brand. She only wanted generic brand.

"No sense spendin' money ya don't need to," she would say. Sharon wouldn't argue. There was no point. The woman wanted expensive cereal but inexpensive milk. It worked in her head and that's all that mattered. Sharon looked at her list. Overhead, a generic radio station played generic light rock music. She wouldn't have paid it much attention if it wasn't for the interruption.

"Attention shoppers. A severe weather watch has been issued for North Alabama. We will keep you advised as the situation develops. Repeat, a severe weather watch has been issued for North Alabama. Thank you." Sharon looked at her watch. 7:45 am. It was still early, but she needed to get to Colleen's house. She didn't want her there by herself for long. With no one to help, it was difficult leaving her alone. She worried the woman would fall and hurt herself or someone would break in and something awful would happen. She looked at the list. She had the milk, which was most important. Colleen needed that for breakfast. Sharon remembered Colleen still had another box of cereal left which should take care of her for now. There were so many things going through Sharon's mind that she wasn't sure what to pay attention to and what to tune out. *Did she need soap? Did she need to get more cereal? Did they have enough toilet paper? Did they have bottled water? Did they have cooking spray?* She took a deep breath. She needed a quick break, but first she needed to pay for the groceries and get out of the store. She walked towards the registers and noticed she wasn't the only one.

As people made their way towards the front of the store so they could check out and leave, many people were entering. Sharon thought back to all the storms since she'd started caring for Colleen. It always seemed when the weather was supposed to be even a little bad, people made a mad dash for the grocery stores to get milk and bread. Sharon was no exception. She could think of plenty of times she'd done the same. She was glad to already be at the store with her groceries though. She looked at her buggy. *Do I have enough? Should I go back and get more just in case?* She shrugged it off and decided to just check out. She looked at the lines again.

Some people had buggies with only a few things in them. Others were just finishing up and would probably use several bags to take care of their groceries. Sharon scanned the numerous registers in hope of finding one that was open. No luck. Her next goal would be to find one with only one person in it with a few items. She spied one out of the corner of her eye. Number 19. She turned her buggy and darted for it in hopes no one would try to do the same. She'd seen it first so it was hers to claim. She moved briskly, mutter under her breath.

"Don't take it. Don't take it. Don't take it. Don't take it. Ah." She let out a sigh of relief. No one else was there. The man in front of her had only six items. She put the bar down to separate their groceries and began unloading her buggy. She thought about Colleen being alone in that house. It wasn't a dangerous house by any means, but it was large enough that she worried Colleen might do something she shouldn't and hurt herself. Sharon pictured her walking through the living room, her foot getting caught on a rug and falling down to remain there until Sharon returned. Maybe she was in the floor in pain wanting someone there to help her. The woman's voice is still fragile and barely intelligible when the person is in the same room with her half listening.

"Good morning. How're you?" the cashier asked. It startled Sharon. She took a deep breath.

"Sorry. I'm good. Just...just a little distracted."

"Ah. You worried about the weather?"

"Weather?" Sharon asked.

"Oh yeah. 'sposed to be bad weather headin' this way."

"Oh", Sharon said. "They're always making a big deal out of nothing. You remember when they closed all the school at 10 in the mornin' just for a storm they *thought* would be here at 2?"

"Oh no," the cashier said. She seemed worried. "I've got relatives in Mississippi that said the weather there is pretty rough. I'm bettin' this ain't gonna work out all that well if people ain't careful." Sharon stopped listening. She thought about Colleen back at home and what she would think about bad weather.

"I felt it," she'd say. "I felt it in my bones. I told ya this'd be bad. I told ya. But ain't nobody list'nin' to an old woman these days. Nope. Not no one." Sharon paid for her groceries and went outside. She looked around. The weather didn't seem that bad. The sky was overcast and it looked as though it'd rained some but nothing that would cause worry. She loaded the car up and set the buggy aside. Her eyes darted around. She looked to see if anyone was watching. She pulled a light and a cigarette out of her purse.

It wasn't a bad vice, she told herself. She knew people who'd done worse and at least she wasn't as bad as them. She took a long pull and let it out. She did her best not to smoke in the car. Colleen did not forgive drinking ("licker") or smoking and chewing ("bacca"). Sharon had endured many lectures on how sinful such things as "bacca" and "licker". She took a pull on the cigarette and flicked it away. There was enough to smoke a little more, but she needed to get back. Colleen needed her back, especially if there was bad weather coming. She got in the car and prayed Colleen didn't know about the weather.

<u>Neil Senior</u>

I bet I'm late for class, he thought. *Not again.* He rubbed his eyes and sat up. His eyes opened. He looked down. Jillian was here. He'd forgotten she'd spent the night last night and was still here. He looked around. There was no way to avoid waking her. He leaned back down and thought about last night and what happened.

They were going to have a party. It was their final semester and time to celebrate. Finals were almost over and they would be free of this horrible school. They didn't have a problem with UA or with Tuscaloosa for that matter. They were just sick of classes, exams, schedules, and everything else they had to do.

Unfortunately, everyone was busy and couldn't make it. He'd begged his friends but no one could make it. So instead, it was just him and Jillian. They'd been together for a long time now, but he was ready to move on. He was going to grad school and she was going to law school. He wasn't sure when he was going to break the news to her. She wouldn't take it well. She would get upset and cry and make a bigger event of it than he wanted to deal with. She would scream and cry and yell and go on and on about every time they said "I love you". He would've been much happier if she'd broken up with him.

It's time, he thought, and he moved to get up. She shifted and he stopped. He felt her grab hold of him and pull him closer.

"Good morning," she said. He closed his eyes.

"Good morning. How did you sleep?"

"Very well, thank you. How about you?"

"Meh. Okay. Listen, I need to get up and go to class. I don't know what time it is but I'm betting I'm late again."

"Oh no, baby! You better get your stuff together. It won't be good if you're late again."

"I know. I need to get a move on."

"I know, sweetie. Are we still having the party tonight?"

"Oh yeah. I'm gonna stop by Tex's place and get us a pick-me-up for the party." Her face lit up.

"Ooo. That's such a good idea. I think we could all use it before finals get started. I really need to be as stress free as possible tonight."

"You're that stressed about your finals?"

"Well, yeah. I mean, why wouldn't I be? If I don't do well I might fail and that'll ruin everything! I'll be stuck here for another year and everything I did for all those years will be for nothing!" He rubbed her side.

"It won't be for nothing. You've worked hard at these classes and you've studied hard. You're gonna be awesome, don't worry about it."

"I guess I'm just nervous like always. Just don't wanna screw anything up, you know?"

"I know, baby. Here, I need to get up and get going. When do you have to be at class?"

"I don't have classes today, remember?" No. He didn't.

"Oh yeah, right. Then how about you get some sleep while I head to class, okay?" She was already asleep. He slipped out of bed and searched for his clothes. It wasn't dark. He found his pants and put them on.

He grabbed his phone and keys from her nightstand and put them in his pocket before looking at her once more. She looked so peaceful there in bed. He took a deep breath.

"How can you be so scared of everything?" he whispered. She moved and startled him. He walked into the living room and rubbed his eyes. Yeah, it was definitely time to end things. They'd been together for a while but he was tired of having to remind her that she was a good student and always doing well in classes. It exhausted him how much he had to make her feel better. He found his bag, still on the floor next to the door. He grabbed it, walked out, and locked the door.

He let out an exhaustive sigh. She was stressing him out. If only he could do it. He wanted to be with her and he didn't. He pulled out his phone. Yeah, it was time to go. He had plenty of time to get to class. He just wanted out of there. He put his phone in his pocket and walked towards his car. He looked back to see if she was watching him through the window. Nope. He unlocked the car and put his stuff inside. He shut the door and wiped his forehead out of habit. He stopped and looked around.

Normally, the walk to his car would cause him to breakout in a sweat. The South was known for its nasty heat. The cloudy feeling brought about by the humidity caused anyone to break out into a sweat. It wasn't as bad right now, though. It had been raining earlier, but things were quiet. He got in the car and looked in the rearview mirror.

He hated to leave her. He did. She was a wonderful girl, no denying that. They'd had some good times and bad times and they'd always stuck it out. But time had moved on and now they were growing apart. It wasn't fair to keep going. He figured tonight after the party would be as good a time as any. It would give him a clean escape but also not cause her to be sad during the party, which was important to her. He cranked the car and pulled out. The radio was blaring country music. It was in the middle of a song he couldn't immediately place. He hummed along as he turned onto McFarland to head towards UA. The song ended and the DJ came over the radio.

"Hey, everyone, we got an update on that weather forecast. For those just joining us, we've been tracking a line of storms over in Mississippi that're lookin' to head this way. This started over in Arkansas but've gotten a lot stronger as they've moved on. We've heard reports of tornadoes touching down in Mississippi but it's unsure if the storm will stay together long enough to affect any of the surrounding areas. I will say this storm is big and not something that needs to be joked with." Neil scoffed. He'd heard it a million times growing up in Alabama and so had everyone else. The weather people always predicted horrible weather that would bring about the destruction of the world as we know it only for next to nothing to happen. It was something that drove him crazy.

In 2005, there was a line of storms moving in from Oklahoma. The weather people jumped on the news that morning and told everyone to stay inside because the storm was nasty and was headed towards them at a powerful speed. Back then, Neil had a Palm Pilot and used it to check the weather. He watched the pixelated image of the storms move very slowly across the states. He was in homeroom at the time. Even though he was only 15, he could see the storms weren't going to move into Cullman, Alabama until much later that evening, but because of the uproar created by the news, school was cancelled. Not long after that, schools became much more rigid about when classes could and couldn't be cancelled. More schools implemented the late-arrival policy instead. That allowed them to count the day as a school day instead of cancelling it altogether and causing the students to be kept over during summer. Nothing happened with that storm except some rain and maybe some power outages. As far as he could remember, no one died because of it. He turned the radio up.

"We are advising everyone to stay indoors tonight. Please find a windowless room as close to the center of your building as possible. The lower the elevation the better. We've received reports of a good bit of damage in the Mississippi area. It's showing a lot of potential to turn into a pretty bad storm as it continues to move this way. Again, please take the proper precautions and-" He cut it off. He wasn't concerned about the weather. He had enough to think about as it was. His phone vibrated. He picked it up and saw it was from Jillian.

"Miss you! Can't wait to see you tonight! ly!" He didn't know how to respond. He pulled up to the turn lane, then looked back at his phone. He backed out of the message opened one to Tex.

"Party 2nite @ my place. U know what to bring." He put the phone down and looked around as he waited for the light to change.

The line to Krispy Kreme on McFarland was huge. Every morning cars were lined up to get donuts. The place was always busy and it wasn't easy to get your orders. He looked up at the sky behind it.

The clouds were gray and it was a little hazy. He couldn't

see well because of all the trees and signs in the way. He wondered about the forecast and if it was true or not. There'd been so many false alarms that now it was difficult to know what was and wasn't being blown out of proportion. It probably was and, like most people, he wasn't going to worry about it.

His phone vibrated. He started to look at it, but stopped. He didn't want to look at another message from Jillian and see her asking if he was okay or why he wasn't responding. It could've been Tex, but he rarely replied about anything. He just kept driving to school and tried to get a better look at the sky.

Hannah Leon

Hannah walked into CVS. She needed to pick up some personal items. She was on her way to school, but was ahead of schedule enough she could make the quick stop. She only had one class today, then it was break time until finals. She felt confident about her grades and wasn't worried about failing anything. There were two exams she needed to study a little harder for to make the grade she wanted.

She hadn't heard from Ryan since he got to work. She figured he was getting busy for the end of the school year. His work had a fairly strict no-texting policy which also kept them from talking.

The store wasn't as full as she expected. She'd heard some news on the radio about there being some potentially bad weather, but she wasn't sure if she believed it. So often the weather was predicted to be terrible but that rarely turned out to be the case. She wasn't going to be crazy and go out or anything tonight, but she didn't really think it would be as bad as they were saying it would be. She found what she needed and walked to the front. A radio behind the cashier played and several people gathered near it.

"Welcome back, folks."

"Quiet everyone," someone said. "Quiet, quiet!"

"So for those of you just joining us, we've been tracking this storm for quite some time now. It's been making its way through Mississippi and looks to be heading this way. We're not sure how bad it's gonna be but we are definitely expecting some heavy rain and rough weather with this storm. We advise you follow all proper precautions and do what you can to take shelter as the weather gets worse. Everyone needs to stay away from windows and stay as low as possible, too. We will keep you updated throughout the day so keep it tuned here at-" the cashier turned it off.

"Sounds like a buncha baloney again," one of the customers said.

"Yeah. They always tryin' ta get people all upset 'n worried 'bout nothin'. It's pro'ly just gonna be another thunderstorm and that's it."

"Well, it's better to be safe than sorry," said the cashier. He seemed cautious rather than worried. Hannah thought that was a good idea. The customers all walked away and she approached the counter.

"How're you doing today, ma'am?"

"Oh fine, thanks," Hannah said. "So what's this about some bad weather later?"

"Well, it seems there's been a pretty big storm headed this way from out west. It's been moving for a while and they reported earlier it was losing steam, but now they're starting to say it's beginning to pick back up again. Not sure what to think about it, but they seem serious."

"Yeah, but they're always reporting bad weather like it's the end of the world." The cashier nodded in agreement, but something on his face told Hannah there was more than that. Something about this storm seemed to have the man worried.

"I guess we'll just all have to wait and see, won't we? You just make sure you're somewhere safe tonight, okay?"

"I will," she said. "Thank you and have a good day!"

"You too." She walked out to her car and looked at the sky. She was near an intersection so it wasn't too difficult to see, but the trees behind Krispy Kreme weren't making it easy. It looked like rain, but nothing really screamed storm or bad weather like they were saying. She got in her car and began leaving. Her phone vibrated. "JILL BFF" it said. She smiled and answered. Jillian had been her best friend since she started going to UA.

"Good morning."

"No, it isn't." Hannah frowned.

"What's wrong?"

"I think Neil is going to breakup with me."

"What? Why do you say that?"

"He's been kind of distance lately. He hasn't really been talking to me or excited to see me like he usually is. He stayed here last night but this morning he seemed so distracted from everything. He rushed out of here and said he had to go to class like I was a one night stand he had to get away from. I just don't know what to do, Hannah."

"Just calm down. You don't know if he's really going to do that or not. Maybe he's just been stressed out from school or something."

"No. No, he wants to leave me. I can feel it. He's sick of being with me and wants to get away and be with someone skinnier and prettier." Hannah tried to hold in her sarcastic sigh.

"Well, why not talk to him? Why don't you guys go out or something and talk about it?"

"Would it do any good at this point?"

"You don't know until you try. For all you know, he could be thinking you're gonna break up with him and he's just nervous about that." There was silence.

"You think?"

"Definitely."

"Well, we are having a little party tonight to celebrate the end of school and all. We decided to just relax before things get hectic. You're welcome to come!"

"I'll think about it. And I think that's the perfect time to talk to him about it."

"You're right. Are you in class?"

"About to be. I'm on University headed towards class right now."

"Oh I got ya. I guess I'll talk to you later then."

"Okay then. Hope you have a good day."

"Thanks! You too!" she said and hung up. Hannah put her phone down and pulled into the parking deck.

She parked and looked at her phone. Still no messages from Ryan. She got out of her car and started towards class. Her phone rang.

<u>Sharon Rogers</u>

Colleen's house was not in the best condition. It needed a paint job, some work on the siding, and a good deal of heavy gardening. Sharon wasn't skilled in any of these things and hated it too. She wanted Colleen to live in a nice home, but it wasn't something Sharon could provide. She unloaded some of the groceries but stopped. She set them on the trunk of her car, pulled out a stick of gum, and put it in her mouth. She'd already had two or three sticks, but she wanted to be certain Colleen wouldn't notice. That was the last thing she needed. She gathered the groceries and walked in the house.

The smell of moth balls hit her as she entered the house. Colleen had used them her whole life. Sometimes the smell got too strong for Sharon, but she did everything she could to avoid making a face in front of Colleen. She just needed to be as calm and collected as possible.

"Who is it?" came the call. Colleen's voice had a tinge of confusion about it. Sharon picked up on it and worried.

"It's just me, Miss Colleen."

"Oh Sharon. I'm so glad it's you. I been worried sick 'bout where you been." Sharon sighed with relief. So far it seemed like today would be a good day.

"I just went to the grocery store to grab a few things for you."

"I didn't think I needed anything."

"Oh, just a few things. Nothing too big. Just wanted to make sure you had everything you needed."

"What else do I need? I've got my health and my house. That's good enough, if you ask me." Sharon didn't bother arguing. Colleen wasn't going to budge on the issue so it was better to just let it alone until she forgot about it.

"That's a good point. I didn't think of that."

"Don't patronize me. I'm not as slow as everyone thinks I am."

"No one thinks you're slow, Miss Colleen."

"Uh huh. They sure do. They all think they can just walk all over me 'cause I'm old 'n don't know what I'm doin'. But I ain't gone yet so they can just hold off for now."

"You're right. You're not gone yet."

"Uh huh. And I ain't plannin' on goin' anytime soon."

Sharon had to think about what Colleen was saying. She wasn't sure what Colleen was talking about. Was she talking about bill collectors or church people or-

"Those people were here again," Colleen said.

"What people?"

"Those people asking for stuff again. I told them a million times I don't want anything they have to offer and I don't want to give them my money, but they're always coming by."

"Who were they, Miss Colleen?"

"You know. Those people that stop by every Saturday. I told them you were out and I couldn't hear anything they wanted until you got back from the bank."

"When was this?" Sharon asked, but she feared she knew the answer.

"Today. They came a knockin' with their Bibles and their kind words and such, but I told them I wasn't interested. They're always trying to sell you something. So annoying when they do that. A person can't get no peace and quiet with all that knocking going on. I just wish they wouldn't leave their bicycles in my garden. I've put so much work into it and I don't need them messing it up again."

Sharon lowered her head as Colleen continued to ramble. Every once in a while she'd have a spell that would cause her to imagine things that happened years ago happening again. She hadn't worked in her garden in years and she rarely got visitors, even from door-to-door salesmen or Jehovah's Witness. People passed right by the worn-down house in favor of those that looked like people with some sort of stable income happened to live there. Sharon both hated and loved the thought.

"What did they do to your garden?" Sharon asked. Colleen looked at her.

"What did who do to my garden? Ain't nobody been here in weeks and I can't take care of my garden like I used to. It's just out there gaining weeds and rotted stuff while I sit in here. Nope. Ain't nobody done nothing to my garden. What are you talking about?"

"Oh nothing," Sharon said. "Guess I just misheard you."

"I guess you did."

"Let me get the rest of the groceries and I'll be right back, okay?" Colleen nodded and Sharon left. She could tell this was going to be a difficult day. The weather wasn't going to help, but the way Colleen was acting definitely showed she wasn't faring well. Sharon gathered the rest of the groceries and locked her car. She still didn't see anything in the sky that looked like the storm people were describing to her. They had to be wrong. If a storm was going to be that bad, wouldn't it already show some signs it was coming? Sharon entered the house.

"Okay, that should do it."

"You certainly got a lot of stuff."

"Well you never know what we might need," Sharon said. She took the groceries into the kitchen and began emptying them. "Have you had a good morning so far?"

"It's supposed to storm later," Colleen said. Sharon stopped sorting the groceries. She said a prayer.

"What makes you say that?" she asked. Colleen didn't listen to the radio and wasn't a fan of the TV, but there was always that chance she turned it on. *Maybe she was having a spell.*

"Just a feeling. I can tell based on how the wind's blowin' outside and the way the sky looks." Sharon looked away so Colleen couldn't see her confusion. Colleen hated looking out the windows because all she could see was the dirt and grime Sharon never saw. Sharon listened for any creaking in the house from the wind, but heard nothing. She wondered how Colleen could know about the weather. "Are you done in there?"

"Almost," Sharon said. "Just trying to get things situated in here. I know you like your kitchen organized and all."

"Yes, yes. I don't like a dirty kitchen. A dirty kitchen's a dirty person. That's what my mother used to say. She didn't like it when people didn't clean up after themselves or didn't take care of things like they should. Nope. She wanted people to be clean and organized just like they should be, which is how I think things should be." Sharon nodded. She'd never seen any pictures of Colleen's family, but she always spoke of her mother and how much she admired and respected her. Not a day had gone by that Colleen hadn't said something about her.

"There we go. Everything in its place."

"Good. I'm sorry about the mess. I was just so tired from cooking last night I couldn't help but go lay down instead of doing the dishes."

"It's okay," Sharon said. "It wasn't all that bad."

"You always take good care of me." Sharon smiled. She knew Colleen wouldn't remember this conversation, but it made her feel better to hear those words.

"We need to check your blood sugar," Sharon said.

"Yes. I suppose we do. Hate it something awful, though."

"I know, but it's better safe than sorry."

"I suppose," Colleen said. She didn't move as Sharon pricked her finger and checked the numbers. Sharon nodded when the machine beeped.

"Looks like you could use a little insulin. You sure you're feeling okay?"

"I feel just fine. Let's get it over with."

"Okay." Sharon prepared everything and gave Colleen her medicine. Colleen winced slightly, but her attention was elsewhere.

"Is the wind picking up?" Sharon walked over to the window.

"Doesn't look like it. And it's just cloudy right now. No rain or anything like that. I think we'll be okay."

"Just don't want the weather to get too bad. Don't like it when it rains hard on my garden. Causes all the plants to get crushed and not be pretty no more. Don't like it when that happens. People won't be as impressed when they visit."

Sharon nodded. She didn't think she would need to tell Colleen what was happening. The weather was probably an exaggeration like usual. She didn't want to get Colleen all up in arms over something that wasn't true. Colleen continued talking about all the people who hadn't visited in years and the things that didn't matter anymore.

Ryan Peterson

The drive to work earlier that morning hadn't been bad. There was a chance of rain today and people were advised to be safe while out on the roads. It had already rained earlier when he was getting ready and more rain was expected. The only bad part of the drive was the I-65/565 junction. When headed north from Rosetta Falls, drivers had to be careful merging.

Alabama drivers rarely let people just change lanes. Usually they had to fight their way over and earn their place in the lane they needed. The drive could be dangerous and several accidents had happened there. Ryan had had so many close calls at that junction.

Hannah hated that he hadn't moved out yet and was still making the drive. He told her many times he couldn't afford to move out yet. His job barely covered his school expenses as it was. He couldn't imagine trying to move out and live on his own at this point. He was saving up, though, in hopes that upon graduating he would be able to find something to help him get out on his own.

He didn't mind his job. He worked for a small program at UAH in a windowless room filling boxes with school supplies. It sounded menial, but it provided money for him to pay for school which was important. He wasn't stretching too much, but there were days when he couldn't go out to eat or spend time with friends like he wanted. Instead, he just brought his lunch and ate by himself in the breakroom. Sometimes one of the workers would join him. That Wednesday, though, everyone had gone out to eat for burgers and would tell him when they got back.

It was still two days until payday so he was going to eat the peanut butter and jelly sandwiches he made the night before. He enjoyed their company, though, so he listened to the radio and worked until they got back. The station stopped playing music and started talking about the weather. He turned it up.

"We've received reports of aggressive weather moving

into Alabama now. There's a large line of storms moving in from the west. The line runs from Arkansas to southern Mississippi. The line seems to be breaking up, but forecasters are saying it still has potential to produce large amounts of rain and hail as it moves across the state. Winds are beginning to pick up and we've received reports of minor accidents out on the roads so we're advising everyone to please be careful when driving and to not be aggressive."

Interesting, he thought. He'd heard them this morning talking about how there was a chance of rain in the forecast, but not that was being made out to be a massive storm outbreak. He wasn't sure whether to believe them or not. He made sure no one was back yet and pulled out his phone to text Hannah.

"You okay? The weather people just said it's getting bad. Have you heard anything like that?"

"Yeah. In class."

"I thought so, but wanted to check on you just in case. Radio sounds intense." They'd gone back to playing classical music for the time being. He walked out of the room to the backdoor. He tried to push the large dock doors open, but they didn't move. He checked the door to see if it was locked, but it wasn't. He pushed harder. It felt like someone was standing on the other side pushing against him. It finally opened. The wind was so strong it caused him to stagger. He looked up.

Earlier that morning, the sky had been an overcast gray that could've meant rain or just the threat of rain. It rarely meant anything certain in the South. Now, the sky was darker and the clouds were moving at an alarming pace. He watched in awe at how fast they moved East. He didn't see any signs of it raining recently, but he could tell it wasn't far away. He shut the door and went back in the room. He picked up his phone.

First message: "Teacher just cancelled class. Said he studied meteorology in school and this was gonna be bad. Headed home." Another message: "You okay?" After several minutes, another message: "Hello?"

"Sorry," he wrote. "Went outside to see what it looked

like. It's starting to look pretty rough out there. Not sure when we'll go home today, though." He heard the backdoor open.

"Dang! That wind is rough!" Dwayne said as he came in.

"Yeah, really," said June, the floor manager. "I thought for sure we weren't gonna make it back. A whole lot of close calls. People not knowing how to drive or signal. How hard is it? It's a little stick on your steering wheel. Just move it in the direction you're going. Good grief. Hey, Ryan?"

"Yes, ma'am?" He looked up. She was holding a Styrofoam to-go box in her hands with the words "Happy, BDay" on it. He smiled.

"Oh man! Thank you!"

"I know you put in the hours to be off tomorrow and Friday, but your Dad spilled the beans about why." He laughed. That didn't surprise him. His Dad had trouble keeping some things to himself. He took the box from June and went into the breakroom. The rest of his coworkers were already there. Randy raised his plastic cup.

"Here's a birthday toast. If I'd somepin better, I'd use it, but I guess water'll hafta do."

"Hey, that's better than nothing," Ryan said. He sat next to Randy.

"Yeah, you didn't tell us it was your birthday, man," Dwayne said. "We coulda got you a little something, you know?" Ryan smiled.

"That's fine. It's nothing big. Just another birthday."

"Yer not turnin' 21, are ya?" Randy asked.

"No. 22."

"Ah. Then yeah, it's nothin'."

"What do you mean?" Dwayne asked. "Just because it's not his 21st birthday it's not important?"

"Course not. After your 21st, the only good birthday is 40 'cause that means yer old."

"Hey," Jon Spencer said as he walked in. "40 isn't old; thank you very much."

"Aw man, you know I's just kiddin'," Randy said. Jon and Randy were Alabama football fans and always argued about how the team was going to do. Randy firmly believed they were going to go undefeated and win the National Championship every year. If they lost, he never acknowledged it. Jon was different. He looked at the team and how they actually played. If they didn't do well, he had no problem calling them out on it. He was not blind to college football like some were. Ryan hated football and tried to avoid the conversations.

"Ryan, have you had their burgers before?" Jon asked. Ryan shook his head. "Oh, then you are definitely in for a treat. This is the biggest, greasiest burger you've ever had before and it is delicious."

"And it being free didn't hurt," June said. She walked in with her sister who also worked with them.

"Hey, that's just a bonus," Jon said. "I don't always eat there for free. Just usually. They like me." Rebecca rolled her eyes.

"You bring them enough business I'm surprised they haven't made you a business partner," she said.

"You're right. I should have a talk with them about that." June sat down and Rebecca got her food from the fridge.

"How bad was it out there?" Rebecca asked. She'd been in her office and hadn't paid any attention to the weather.

"Not really bad," Jon said. "You can tell it's headed this way, though. Wind's starting to pick up and clouds are really moving in now. Might need to call the wife and make sure she's good. Anyone know of schools letting out?"

"They didn't say anything on the radio," Ryan said. "I've been listening since you guys left. Right now it's just classical music, but they were interrupting it all morning with weather updates. Apparently it's getting worse."

"Yeah," June said. "I was listening to the radio this morning and thinkin' it couldn't be as bad as they're saying, but now that I've driven in it, I'm thinking it could be pretty close."

"Well, I better call Tracy and see if she's heard anything about the schools or the kids." Jon closed his to-go box and left the room.

"Hey," Rebecca said. "Where's Dwayne?" They all looked around the room.

"His food is still here so he couldn't have gone far," Randy said. "Maybe he went to the bathroom. I'll go check."

"You're gonna go to the bathroom to see if another guy is in there?" June asked.

"Hey," he said. "Dwayne ain't exactly the brightest knife in the box...or whatever. I'll go check." They laughed as he walked out.

"This is really good," Ryan said of his burger. "Thanks again, June."

"Figured I'd treat you since you won't be here for your actual birthday." Her phone vibrated on the table. She looked at it and let out a sigh. "It's Dwayne. Hello?" Rebecca and Ryan waited silently. "What? What do you mean they won't let you leave the basement?" Pause. "If you're trying to be funny, it's really not working." Pause. "All right, hold on." She hung up. "Looks like Dwayne went down to the basement for something he randomly remembered and now school officials aren't letting him leave the basement. I'm gonna go check on him." She walked out.

"So do you have any plans with Hannah for your birthday?" Rebecca asked.

"Not really. We might do something when she gets back. UA runs longer than we do."

"Does she graduate this year?"

"No. She's two years behind me so she's got a little longer."

"Well, that's okay."

"He's not in the bathroom," Randy said, causing Rebecca to jump.

"Well, hello to you, too," she said.

"Oh. Right. Sorry. Was just hungry and wanted to get back. Kinda weird lookin' for a guy in the bathroom." Ryan laughed. Jon came back in.

"There's a warning out right now and some of the schools

are closing early," he said. "None are out yet but they called the parents to let them know. Athens State and Calhoun are already closing and I think Oakwood and Alabama A&M are planning to close too."

"Any word on if UAH is or not?" Ryan asked. Jon gave him a look.

"You know UAH ain't gonna close until after all the other schools close. That's just how they are." Rebecca's phone rang.

"It's June," she said. "Hello?" Pause. "Seriously?" Pause. "Okay, we'll stay in the breakroom." Pause. "Okay, bye." She set her phone on the table. "So apparently some idiot down there won't let anyone leave and is blocking off the entrance. Someone already threatened to leave and the guy said he had no trouble knocking anyone back if they tried to go passed him."

"Seriously?" Jon asked.

"That's what she said."

"That's ridiculous," he said. "You can't force people to stay in the basement if they don't want to. They might can keep them from working, but you can't stop them from leaving a floor of the building they're in." Rebecca shrugged.

"I don't know," she said. "Maybe they'll let us leave soon."

"Well, I'm gonna leave when I want 'cause they can't keep me here," Randy said.

"Calm down," Rebecca said. "I'm sure they're gonna let everyone go soon." Randy continued eating as Ryan pulled out his phone.

<u>Hannah Leon</u>

"What is it?" Alycia asked. Hannah looked up from her phone.

"What?" she asked.

"I said 'what is it'. You look worried is all."

"Oh. Sorry. Ryan just sent me a text saying schools up there are letting out and they can't leave the university right now for safety reasons."

"That's weird," Alycia said. "I think our order is up." Hannah got up and walked to the counter. Since class had let out, she decided to make up for not having breakfast by going to Milo's to eat. Jillian was in a depressed mood and wasn't interested in going out to eat. Thankfully, Alycia was starving and craving some sweet tea.

She was in the same program as Hannah and they'd met while working together in the admin offices. They hadn't spoken a lot during their first few weeks together because they worked different times. She often took up the morning and Hannah came in after lunch. During the registration rush one semester, they worked together to help several students undo the damage done to their school schedules and had remained friends. She picked their food up from the counter and took it back to their seats.

"Oh man," Alycia said. "I've been cravin' me some Milo's tea for a while!"

"I can't get Ryan to come here."

"Really? Why not?"

"He hates the tea they sell in the jugs in stores and thinks that's how all their tea is."

"Oh no. You gonna have to break him of that. They sell people short in stores over that crappy stuff. He needs to get in here and *really* try some tea."

"He has pretty high standards for his tea. His grandmother makes tea that's pretty sweet. His brothers love it, too."

"How many brothers does he have?"

"Two younger brothers. They're twins."

"Oh boy," she said with a grin.

"What?"

"You know twins are usually a genetic thing, right?"

"Hey now. Twins aren't that much trouble." Alycia just shrugged.

"I would be more concerned about twin little brothers. That sounds like twice as much a pain."

"Uh huh," Hannah said. They laughed. "So what do you think about this weather they're reporting?" Alycia took a moment to think.

"Well," she said. "I've heard a lot about how bad it's supposed to get and how some people went from 'it shouldn't be too bad' to 'this is some of the worst we're gonna get ever.' But I'm not all that worried about it."

"I don't think most people are," Hannah said. "Ryan texted me early about it but didn't say how things were up there until a minute ago. I'm surprised schools are letting out right now."

"Yeah. Especially all the way up there. Did he say what the weathermen are saying up there?"

"No. Just that the weather is bad and all," Hannah said. "Nothing specific. I'm kinda worried about him now." Alycia took a long sip of her drink.

"I wouldn't worry too much," Alycia said. "We've all been through this before. Weather is bad nearby so clearly it's gonna be bad here. Sometimes they aren't kidding, but they usually are. I'm still gonna go in the closet when it gets later this evening but I'm not worried anything really bad is gonna happen."

"Did you hear from your parents?" Hannah asked.

"Yeah. They just wanted to make sure I'm gonna be safe. I told them I plan on just staying in my apartment and being ready to jump to safety if I need to."

"Did that make them feel better?" Hannah asked. Alycia just gave her a look, but didn't say anything. "Right, right." She felt uneasy. She'd heard so many times that the weather wasn't always predictable and could easily be misread. She wondered what the point in reading and studying it was if it could be misunderstood. Alycia stood up.

"I'm getting a refill. You want anything?"

"Yeah. Diet Coke please?"

"Sure." Hannah sat there and looked out the window. What she could see of the sky had definitely darkened. She moved her head in hopes to see more, but the trees across the street blocked the rest of her view. She went back to her food as Alycia walked up.

"Here ya go," she said.

"Thanks. I can't really tell how bad the weather is out there."

"Yeah. I looked around on my way here while listening to the radio but couldn't tell anything either. It seems to be doing okay for now, but don't know how long that'll hold up." Hannah nodded in agreement as she drank.

"What are you doing tonight?" she asked.

"I'm staying with some friends," Alycia said. "We've been planning a girls' night kinda thing and I need it."

"But it's Wednesday."

"I know, but sometimes you just need to take a break and relax, you know? You can't just keep going and going. You gotta take it easy and breathe a little." Hannah thought about that for a moment. So often her life was wrapped up in school she forgot about kicking back and relaxing. "You know Jillian is having a party tonight?"

"Yeah," Hannah said. "I'm not sure if I'm gonna go or not."

"You should. I mean, at least you won't be alone if anything happens with the weather, right?" Hannah hadn't thought about that. She'd never worried about the weather before and wasn't all that concerned now. Still, it would be nice to have people around just in case.

"But you know how Jillian is when she's down in the dumps. And she's really upset about this whole Neil thing. I'm not sure if she's just being crazy or if she really thinks he wants out."

"It wouldn't surprise me if it was all in her head," Alycia said. "This happens every once in a while."

"Yeah, but still. If it is legit, she's gonna be a pain." Alycia nodded. Hannah understood insecurity, but sometimes Jillian made even her crazy. Wondering if everyone around you is saying or thinking something negative about you must be stressful.

"So you gonna go?" Alycia asked.

"I don't know. I'll probably just go so I won't be alone."

"Good. I was gonna be worried about you."

Neil Senior

"I don't know," Neil said. "I mean, she's getting to be so needy lately. I'm not sure if I can handle it anymore." He was at his apartment now. When classes were cancelled he decided not to go back to Jillian's and just told her he was meeting up with friends to get ready for the party that night. "Which wasn't untrue," he explained to Tex and Andrew.

"Neil," Tex said with his strong Southern accent. "We both know what you been talkin' 'bout doin' with this girl for a long time now. Every time she needs just a little love you go and do this thing where you start questionin' all of life and all the stuff in it and what not. You really need to just chill and realize she's the one you need to be with and just leave it at that." Neil shook his head.

"Naw, man. It's not that simple. She's probably wanting everything right now and I'm not ready for that, man. I don't need that on me. We're both gonna graduate next week and then who knows what'll happen." Andrew rolled his eyes.

"Man. I'm just gonna be honest with you. Shut up and grow some."

"What?"

"Man, you're always talkin' about how worried you are with this and that. But every time we sit here and listen for a few hours, we tell you the same thing and you do the same thing. It's getting old. You need to get it together or something."

"What do you always tell me?"

"We always tell you to shut up and be happy you have her and you always do that," Tex said. Neil thought about their relationship and watched it play on the off-white carpet beneath him. He watched as they met, talked, dated, fell in love, broke up, got back together, broke up again, and came back together. He could see how no matter what they did, it always came back around to them being together. He smiled.

"What?" Andrew asked. Neil laughed.

"You're right. I *do* always get back with her. Guess maybe one day I'll shut up and stay with her, right?"

"If prayers are answered," Tex said. Neil rolled his eyes.

"Come on. I'm not that bad." They both stopped what they were doing and looked right at him. It made him slightly uncomfortable so he took a sip of his drink. "You guys are right. I need to go ahead and invite her over so we can get this party started."

"That's what I'm talkin' about," Tex said. "All right. I'm gonna take Andrew and go get a little something-something for the party and then we'll be back here. You get your girl on the phone and get her over here. I know she's gonna be happier to listen to you than us."

"Gee thanks," Neil said. He pulled out his phone and called Jillian. The phone barely rang once when he heard her.

"Hello!" she said.

"Hey. How're you doing?"

"I'm good. You okay?"

"Yeah, why wouldn't I be?"

"Well, I dunno. Just hadn't heard from you so I was curious."

"Oh no. Everything's fine. You okay and all?"

"Yeah. Just worried about you was all."

"Well I'm fine, I promise. Hey, you wanna go ahead and come over here? Tex and Andrew just stopped by with beer and are gonna be back in a few minutes with some other party stuff."

"Oh," she said. "That sounds nice, actually. When will they get there?"

"Not sure, but you can go ahead and head over if you want."

"Definitely! See you soon."

"All righty."

"Hey, is it okay if Hannah comes over?" Neil thought for a moment. *Hannah. Hannah. Who was Hannah?*

"Yeah, sure," he said. "Is she gonna be okay with the weed and stuff?"

"Oh yeah. Hannah won't mind. She just doesn't wanna be alone during all this weather stuff and I thought we could provide her with entertainment to distract her."

"Sounds good to me. I'll see you when you get here."

"Okay. I love you," she said.

"I love you too," he said and hung up the phone. He walked over to his computer and pulled up the weather.

The radar showed a large patch of red and yellow west of Tuscaloosa and the path it would take once it crossed the state line. He watched the last three hours on loop.

The storm had grown quickly and slowed down its movements. All the reports he now read said the storm would be one for the record books, which was a major change from what he'd heard that morning. He wondered if they really needed to be partying tonight with this kind of weather. He closed the browser and looked around his apartment. He wanted to figure out where they could go in case something did happen.

When growing up, his mother was always worried about every little storm. If the weather people said it would be bad, she pulled them out of school immediately and they all got in the little storm cellar his stepfather made and waited it out. He remembered he damp feel of it. He didn't like being trapped in such a small space and wasn't looking forward to possibly doing it again during the storm, but he didn't really have a choice. If the storm was going to be as bad as they said, he needed to be ready.

He had a fairly large closet that could hold two people and people could fit in the bathroom if worse came to worse. He doubted things would get that bad, but at least he could tell them when they got here not to worry because he'd already thought of these things. He opened the closet. Except for some clothes he'd hung up only to make Jillian happy, it was bare. He wasn't one for keeping extra stuff and figured it wouldn't do any good to keep things stored in his closet if he wasn't going to use it.

Jillian, on the other hand, was a packrat and kept everything he had ever given her in their relationship. She was much more sentimental about things than he was and there was no reason he should say anything that might upset her. He pushed all the clothes to one end of the pole they hung on to make more room. He heard a knock at the door and closed his closet.

"I'm coming!" he said.

"It's just me," Jillian said. He worried maybe she'd figured him out. He didn't want her thinking such things, especially now since he was on the rocks about the decision.

It wasn't that he was still unsure. His friends had made it clear he needed to stay with her since they belonged together. He realized they weren't just saying that to put up with him. True, he'd pushed them so far that now he felt he'd annoyed them and they weren't going to come back. At the same time, he felt maybe they were right and he needed to see just how good he had it with Jillian. He opened the door and smiled at her.

"Well hello there," he said. "Would you like to come in?"

"Yes, please," she said. As she entered, he looked at the sky. Everything was much darker now and he could see the clouds coming. They spread across the horizon, blocking out any suggestion there should be sun behind them. For the first time that day, he was anxious.

"You okay?" Jillian asked. Neil took a deep breath.

"Huh? Oh sorry. I was just...noticing the clouds up there. I hadn't noticed how dark they'd gotten until now." He felt her push against him and put her arms around his waist.

"Yeah. It's gotten bad lately, hasn't it?"

"Yeah," he said. "But sometimes things get bad for a while, but then they get better." He looked down. She smiled as tears were forming.

"But they get better, don't they?" He kissed her.

The car honking startled them both. They looked up to see Andrew waving wildly at them as Tex pulled into a parking spot.

"Look at the little lovebirds!" Andrew yelled as he got out. "We figured we'd give you nuff time to make up and all that."

"Thank you," Neil yelled back. He pulled Jillian inside

and left the door cracked.

"Do you think we're gonna be safe here?" she asked. He nodded.

"Oh yeah. I've made room in the closet if we need to go in there and there's definitely room in the bathroom if someone wants in there."

"I think I'd want in there. I don't want to get caught in the middle of a storm and need to go to the bathroom." Neil chuckled.

"If we have a tornado over us, I doubt peeing will be the first thing to come to mind." She gave him a funny look.

"Well, how about just in case?"

"Sounds good enough to me," he said. "Hey, when is Hannah getting here?"

"I'm not sure. She said she wanted to be here soon, but she was talking to Ryan first. Wanted to make sure he knew she was going to be okay."

"I guess that's fair. I don't know her that well so it'll be good to get to know her better. And you said she'd be okay with the weed, right?"

"Yup." The door opened and Tex and Andrew walked in.

"Wind's blowin' hard," Andrew said. "We could hear it inside Tex's car it was so loud!"

"Yeah," Tex said. "I'm glad we're stayin' indoors tonight 'cause that thing outside ain't pretty."

"Don't worry," Neil said. I've already made sure we've got places we can stay and if we need to. It's gotten a lot darker but I still don't think we have much to worry about."

"Cool, cool," Andrew said. "We still waiting on one more?"

"Yeah, but we can go ahead and light up," Jillian said. "I need a good one right now." They gathered around the table as Tex divided it up among the four of them.

Ryan Peterson

"How much longer you think this is gonna take?" Randy asked.

"I'm not sure," Rebecca said. She held up her phone. "June said they're still not allowed to leave the basement yet. She's getting frustrated, but hasn't tackled whoever's blocking the door just yet. She's probably thinking about it." They all laughed.

"That's just weird how it snuck up on everyone," Jon said. "I figured we would've at least gotten some sort of warning, right?"

"They did say something about it," Ryan said. "But they're wrong so often it's hard to know when they're being serious or when they're overreacting." Randy nodded.

"Yeah, I mean, they overreact more than not. So yeah." June quickly entered.

"Okay, everyone. University is now closed. Everyone get everything you need and get out of here while we have a chance. The guy downstairs said if we aren't gone before they upgraded our tornado watch to a warning, we'll be stuck here. So grab your stuff and get to your cars quick." No one moved. Ryan wasn't sure if she was being serious or not. He started picking up his stuff. Everyone began to move too. Dwayne entered.

"Gosh. Those guys downstairs were intense."

"Only you would manage to get stuck downstairs, Dwayne," Randy said. "How'd you manage to do that anyway?"

"I dunno. I just needed to get something and didn't think they were gonna go all 'Oh no! You can't leave or we'll beat you up' kinda stuff."

"Did they really threaten to beat you up?" Randy asked.

"Well, no. Not really. I was just being sarcastic, guys. Come on."

"Hey," June said. "Less talking, more moving. We need to get out of here before they try to trap us."

"Thank you for the burger, June," Ryan said.

"You're welcome. Hope your birthday is good." She picked up the rest of her stuff and went to help Rebecca. Ryan left the room and saw Jon already headed out the door.

"They ain't gonna keep me here," he said. "Hey, you have a safe drive. I know Rosetta Falls is a bit of a drive from here."

"Thanks. You be safe too," Ryan said. He walked outside and looked up. The building and trees behind his work blocked off most of the sky but he figured he'd get a good look at it on his drive home. There were several place, including the bridge, where he could get a clear look at the sky.

He walked to his clunky green car. People were hurrying to their cars to get away. Many of them had worried looks on their faces. Others were on their cellphones yelling at spouses about picking children up or getting groceries just in case.

Dad had an appointment earlier and already left. He got in the car and left. He saw Rebecca and June at the door hurrying people out. They were talking about something, but Ryan couldn't hear them. Dwayne lightly walked out of the building as if he still didn't know there was a storm coming. Randy was already in his truck and leaving as Ryan pulled away. He changed lanes then got on I-565. He looked at the sky.

The darkness of the clouds was a sharp contrast to what he'd seen earlier. An endless sea of dark grey shown from one edge of his view to the other. The clouds seemed to be building strength as they made their way towards their destination. He saw no lightning, heard no thunder, and felt no rain, but something about the clouds caused him to feel uncomfortable. He heard a honk behind him as he signaled to get over.

As he merged lanes, he saw many more headed home. 565 was packed with people changing lanes without signaling or lights on. He did his best to be careful and make sure no one else honked at him.

Cars were flying past him to get home to safety. Ryan only went above the speed limit when it was absolutely necessary. He'd never gotten a ticket, never been in an accident, and never wanted either to happen. He watched carefully as he drove. The lane he was in would take him straight to I-65 without having to get over anymore. He slowed down. The exit ramp was backed up a long way and several cars were in his lane trying to get over. He wanted to make sure he didn't hit any of them and gave people behind him plenty of time to stop if necessary. He changed lanes to avoid the traffic. His phone rang. He reached for it carefully as he kept driving. *Hannah.*

"Hello," he said.

"Hey. Are you okay?"

"Yeah, I'm fine. What's up?"

"They're saying the weather here is pretty bad so I thought I'd talk to you if you can."

"Yeah. UAH finally closed so I'm headed home. Traffic is nasty right now. Madison is really backed up."

"I guess a lot of people let out at once."

"Yeah. That's what it sounded like earlier."

"I heard this is supposed to be one for the record books."

"Wait, what?"

"I know. Everyone here has been kinda 'meh' about the whole thing like it's just another storm or something. I mean, we get them all the time so I'm not really all that worried, but I'm definitely a little concerned."

"I understand. At least you're safe, right?"

"Yeah, I guess." There was a pause.

"Are you okay?" he asked.

"I'm just worried. No one seems to care."

"I know, but it'll be fine. How has your day been, otherwise?"

"Pretty good. Hasn't been very productive because of everyone closing and what not. I tried to get stuff done at home but there's nothing I can really do. With finals and all about to start, most students are busy studying for that."

"Well, why not try enjoying the little break you're getting? I know you love having a lot of things to do, but maybe it'll be nice to not have anything for once, right?" He didn't get a response. "Hannah?"

"Sorry. Jillian just texted me and asked if I was coming over or not."

"Ah. Are you?"

"I dunno. I don't think so, but I'm not sure. I don't want to be alone or anything like that."

"I understand. It might be better if you just stay at your place, though. I mean, that way you're with all your stuff and you don't have to worry about not having something you need."

"Well, if I need something, I can just go get it in the morning, right?"

"Maybe. I dunno. I just think it'd be a better idea if you stayed at home tonight."

"I'll think about it." Ryan merged onto the loop for I-65. As he went around, he saw the clouds again. They were much larger now and much darker.

"Wow..." he whispered.

"What?"

"Oh. Sorry. I was just looking at the clouds and all. You know the junction?"

"Yeah?"

"I just went around it and saw the clouds. They look scary. They definitely weren't like that this morning."

"What did it look like this morning?"

"You know. Just overcast and maybe a little like some rain, but nothing like this."

"Yeah, it's the same way here. It's starting to look really bad now. I'm not sure how fast it's moving but it seems like it's moving fast."

"It probably is. North Alabama was under a tornado watch briefly which is why we were able to leave. It might be under a warning now, though."

"You think?"

"Definitely. Those clouds look pretty rough, if you ask me. Have you looked at any down there?"

"Not really. I came home and haven't look outside. Been getting things together and what not."

"I wish you wouldn't spend the night."

"But I don't want to be alone if it gets bad."

"I know you don't, but it'd be better to be at your place and you can call me if you need someone to talk to." There was a pause. He figured she was still hesitant, but he didn't want to push her on the matter. "You there?"

"Yeah. I'll decide what I'm doing and I'll let you know, okay?"

"Okay. Hey, I'm at my exit so I'll send you a text when I get home, okay?"

"Okay. Thank you."

"Be safe," he said and he hung up.

The light was green as he got off the interstate. He kept going straight and looked at the sky to the east. It looked just like it had this morning with only a little bit changed. The clouds were moving away from him at a much faster rate, but it seemed like nothing had happened. He looked in his side mirror. He didn't notice the rain beginning to fall. All he could see were the clouds.

<u>Sharon Rogers</u>

Sharon watched Colleen. The sky had darkened and she knew what was coming. She wanted to say something, but wasn't sure how to say it. Colleen was watching something on the TV and oblivious to whatever was going on in the world around her. Sharon wasn't even sure what show was on, but Colleen seemed enthralled with it. Sharon walked to the windows and looked out.

The clouds were there now. Big, black, and powerful looking clouds. She watched the lightning clash and she counted. "1. 2. 3. 4. 5. 6. 7. 8. 9. 10." *Soft thunder*. Yup. It was getting closer. She walked over to Colleen and sat down next to her.

"Miss Colleen," she said.

"Did you hear that racket?"

"Yes, I did."

"Kids today really need to keep it down. There's innocent people around here."

"Listen," Sharon said. She felt as though she were addressing a child but did her best to conceal that in her voice. "There's a big storm coming. It's supposed to be pretty bad. I can't leave and come back because it's too dangerous so I'm just gonna stay the night with you, okay?" Colleen looked at her funny.

"Why you gonna do that? Ain't nothing wrong with a little bit of rain. Doesn't seem right you putting yourself out and all just 'cause you're a little scared about driving in some bad weather."

"I'm not worried about driving in bad weather. I'm worried I won't be able to get back to you."

"I been doin' just fine all these years without you sleeping in my house and I'm sure I can do fine again."

"How about I sleep in the guest room?"

"Oh no, can't have that. Never know when someone will stop in and need a place to sleep. Lots of times relatives just surprise you with them showing up and it's not good if you can't take care of them."

"Well, if someone shows up I'll be sure to give them the bed, okay?"

"Who's gonna show up?" she asked. "I wasn't expecting any company. You just go ahead and sleep in there if you need to. Don't wanna put you out or anything."

"Sounds good to me." Sharon walked back into the kitchen and looked at her. In a few seconds they'd had a conversation that probably went all the way back to the 1960s with Colleen remembering a time when people dropped by all the time and were welcomed with open arms.

Colleen watched the TV without paying any heed to Sharon or Sharon's thoughts. She seemed lost in whatever decade she found comfort.

"Sharon?" Colleen called, snapping Sharon back from her thoughts.

"Yes, ma'am?"

"What were you thinking of making for dinner?" she asked. Sharon hadn't given dinner any thoughts. It was a little early to be thinking about that right now, but maybe she could go ahead and get things going.

"I'm not sure," she said. "What are you in the mood for?"

"Oh I don't know. We've got something in the freezer, I'm sure. Maybe we could have some of that chicken from last night."

"I'll have to check and see if there's any left." Knowing Colleen remembered what they had for dinner the night before gave Sharon a bit of hope. She opened the fridge. "Yeah, it looks like we have some left. Would you like some of that?"

"Yeah. No need to hafta go to any trouble."

Sharon listened to Colleen mutter to whatever she was watching on TV as the clouds continued to move.

Ryan Peterson

Ryan pulled into the driveway and parked his car away from the trees lining the west side of his house. It wasn't that he thought something *would* happen. He just didn't want to chance it if it did happen. He was in front of the house, facing towards the wide paneling along the side. He looked west and saw the clouds. They were much closer than before and seemed darker, though that could've been the time of day. He looked at his watch. 4:30 pm. It couldn't have been the time a day. There was still supposed to be a few more hours of light. Rain sprinkled his windshield as he grabbed his things to go inside.

He walked around the addition to the backdoor. He noticed the dog pen was empty, which was unusual. He opened the door.

"Hey. Where's the dog?" he said.

"He's in here," his twin brothers called out in unison. Ken and Brandon were both 11 years younger than him. His parents had opted out of giving them cute names that matched and instead chose names that allowed them to be individuals. However, they'd grown up being the kind of twins that wanted to match and dress alike and pull tricks on people using their identical looks.

"Why is he in here?"

"Causth Mom sthaid we couldn't leave him out there if it rainsth," Brandon said. His lisp helped tell them apart.

"Got ya. I guess that makes sense." He walked into the dining room to see Mom. "Do you think it's gonna get that bad?"

"Well," she said. "It could. I'm kind of skeptical myself, but the weather people seem pretty adamant about it so it's better to be safe than sorry." Ryan nodded.

"Where's dad?" he asked.

"Up the hill with your grandparents. They're talking about what to do in case something happens."

The road Ryan lived on was short and formed a loop called O'Connor Circle. Its residents had lived there for years and many of their descendants moved back to take their place in the tight-knit community. While most of the loop was flat, the center of Ryan's road went up a hill past a house his grandparents inherited from his great-grandparents.

"How are they doing?" he asked.

"I suppose they're doing well. They've been having trouble with that new tank-less water heater they installed in the house."

"Weren't we thinking about getting one of those?" he asked. She gave him a look. "Ah. Got ya. So what's for dinner?"

"We left you some Wal-Mart chicken in the microwave. We all already ate but figured you were stuck in some traffic so we left it there for you." He went to the microwave and saw a plate of fried tenders and potato wedges fixed for him.

"How long have they been in there?"

"Only a few minutes, but you might wanna warm them." He put the time in. It seemed like an early time to eat dinner but he was hungry. *Wait!* He pulled out his phone and text Hannah.

"Home." The microwave beeped. He took his food out and set it on the table before getting the ketchup from the fridge. The old part of the house was small. The fridge and freezer were right next to the dining room table so one of them could just lean back, open the fridge, get what they want, and close it back. Mom frowned heavily on this so they tried not to do it. He got the ketchup and grabbed a can of Dr. Pepper too. His phone buzzed.

"Took you long enough. I think I'm gonna go stay with Jillian. Really don't wanna be alone." He shook his head. He knew it sounded strange. He couldn't figure out how to describe it to her. For whatever reason, he just felt better knowing she was safe at her place. Her being somewhere he didn't know or hadn't been wasn't comforting. He just wanted her somewhere where he knew what it looked like. Where he could picture her safe. He couldn't explain why.

"Maybe you should stay home," he wrote. "It might be a

good idea. You don't have to if you don't want to." He popped open the can and took a big gulp.

"You better eat all that 'cause we saved it for you," Ken said.

"Oh don't worry. I plan on it." *Buzz.* Ryan looked at his phone.

"I can't, Ryan. I don't want to. I'm already scared as it is." He let out an exhausted sigh.

"Okay. Just please be safe!" His brothers gasped. Ryan looked up from his phone and realized the power was out.

"Ooo!" "Ahh!" Ken and Brandon said. They were making ghost noises to try and scare Ryan. He rolled his eyes at them and let out a chuckle.

"Don't worry," Mom said. "I'm sure it'll be back on shortly. It's probably just from all the rough weather. Everyone calm down." Ryan hit send on his phone. A message flashed across the screen.

You are no longer in service. Your message will be sent once service has been restored.

Ryan moved his phone around to see if maybe it was just where he was sitting. Nothing happened and the signal did not return.

"No, Jack, please," she says. "Why aren't you home yet?"

"I promise I'm trying. Traffic is backed up and it's almost impossible to get into Northport. McFarland is a mess. I'm not sure if I'm gonna be able to get to the house anytime soon."

"But I'm scared," she says. "There's no one else here. All the sounds are driving me crazy and they aren't getting any softer."

"Aww. *Mi mariposita,* I promise I'm trying. The interstate was just as bad as rush hour traffic and I wasn't expecting it to be."

"I told you not to go to that seminar. I told you it would just cause trouble."

"*Cariña,* you could not have known this would happen. Sometimes bad things happen, but just calm down. I promise I'll be there soon." She doesn't reply immediately and cries.

"*Lo siento,*" she says.

"Aww, no. No. What's wrong?"

"I don't mean to be upset with you, *querido,* I just need you to be here."

"I'll be there as soon as I can, I promise."

"Promise me you'll be safe."

"*Cariño,* I-"

"Promise!" He pauses.

"*Juro ser seguro.*" I swear to you.

"*Gracias,*" she says. "I love you."

"I love you too." They hang up. She misses him. The humming outside bothers her. It's not loud, but persistent. It continues to bother her. She wants it to go, but it remains. She climbs into bed and covers her head with a pillow. The sound quietens. Her tears stain their bare mattress as she tries to hide from the storm. *It wasn't supposed to be this bad.* She hates the lightning, but prefers it over the humming. Persistent and seems to poke at her.

She thinks about what she said. If he is on McFarland, he can't be far. She lives just past 15th street. She peeks out from under the pillow. She wants to look outside. She wants to see what's causing the dreadful sound. It can't be anything big. Maybe it is and just not close by. She tries to place the sound, but nothing comes to mind. It feels like a large choir of men far away humming the same note.

Why isn't he here yet? She needs him. She isn't used to this kind of weather. Tornadoes. Storms. Lightning. Thunder. It scares her. Scares her. She takes deep breaths in hopes it will calm her down. She walks into the bathroom, shuts the door, and crouches down.

The Spencers

"Come on, girls," Jon says. "We've got to get downstairs."

"But why?" Lisa asks.

"Yeah," Laura says. "The power goes out all the time."

"Right, but you girls have been told all day this one was gonna be bad. We need to get downstairs before it really starts hitting. You girls go on downstairs to the shelter and I'll get your mother." They both go down as Jon shuts the door. "Where are you honey?" Tracy walks out of the den.

"Do you really think it's gonna be that bad?" she asks, frantic and trying to find some comfort in Jon. She hates bad weather of any kind and refuses to drive in any conditions but sunny. "It just seems like a bit of overkill to go running downstairs just to avoid what could just be a bit of stormy weather."

"If it was just a little bit of stormy weather, you know UAH wouldn't have closed when they did. They don't close for anything unless they absolutely have to and, Tracy, I think they had to."

"But maybe the head person told them they had to because they were putting people's lives in danger." He takes her in his arms and hugs her.

"Honey," he says softly. "You realize some of the country's top weather scientists work on campus. I don't think they'd be calling it like this if they weren't positive something was gonna happen. But we have a storm shelter and we are going to be fine. You need to get down there with the girls so they don't freak out and I'll double check the rest of the house, okay?" No answer. "Okay, Tracy?"

"Okay, Jon. Please be careful."

"I will." He kisses her forehead. She goes downstairs and shuts the door.

He looks around the house. He goes upstairs to the second floor. All windows tightly shut and no candles still burning. He goes to their bedroom. One candle Tracy left on in their bedroom. He blows it out and checks the window in the room before walking down the hall. No candles in the hallway. He checks all the windows. He goes to the girls' rooms. Laura's door is closed. He peeks inside and sees no burning candles. He checks her window and leaves. He goes to Lisa's room. Two lit candles on her desk and window curtains pulled back with blinds up. He blows out both, walks to lower the blinds, and stops.

A cyclone falls from the sky. It rotates and all the debris picked up time follows. Dark gray, not black. It forms with aggression. It moves with purpose like a hungry animal moving towards food. Jon stares.

It seems headed straight for him. Not the houses, not the neighborhood, but him. His breath quickens. He turns from the window and runs down the hall. He takes the stairs four at a time and lands hard on his right ankle.

"AH!" he yells, but stops. He doesn't want the family to try coming back up the stairs with that tornado heading this way. He stands and stretches the ankle out as best he can. He grimaces and tries to endure the pain. It hurts when he puts pressure on it. He needs to check the rest of the house. He goes to the living room and sees two candles. He makes his way towards them and blows them out. He moves to the guest rooms. Nothing.

He moves back through the living room and looks out the patio at the cyclone. It's close to touching down. He reaches the top of the stairs leading to the shelter. Tracy stands next to it.

"Everyone in there?" he yells. The pain grows as he descends the steps.

"What's going on, Da-"

"Girls, Tracy, please. This one is bad and we need to be safe."

"But, Jon, why are you being so-"

"Please, Tracy. Just trust me." She enters the small shelter door and Jon follows her and slams it shut.

"Jon, wha...what happened?" Tracy asks. He doesn't answer. He pulls Tracy and the girls close to him and prays.

<u>Neil Senior</u>

"Do you guys hear that?" Neil asks. He's high and unsure if what he sees and hears is real. Maybe he isn't hearing or seeing anything. Maybe it's all a dream.

"No, man," Tex says. "What're you hearin'?"

"I'm," he starts, but can't remember what he wants to say. Something about...but not sure. Maybe...but not that either. "I dunno, man. But I...oh yeah! I hear something. Something loud. It's like..."

"A low hum," Jillian says. "Is that it?"

"Yeah! That's it! A hum! Anyone else hear it?"

"Naw, man. I dunno what you're talkin' 'bout," Andrew says. On his back staring at the ceiling.

"Guys, I'm telling you I heard something and it didn't sound good. It didn't sound good at all. It was like a low hum like Jillian said. Come on, guys, you had to hear it."

"Hey," Andrew says. He points to the ceiling. "The fat people upstairs made some giant cracks in your ceilin'. You should sue 'em."

"I live on the top floor, stupid," he says. Neil begins to come out of his high. He feels nauseated. The combination of that and the strange sound hurts. He loses orientation and staggers to the bathroom. The feeling leaves, but not the sound. It gets louder. He twitches his head to one side to find it. He opens the bathroom door and tries to flip on the switch.

"Guys, the power is out."

"What?" Jillian asks. "When did that happen?"

"I dunno, but it did. You hear me, Tex?" No response.

"I think he and Andrew passed out." Neil stares into the darkness of the bathroom. He feels the pieces of the puzzle he saw as one big blur take shape. His eyes widen.

"Jillian!" he yells

"What?" she asks.

"Get in here with me!"

"Wha-?"

"Just get in here!"

"Everything ok-"

"Just get in here!" She moves in the darkness. He waits until he feels her hands against his back. He pulls her into the bathroom and shuts the door. He pulls her close in the darkness and sits on the floor.

"What's wrong, Neil?"

"We need to stay in here."

"What? You don't think there's-"

"Yeah. I think there is. Something about it doesn't seem right. And that annoying hum won't go away."

"But that could just be the weed, baby."

"I'm not high anymore."

"How do you know?"

"Trust me. I'm not high and something is wrong." She cries.

"Neil, hold me."

"I'm here. Don't worry."

"I'm so scared."

"Shh. We're gonna be okay."

"Are we?" No answer. The hum grows louder. *Was it something outside?* A swishing sound follows. The hum never changes pitch. The swishing moves back and forth. He pulls her closer as she cries. He listens for Tex and Andrew to say something but nothing. *Too late to wake them,* he thinks. *I can't leave Jillian now.*

Neil winces. The hum becomes like a buzz inside him. He can't recall thunder or lightning. He remembers the rain picking up and being strong, but sketchy. Details refuse to form. Maybe if he thinks harder he can remember. Jillian shifts.

"It's getting louder!"

"I know!"

CRASH! He jumps. Jillian grabs tighter.

"What was that?!"

"I don't know!" *SLAM!* They hear voices, but can't make them out. Sounds muffled by the hum and swishing. *THUD!*

Neil listens for movement outside the door. He opens his eyes, but no good. Pitch black. Covers ears. Head throbs.

Unsafe. Loud. Constant. Shaking. Crying.
CRASH
BANG
SLAM
SCREAM

THE AFTERMATH

<u>The Spencers</u>

What time is it? Is it over? What happened? Jon's phone died during the night and he had no idea how long they'd been in the storm cellar. He shifted in the darkness and immediately felt stiff. He wanted to stretch, but had no room.

He moved carefully up the stairs. His ankle still hurt from the fall. He reached the top of the stairs and pushed the storm cellar door open slightly. When nothing happened, he pushed the door open all the way. Everything looked fine. The truck was there as was the garage. *Things look safe*, he thought.

"How does it look?" Tracy whispered. He turned to see her leaning towards him.

"It looks good so far," he whispered. "I'm gonna go look outside. I need to stretch too."

"Be careful." Laura shifted and sat up.

"What time is it?" she asked. Jon went back down.

"Don't know yet," Jon said. "You okay?"

"Meh. Didn't sleep well. It's really cramped in here."

"Yeah," Jon said. He rubbed his neck. "Not a five-star hotel, that's for sure."

"Lisa seems to have slept pretty well." They looked at her. She wasn't making any movements. They smiled.

"You gonna go check the inside of the house?" Jon asked.

"Yeah," Tracy said. "I'll do that."

"All right," Jon said. He stepped into the garage. Except for the light shining through the slits of the garage door, it was dark. He opened the side door and walked outside.

The sun hurt his eyes. He looked at his watch. 7:33 am. He put his hand to his head to block the sun and looked around. The neighbors were carrying luggage and other things to their cars. Jon saw his next door neighbor Michael outside.

"Hey," Jon said.

"Oh hey," Michael said. "You guys make it okay?"

"Yeah. We stayed in the shelter all night."

"Smart. I'm gonna have to get one of those in case this

happens again."

"Yeah," Jon said. "Where are you all going?"

"South Carolina. My brother owns an inn up there and we're going to stay with him until the power comes back."

"The power's still out?"

"Oh man. Guess you guys haven't heard?" Jon shook his head. "Oh yeah. Whole area is out. No clue when it's gonna be back either. Some say a few days. Some say a few weeks. I don't know about you, but we're getting' out of here. Just seems crazy to wait around for power to come back when you could just go somewhere else and get what you need."

"I hear you," Jon said. "They really said 'weeks'?"

"Yup. Dunno if it's gonna be that bad, but there's no telling."

"You're right." Jon looked around. Now he understood why people were leaving.

"Well, hey, we gotta get on the road. You guys be safe wherever you go, okay?"

"Yeah. Thanks. You too." They shook hands and Jon walked away. He entered the side door and into the house.

"There's no power," Tracy said almost immediately.

"I know," Jon said and told her what Michael said.

"Weeks?"

"That's what he said."

"But...weeks? Can it be that bad?"

"I don't know, babe. I didn't think the storms could be as bad as they were saying and see where that got us."

"Well, that's never happened before. Of course we were suspicious. Why...how is it out for that long?"

"Honey, I don't know. I do know our neighbors and packing up and going somewhere. Michael said they're going to South Carolina to stay with his brother."

"They're all leaving?"

"Yup."

"But...are we gonna do that?"

"I don't know. I think it'd be a good idea, though."

"Come on, Jon. Where are we gonna go?"

"We could stay with your parents."

"Jon, my parents can't take us in for weeks and weeks. They...they're older and I really don't think we should put that kind of burden on them."

"Well, we could stay with my parents, but the cemetery caretaker smells funny and doesn't like football." Tracy stared at him and he panicked. Maybe it wasn't the best time for a joke of that color. She smiled.

"You're terrible." Jon smiled.

"Want me to call Gran and Pop or do you?" he asked.

"You can call them," Tracy said. "I'm gonna go check on the girls. They both went upstairs after you left."

"Oh, is your phone charged?"

"No. It died last night."

"It's all right. I'll go out to the truck and charge it."

"Just use the landline."

"Can't. All our phones are cordless."

"Of course. Why didn't we think of that?" Jon shrugged and went in the garage to his truck. He climbed in and plugged his phone into the charger. It charged without having the truck on so he didn't have to lift the garage door. He waited for his phone to boot.

"Hey Jon," Tracy said.

"Yeah?"

"Does that mean the security system is down too?"

"Yeah. It does." Tracy nodded.

"Okay," she said. "Let me know what they say." She left the garage and walked upstairs. The girls went right up to their rooms after she woke them up. She still hadn't been upstairs yet and didn't know what to expect. She walked down the hall to their rooms.

"Hey, girls," she said. "Everyone okay in here?"

"No," Laura said.

"I guess," Lisa said.

"Did anything get damaged?"

"No," Laura said. "But there's no power and my phone is dead. I can't see if anyone else is okay."

"Well, I'm sure they are. You can charge it in the truck and see then."

"In the truck?" Lisa said. "Are we going somewhere?"

"Well," Tracy said. "I think so. Right now your dad is downstairs talking to Gran and Pop to see if we can come and stay with them a few days."

"Why are we leaving?" Laura asked.

"Because Dad talked with the neighbors. They said power is out all over the place and they don't know how long it will take for it to get back up."

"Wow…"

"Yup. So we thought it would be a better idea to go stay somewhere until the power comes back." The girls pondered this.

"How will we know when the power is back?" Jon entered.

"I'll be checking the security cameras online," Jon said. They turned to look at him. "Once the power is back, they'll turn back on and we can see."

"What did they say?" Tracy asked.

"They said that was fine and they were happy to open the doors to Laura and Lisa and we were welcome too." Tracy laughed.

"Yeah, right. All right. Guess we all better get packing." Tracy and Jon left the room.

"Do you want to use my phone?" Lisa asked Laura. "It's still pretty charged. I turned it off last night after the power went out and forgot to turn it back on."

"No," Laura said. "That's okay. I'll just charge it in the car."

"Okay. I'm gonna go pack."

"Let me know if you need any help," Laura said.

Ryan Peterson

The silence caused his ears to ring. He opened his eyes in disbelief. The sun peeked through his windows. He pushed the covers back, sat up, and placed his feet on the plywood floor. He looked for his house shoes but realized in the hustle last night he forgot them in the old part of the house. He looked out the window at the brightest blue sky he'd ever seen.

He tried turning on the small lamp in his room. Still nothing. He sat on his bed and turn on his phone. He'd worried it would die during the night if the power stayed off so he left it off. He watched the screen go through its motions and he wondered what time it was. The sun was still rising so it couldn't have been too early, but it was definitely later than he usually got up. The eerie stillness of the air caused his ringing to grow louder. His phone beeped at him. Still no signal. There was plenty of battery left so he didn't turn it off. For some reason, it wasn't showing the time. He got dressed.

There were no sounds or signs anyone in the other part of the house was awake. He walked around the hall and down the stairs.

"LOOK WHO'S UP!" He stumbled and almost lost his footing on the next steps. Mom stood at the window that connected the two portions of the house. "About time you woke up."

"Yeah," he said. He cleared some of the sleep away from his throat. "What time is it?"

"About 7 or so. Dad left early this morning to go get gas. He managed to get a battery-powered radio working and heard some of the reports. Seems some tornadoes came through yesterday and took out a large part of the power lines connected to Browns Ferry."

"The nuclear plant?"

"Uh-huh. Kinda crazy it took out so many, but they said yesterday was the worst tornado outbreak in history. I'm not sure I agree since I remember the big outbreak in the 70s, but I suppose it's possible."

"Did they say how many?"

"Nope, but most of North Alabama is without power right now. Seems it's pretty bad."

"You said Dad was getting fuel?"

"Yeah. For the generator. He's hoping we'll get enough power to support us a little until this gets fixed. I think he's expecting we'll be without power for a few days."

"How'd the people broadcast on the radio if there's no power?"

"He tuned into some station in Birmingham. They got hit pretty hard too, but they still have power in most places. I don't know when he'll be back."

"Do we have anything for breakfast?"

"We still have some milk and cereal so you should be good for that at least. We used as much ice as we could to keep it fresh."

"Sounds good to me." He turned to walk outside.

"Oh, by the way," she said. He looked at her.

"What?" She smiled.

"Happy birthday." He chuckled.

"Yeah, thank you."

"Hey, it could be worse, right? We didn't get any major damage from the storm so I think that's a good thing."

"Yeah, I guess. How long has Dad been gone?" She pursed her lips.

"I'm not sure," she said. "It's been at least an hour or so. Power is out everywhere so there's no telling where he had to go."

"Did he call?"

"Why? Do you have signal?" He shook his head. "Strange."

"How are the grandparents? Has anyone checked on them?"

"The twins are up there with them right now. Your Dad went up there to get some gas cans to fill them up as well. Not sure how many he got so that might take him awhile. Will you go up there and get your brothers? I need their help."

"Okie dokie. Do we need to give the grandparents anything?" he asked.

"I don't think so," she said. "Just get the twins to come home and we'll be good I think."

"Okie dokie," he said, and he walked outside.

A strange coolness brushed against him. Everything outside seemed hushed and still. There was a breeze just light enough to ruffle the trees. It seemed like something out of a picture book. The colors were brighter than usual. Everything seemed to be much stronger and brighter than yesterday. He walked through the front yard and looked around. There was little evidence anything bad had happened. At most, he could see a few limbs had fallen, but those came from old trees. He walked to the road and began going up the hill.

The pasture to the left had no cows in it today. Normally, the cows would all be staring at him as they tried to figure out where he came from and why he was there. Ryan figured they were still locked up until they were sure nothing had fallen and messed up the fences. He walked up the hill and looked at the trees towering above it. None of them seemed to have fallen or been damaged. They'd lost a lot of leaves which now covered the road. He walked into the driveway and saw his cousin Max's car. He walked up to the door and entered.

"Hello? Anyone home?" The twins came around the corner with Max.

"There you are!" Ken said. "Did you sleep through everything?"

"Pretty much," he said.

"Happy birthday," Max said. "Kind of a strange way to celebrate it."

"Believe me, I know. How are things in Madison?"

"They're okay. We're without power so we're not sure what we're gonna do."

"Is everyone without power?"

"Oh yeah," Max said. "It's a mess from here to Madison. Lights are out and people have no idea how to drive when the lights aren't working. I saw three accidents just on my way here."

"That's just crazy."

"Yeah. It's a four-way stop, people. Not that difficult. But they were just going through it like they had a green light."

"Good grief," Ryan said. His grandfather entered the room.

"Good mornin'," he said. "Nice to see you survived that bad weather we all had." He spoke in a slow, deep Southern drawl that showed some exhaustion from the night before.

"Yeah. I actually slept through it all. I'm still surprised we don't have power or anything."

"Last your dad said was most of North Alabama is without power. They're probably tryin' to get everything at the plant all fixed and what have you."

"How're y'all doing?"

"Oh, fine fine. We made it through the night and are just trying to get things together and all. Gotta make sure we got enough food so we don't starve." He let out a rough laugh. "Wouldn't be the best thing if we survived the storm but didn't have food to eat."

"Oh yeah. Hey, did Dad go get gas for you?"

"Yeah. He, uh, came up early this morning to check on things here and said he was goin' up to Athens to try and get some gas if they had it there."

"That's 30 minutes away!"

"He might've decided it was easier to go all the way up there and look or just figured there was nothin' around here to go see. No telling."

"Yeah," Ryan said. "But I need Ken and Brandon. Mom wants us all at home to help her with something." The twins dropped their shoulders.

"Aww."

"Do we hafta?" Ryan nodded.

"Yeah, you do. Let's go. We'll see you later, Papaw. Give Mamaw our best."

"Will do. She's in the bedroom right now."

"Okie dokie. See you, Max."

"See ya. Hey, how's Hannah?" Ryan stopped.

"I don't know, but I think she's okay. I mean, she was all the way down there so she should be fine, right?" Max's face went a pale as he shook his head.

"Tuscaloosa was hit pretty hard."

"What?"

"Yeah. I think it's pretty bad down there. You might wanna check on her." Ryan swallowed past the burning sensation forming in his throat. How could he have known? He hadn't heard anything or been told anything about what happened in Tuscaloosa.

"Thanks," he muttered. "Come on, guys. Let's go." He walked quickly out of the house and down the driveway.

"Sthlow down!" Brandon said, but Ryan couldn't. He would stop every few seconds and wait for them to catch up, and then he would walk again. They did this all the way back home.

Ryan was completely on autopilot. It hadn't occurred to him she could be hurt or worse. Why hadn't he thought of her when he woke up? He needed to find some way to get in touch with her so he could find out what really happened. He saw Dad's car in the driveway and did his best not to pick up the pace. When they got to the driveway, he took off running.

"You guys can make it from here," he said to the twins. He entered the addition and went straight to the window. His parents stood there talking.

"Hey," he said. They jumped.

"Hey," Dad said. "You okay?"

"How are things out there?" he asked.

"Well. They ain't good," Dad said. "I-65 northbound was backed up a long ways. Gas stations have limits and some have spiked their prices."

"Spiked their prices?"

"Yeah."

"How high?"

"$1 or $2 extra. Kinda like when those hurricanes went through the gulf a few years ago. Nothing from here to the exit has power. It looks like some of Limestone County along the Dawson City exit has power, but not everything. Most places are shut down, but that could be because of the weather. I found some old Mom and Pop shops I remember from when I worked up there and got gas from them. We should be good for a while."

"Did you have signal?"

"I did when I got to the exit, but it was pretty spotty. I think there's a tower in Dawson City with power, but I didn't want to drive all the way in there. Streets are bad enough outside the city."

"Are they really?"

"Oh yeah. The exit intersection has two accidents on it right now. People don't know how to drive without traffic lights."

"Yeah. That's what Max was saying."

"Max?" Mom asked.

"Yeah. He's up with the grandparents. Said they don't have power in Madison either but he wanted to check on us so he drove down."

"That was nice of him," Mom said. "Did he say if he would stop by?" Ryan shook his head.

"Hey, I need to drive towards Dawson City and get signal so I can call Hannah."

"Now?" Dad asked.

"Yeah. Max said Tuscaloosa was hit really bad and I have to make sure she's okay."

"They were saying on the radio it was pretty bad but didn't give any details."

"Okay. I'll try to get where I can get signal but won't go too far."

"Good. Yeah, there's signal right after the bridge but I didn't stay long enough because I saw there was no power." Ryan went upstairs to get his keys and wallet. His thoughts surrounded Hannah.

Maybe she's okay. She's got to be okay. He grabbed his stuff, went downstairs, and out the door. He jumped in his car and almost forgot to put his seatbelt on. His Dad came around the house and waved him down. He rolled the window down.

"Hey, be careful. Traffic really *is* that bad out there. People aren't watching what they're supposed to be doing. Just take your time and don't rush anything, okay?"

"Don't worry, I got it," Ryan said before rolling up his window and backing up. He was really worried now and wanted to get to her and find out how she was. He pulled out of the driveway and turned left. He reached the end of the road and looked both ways. He thought about all the routes he could take and what would be the best way to get there. He thought about going to Rosetta Falls and trying to get signal there.

With Rosetta Falls being such a small town, traffic probably wouldn't be as bad and he could safely make it in and out of town. *What if they don't have signal?* He looked at his gas gauge. Just over half. Even with that in mind, he didn't know how long it would be until power was back and gas stations would be up and running with normal prices again. He turned towards Dawson City.

He pulled his phone out of his pocket and kept it in his hand. *How could I have been so stupid and not thought of her? Why wasn't that the first thing? Just a simple "How is she?" was all.* He felt horrible she wasn't the first thing that came to mind. He tried to shake it off and focus on the drive.

There were tree limbs down on both sides of the road. People were outside their homes gathering trash, limbs, and other things blown by the wind. Ryan watched as neighbors worked together to get their yards cleaned up. He reached the main highway and stopped.

There was no traffic, which was unusual. He looked at the gas station across the street and saw it was locked up with two big signs in front of it.

"NO POWER!" and "STAY STRONG!" He checked both ways before turning towards Dawson City. His phone stayed silent. He checked it to make sure it was on vibrate and put his attention back to driving.

He drove over the hill and saw more limbs down in ditches and leaves spread out across the road. He wondered if people had already been out on the roads in search of gas. He checked his phone again. Nothing. He wished he could get in touch with her already. He took a deep breath and tried to relax.

He came to the first intersection with lights out. He treated it like a four-way stop, then proceeded. He could see the bridge for I-65 now. He was almost there. He pulled up to the first exit intersection. The truck across from him was already stopped and waiting to see if Ryan stopped. Ryan waved him on and the truck got on the interstate. Ryan moved through to the next light. He reached it and stopped. There was no one there so he started to go through. Out of the corner of his right eye, he saw something blue barreling down the exit ramp.

He's not going to stop! Ryan thought. He started to zoom through the light, but realized he couldn't make it in time. He wanted to back up, but there was nothing he could do. He slammed on his brakes and shut his eyes tight. The car's horn sounded and Ryan opened his eyes. The blue car's tires squealed as the driver tried to stop. He was going too fast. He swerved through the light as far out in front of Ryan as he could. He entered some of the median then tried swerving back to head the way Ryan came.

Ryan looked at the driver, who flipped him off. Ryan shook his head and drove through the light. He pulled into the parking lot of a restaurant and went around to the back. He let out a loud sigh and realized he was both shaking and sweating. He wiped the sweat from his head and tried to calm down.

BUZZ! He jumped. *BUZZ! BUZZ! BUZZ!* His phone continued to vibrate at an alarming rate. He quickly swiped away the message notifications. "Happy Birthday" and "Are you okay?" was mostly what he saw. He went to contacts and selected Hannah.

<u>Hannah Leon</u>

She sat in her car. The parking lot was almost empty. People had left or were already heading home. She hadn't heard from anyone all morning. She tried calling friends and family, but no one answered. She didn't want to leave yet. The vibration scared her, then she realized what it was. She looked for her phone. She had dropped it. She looked all around her. The vibrations kept going. She found it and grabbed it without even bothering to see who it was.

"Hello?" she asked.

"Hey, beautiful." She started crying and heard him chuckle. "I thought that's what might happen. Are you okay?"

"No," she said. "No, I'm not. No one's called me. I can't get ahold of Jillian or anyone else. My parents aren't answering the phone. I've been terrified of what's going on outside but I can't go look. I'm just worried and nervous and upset and I'm just so glad to hear from you. I miss you so much!"

"I miss you too. I'm okay, you're okay, and I'm sure your parents are okay. Don't worry."

"But why haven't I heard from them?"

"They probably don't have signal."

"What?" There was a moment of silence. She panicked. "Hello? Are you there?"

"I'm here."

"I thought the call dropped. I was so scared."

"No, no. I'm sorry. It's my fault. I forgot you didn't know about what's going on up here." He told her about the tornadoes and Browns Ferry and the long gas lines that had people on edge. He told her about his near-death experience. She stopped crying.

"So my parents probably don't have signal?"

"I doubt it. My cousin drove down to check on us and he said they didn't have anything either and I think he lives pretty close to your family. What happened last night?" She let out a light laugh.

"Well," she said. "I tried calling you a few times, but it

said you weren't in service. Didn't even try sending me to voicemail. Just said you weren't in service. So I gave up and started to get my things together and go over to Jillian's, but I knew you didn't want me to. I tried so hard. I didn't want to be alone, but I started thinking you were right, so I stayed home at first."

"At first?" he asked.

"Uh huh. At first. But then it started getting bad quick and I didn't want to be alone anymore. I heard a commotion from the people below me and realized someone was home. I grabbed my coat, purse, and phone in case you called back, locked my apartment, and went downstairs. When they opened the door, it was a group of guys just sitting around watching something on TV. They all looked at me kinda funny. I mean, I probably looked like a mess, but they didn't seem to mind. I asked if I could come in until the storm passes. They asked if everything was okay and I said no. Ryan, they had no clue about the tornadoes."

"Seriously?"

"Seriously. I told them about it and they looked outside like I was crazy. They let me in and I stayed there until the power went out."

"When was that?"

"I don't remember," she said. "So I went back upstairs to my apartment and texted my parents and Jillian but no one responded so I just went to bed. No one was replying or messaging me or anything! It was like everyone disappeared or something!"

"Shh," Ryan said. "It's okay, now."

"Yeah," she said.

"And I'm sure everyone is fine. I haven't been able to hear anything specific, but Max said Tuscaloosa was hit pretty hard."

"Really?"

"Yeah. That's why I rushed to where I had signal quick. I wanted to make sure you weren't hurt or anything."

"Thank you, Ryan. That means a lot to me."

"I need to get home," Ryan said. "We're gonna try and get the house hooked up to a generator and have at least a little bit of power." She bit her lip and tried to keep the tears inside.

"Okay. Promise you'll call me again when you can."

"I'll try. Right now the only way I can get to you is at the Dawson City exit. I don't have signal back at the house, remember?"

"Oh. Right. Well, I'm probably gonna come home today or tomorrow. I already don't have power and I just want to be home."

"That's a good idea. You can stop by the house on your way home if you want."

"Thanks. I really want to see you. I miss you."

"I miss you too. Don't worry."

"I'll talk to you later," she said.

"Sounds good."

She hung up. She looked at the phone for a second in hopes of a text or another phone call, but got neither. She looked around as she walked back to her apartment. There was a lot of water and several limbs on the ground, but it didn't seem like what Ryan had just said. She couldn't see any damage done to her apartment or the one next to hers. The few cars around her seemed to be safe. She wondered how the damage could be so bad if she wasn't seeing anything around her. If Tuscaloosa was hit as bad as they claimed, why couldn't she see it here? Surely she hadn't dodged it all. She walked inside.

Could things really be as bad as Ryan said? Maybe she should find out.

Sharon Rogers

She put her head down on the steering wheel of her car and let out a sigh. She'd been everywhere. Nothing was open. All the grocery stores had no power. The tornadoes had left a wealth of destruction. She'd walked up to the glass doors and looked inside, but there was no one to help. She needed to get some things for Colleen. Most importantly, she needed to find some insulin. Her thoughts raced as she took a deep breath. She thought back to their morning conversation.

"Why isn't anything working?" Colleen asked.

"Because the power is out," she said.

"Well then why do I bother payin' for it if it ain't gonna work? Don't do me any good and it's a waste of money, if you ask me."

"I know, Colleen. I'm sure they're working on getting it up and going soon. Don't worry."

"I'm not worried. I grew up in a time before we had electricity all the time. We used to hafta go days without it 'cause the companies weren't set up all fancy like they are now. We'd just have to entertain ourselves as best we could 'cause that's just what you did. You probably don't understand what I'm talking about but I promise you that's how it was."

"I believe you, Colleen."

"Don't you patronize me," she said. "I didn't ask you for your sympathy. I'm just telling you a story. You just listen. You don't hafta comment on everything I say. Just listen."

"I'm sorry," she said. Anytime Colleen left her comfort zone, she grew somewhat hostile.

"Anyway, I don't know how we're supposed to keep things up and going with this. We're supposed to have visitors soon and I don't want them showing up with my house in a wreck." She got up from her chair. "It's just awful, isn't it? Nothing's clean. Dishes are piled up. How am I supposed to entertain guests when my house is in such a nasty shape?"

"I'll get it cleaned up for you," Sharon said. "Don't worry about the guests." Colleen snorted.

"'Don't worry about the guests.' Well someone hasta worry about 'em 'cause you sure ain't. How can I not worry about the guests when we don't even have food for them?"

"With the power out, it'll probably just be the two of us," she said. She did her best not to contradict Colleen's slips straight out. That could cause her anguish and shock her back into reality. Sharon didn't want that. "How about you go lie down and I'll run to the store to try and find us something, okay?"

"But we don't know what they want so that's not gonna do us any good."

"It could help though. It'd be better than what we have now, right?" She'd helped Colleen into bed and left for help.

Now she'd been to four stores and still no sign of any open. What was she going to tell Colleen? If she said none were open, Colleen would probably start talking like the world was ending or maybe have an episode. She lifted her head off the steering wheel, let out a sigh, and tried to think of something. She still had no cell signal so she couldn't call around and ask places if they had insulin. She thought about driving to Athens in hopes they would have something, but that was a decent drive and she'd already been out a while. She couldn't just leave Colleen in bed waiting on her to get back.

She pulled out a cigarette, lit it, and took a long pull. It was her car, not Colleen's, so she didn't worry about smoking in it now. She needed the fix. The stress from Colleen and the tornadoes was a lot to handle. She wanted to take her mind off things for a moment or two. As she exhaled, she wished she had a cup of coffee. Nothing was more satisfying than a cigarette and cup of black coffee with two sugars. The cigarette burned up faster than she wanted and she needed to get going. She flipped the butt out the window.

She cranked the car and listened to the static from her radio. She flipped through radio stations in hopes of finding a medical place or some updates playing. She needed something more than her worries to fill the silence.

Nothing. She wondered if maybe her car wasn't close enough to pick up any of the stations. Or maybe their power was so low she wouldn't be able to get any of them. That was possible. Could they cover their usual range with a backup generator or were they stuck to a certain distance? She drove to University Drive and looked both ways.

She wanted to get insulin and other things, but didn't know if anything was still open. There was the off-chance those places were out of power too. She headed towards Colleen's place. She needed to think about what she was going to tell Colleen.

She could tell the truth and say the power was out all over town, but she didn't want to do that. There was no way of knowing what kind of impact that would have on Colleen. She could take it and be understanding or she could get worked up over all the uncertainty. Sharon rubbed her head. It was a big decision. To lie to someone you love to protect them or tell them the cold truth without knowing the outcome.

Sharon weighed the possibilities. What would happen is she told Colleen? Colleen would probably start talking about how reliable things used to be and how there's no pride in work anymore. Then she'd think of something bad that once happened when the power was out, leading her to worry about something bad happening now. Sharon would do her best to calm her down and convince her everything would be okay. She knew she didn't want to deal with this, but at the same time felt obligated to be honest. She came to an intersection and stopped.

Ahead of her, she saw a gas station with many people standing outside it yelling at each other and trying to maneuver into one of the free pumps. There was a sign clearly stating the gas station only had enough gas for a few people, but the line ran down the long stretch of road. Sharon had never seen anything like that. People were almost fighting just to get some gas.

She drove on through the intersection carefully to ensure no one was trying to cut her off or get there first. While she didn't want to leave Colleen all alone for too long, being hit at an intersection would not have been good either. She needed to be as safe as possible. She tried the radio again. Still nothing. *How long is it going to take to get them up?*

She continued to stop and go with each traffic light. Sometimes she saw a car already at the intersection waiting to see if she would stop. Sharon had always had the small fear of being hit by someone as they were driving, but hadn't been as scared as she was now. She realized how thankful she was for traffic lights.

She passed the dozens of restaurants and stores all with empty parking lots and no lights. She saw a few people pulling up to gas stations and looking around to see if anyone was there. She turned off University Drive onto the little road leading to Colleen's house. She still had no idea what to say. The woman would probably be in her bed waiting for an explanation Sharon didn't have. She turned into the driveway, turned off the car, and sat there for a moment. She needed something. Colleen could ask a simple question and knock down her lies. She had no choice. She got out of the car, locked it, shut the door, and walked to the house. It was only a few steps, but if felt like so much more. She knocked on the door before entering.

"Hey, Colleen. It's just me," she said. Sharon shut the door behind her and walked through the house. "Colleen?" There was no answer. Her pulse quickened and her mouth went dry. She moved as quickly and quietly as she could. She didn't want to startle Colleen if she just didn't hear her, but at the same time no response was a bad response. She reached Colleen's bedroom door and carefully pushed it open. "Colleen?" she asked. Colleen was on her back in bed. Her eyes were shut and she was shaking her head.

"I don't..." she said. "I don't...tell them I don't want any..."

"It's just me," Sharon said. "It's just Sharon."

"Tell those salesmen to leave my house alone. I don't want to sell. I'm not ready to sell," Sharon entered the room now and moved to the bed. She sat next to Colleen.

"Miss Colleen?" she said. Colleen opened her eyes. It was as if she was looking through Sharon. Her eyes seemed to be looking beyond the room and outside of it. Her pupils were dilated. Sharon picked up the small towel from the nightstand and wiped Colleen's mouth with it. "Can you hear me?" Colleen blinked as if being pulled from a daydream. She saw Sharon.

"There you are," she said. "I've been waiting on you. I didn't think you were going to show up today." Sharon started to respond and waited a moment. She didn't want to answer incorrectly and perhaps cause some trouble.

"Oh," she said. "You know me. I couldn't miss the chance to spend time with you."

"Oh, well that's sweet. How are you doing?"

"I'm doing pretty good. How're you?"

"Oh, just fine and dandy for an old woman," she said with a breathy laugh. "When you get to be my age every day is a fine and dandy one." Sharon smiled.

"Do you want to get up?" Colleen paused before responding. She seemed to be mulling it over.

"Yeah, I reckon I better. No sense in staying in bed all day. I need to use the commode anyway." Sharon got off the bed and held Colleen's arms as she moved herself out of the bed. Sharon put both hands around the small arm and felt of it.

"Are you feeling okay, Miss Colleen?" she asked.

"Well yes. Why do you ask?"

"Just wanted to make sure," she said, but she could feel how warm Colleen was. The small woman never felt warm because of her poor circulation. Sharon prayed it wasn't a fever. She tried to think about what was in the house. She began getting angry with herself.

I should've tried to go to Athens, she thought. *I should've gotten insulin and whatever else I needed while I could. Now what am I going to do?* Her mind raced. Even if she had gone to Athens, there was no guarantee she would've found what she needed. She would've just gotten home and found Colleen sick and needing medicine. She needed to focus. She needed to help Colleen sit up. She shifted her weight to counter Colleen and helped her put her feet on the floor. Colleen took a few deep breaths.

"What's that?" she asked.

"What's what?"

"That...that smell. I can't tell what it is but I can smell it." The hair on Sharon's neck stood up. She wasn't expecting to be this close to Colleen until her clothes had aired out a little. She tried not to panic. "Must have been those salesmen. They always have a smell about them. Just wish they'd leave me alone." Sharon sighed.

"I know what you mean," she said. "Maybe they'll stay away now."

"Ha. Not likely." Colleen didn't move.

"Miss Colleen?" Sharon asked. Colleen seemed to be looking off again.

"My daddy smoked a pipe," she said. "He...he always smoked it on the porch in the evening after dinner when we were supposed to be in bed. Sometimes, when I had nightmares or something, I'd go out there to him and would find him. The smell was...was so different. I really liked it. I liked it a lot. It had a strong smell about it that wasn't dirty. I would go to him crying and he...he would take me and hold me in his lap while he smoked. There was nothing quite like it, really. But he was always there for me and rocked me to sleep. So many times."

"That sounds nice," Sharon said.

"What does, dear?" Colleen asked.

"About your father."

"What about my father?"

"With the pi-" Sharon stopped. She realized what was happening. "I was just thinking he must have been a nice man."

"Oh he was," Colleen said. "He was such a nice man. I really do miss him." Sharon waited for a minute to see what would happen. When Colleen didn't continue, Sharon moved.

"Wait," Sharon said. "Miss Colleen I forgot to set the seat up."

"You don't have it all ready?"

"No. You're moving faster than I expected this morning." Colleen chuckled.

"Guess I must really have to go."

"Guess so," Sharon said with a pained smile and walked into the bathroom. The toilet sat too low for Colleen. Colleen still liked taking care of herself in the bathroom and Sharon didn't want to take that away from her.

She moved quickly to the bathroom and tried to turn the lights on out of habit. She flipped the switch back down and turned on the flashlight she'd put in there the night before. She took her jacket off and smelled her sweatshirt under it. She couldn't tell if it smelled or not. She wasn't wearing an undershirt today because it was warm but she didn't want Colleen to suspect anything. She decided it wasn't important. She turned from the mirror. In the tub was an elevated chair with a large hole. A cylinder was in the hole to ensure all the contents didn't get in the floor. She checked to ensure it was clean. She lifted the seat up and carefully placed it over the toilet. She lined it up and walked back into the bedroom.

Colleen appeared to have no strength to lift herself. Sharon worried about leaving her in the bathroom alone.

"All right," she said. "It's ready when you are." She lifted Colleen, who now felt warmer. Sharon struggled against the worrying pounding her head. She didn't have time to be worried about anything and it would do Colleen no good to worry. Colleen didn't realize she felt bad and would probably have trouble concentrating, then start yelling and arguing and would've become unruly and been much more difficult to handle. They moved slowly towards the bathroom. Colleen had most of her weight on Sharon now which was a bad sign. Sharon tried to walk like they usually did so Colleen wouldn't suspect anything.

They reached the door and Sharon awkwardly tried to maneuver herself around Colleen so it would feel like she wasn't helping as much. They entered the bathroom. Sharon looked at Colleen in the mirror and saw the sweat rushing down her face. She got her to the chair.

"Do you need any help with your pajamas?" she asked then wished she hadn't. Colleen's pride meant a lot to her.

"I...I think I do. I'm not...not feeling as strong as...I usually do."

"That's fine," Sharon said. "I'm happy to help when you need me."

"I know you are," she said. "You're always so nice to help me. I...I can't th-thank you enough some...sometimes for all you do."

"Oh, don't worry about that." She got the pajama bottoms down and helped Colleen onto the chair. It was strange to her. Colleen was always adamant about her independence. There were things she wanted to do herself to prove to herself she was strong. Sharon tore some toilet paper off the roll and handed it to her. "I'll be right outside when you need me, okay?" Colleen nodded. Sharon did her best to walk out calmly. She felt a lump in her throat. "Hey Colleen?"

"Yes, dear?"

"Do...do you want me to stay with you?" There was no response. Sharon started to shut the door.

"That would be nice, actually." Sharon let out a sigh and tried to casually re-enter. She felt the lump grow as she tried to suppress it and keep her emotions in check.

"I just thought maybe I'd be here if you needed anything."

"I don't think I'll be needing anything. It's just so dark in here. Can't stand being in the dark by myself for too long."

"Gets kinda scary, doesn't it?"

"Not scary. Oh no, young lady. Just don't like being in the dark too long. You keep blinking and nothing changes and I just don't like that."

"I guess that makes sense. I wouldn't like that either."

"We used to have an outhouse and it would get so dark out there. I hated having to go in that thing at night. I tried to get out there and use it before one of my brothers, but they knew I didn't like the dark. Sometimes they would all be lined up in front of me and wait until it was dark enough. They'd just all walk away when they thought it was time. Some of them wouldn't even use the bathroom."

"That's not nice."

"That's just how brothers are, dear. They can be a real pain sometimes."

"Did they always do stuff like that to you?"

"Oh, yes. When you're the only girl among a bunch of boys, you gotta learn to fight for your own right and do whatever you gotta do. That's why I got so tough and outlived 'em all. They just didn't know they were gonna end up making me so strong."

"And you certainly are strong, Miss Colleen."

"I think I'm about done, dear," Colleen said.

"Okay. Give me just a second." Sharon opened the door to bring in some light to help her see. She picked up the toilet paper and handed it to Colleen. She turned around to fiddle with her hands to give Colleen some privacy.

"There we go."

"You want some food?"

"No," Colleen said. "I think I wanna go lay down for a little longer." Sharon nodded.

"Okay. Let's get you back in bed then." She helped Colleen off the seat, dressed her, and they shuffled back into the bathroom.

"Sometimes this walk just seems so long," Colleen said.

"But that just makes it better when we make it, right?" She asked.

"I suppose so. Makes it harder to wanna go, though." Sharon chuckled.

"Well, don't worry about that. I'll always be here to help when you need it." Sharon lifted her back into the bed and pulled the bedding over her. She brushed some of Colleen's hair out of her face and felt her head. "How's that feel?"

"That feels mighty good. I think I'm gonna take a little nap, if that's okay."

"I think that's a good idea. I'll just go clean up in the bathroom, okay?" There was no response. Colleen's eyes were closed. Sharon kissed her fingers and placed them on Colleen's cheek before leaving to clean the bathroom.

<u>Hannah Leon</u>

Hannah gathered her things. No one had contacted her other than Ryan and everything had been quiet. People were probably recovering from the weather and staying in their homes. Some may not have power back yet and their phones could be dead. Some could just be so swamped with getting in touch with family they were too overwhelmed. Any number of reasons were possible. She smiled in the mirror as best she could and walked outside.

A slight chill hit her. Not cold, but stillness. It wasn't silent, but quieter than usual. She couldn't place what was missing. She locked her door behind her and walked to her car. No one was outside. The parking had been full the night before and was now almost empty. People were leaving and trying to get home as quick as they could. Maybe they were just being crazy or maybe they were doing the right thing. She didn't know. Something about just getting up and leaving bothered her. She didn't want to be on the road during the mad rush from Tuscaloosa to wherever. I-20 was probably backed up for miles and I-65 was probably worse. She got in her car and turned the key to start the radio.

The station she usually listened to was static. She went through her memory keys but found nothing. She finally pressed "Seek" in hopes something would show up. She got it.

"...and do whatever they can to remain safe. People of Tuscaloosa County. We are asking everyone to please remain in their homes if they are livable and to avoid driving on the major roads. McFarland is currently closed in the sections hit worst by the tornadoes. Crews are working those areas and helping families as best they can. Some areas are without power and are currently being serviced. We are doing everything we can to get things up and running here. Again, we are asking everyone to please remain in their homes and do whatever they can to remain safe."

Hannah sat there as the broadcast repeated itself. *It couldn't have been that bad, right? How could the area have been hit so hard? Had the weather been worse than they expected? How bad was the storm anyway?* The questions continued. She wasn't sure about what Ryan told her. He'd heard it from someone who heard it from someone and so on. She looked up and down her road. No cars were out right now. What was she supposed to do? The staleness of her apartment could be felt in her car. She didn't want to stay there right now. It didn't feel right. She got out of her car, locked it, and began walking.

At first, she had no destination. She wasn't going anywhere to get anything. She wasn't trying to see the damage first hand. In fact, all she really wanted was to walk. Maybe that would help her take her mind off of things. She still hadn't heard from her parents. She hadn't heard from her friends. Maybe her apartment was preventing her from getting any kind of signal. Stranger things had happened. She walked to the entrance of her apartment complex and looked both ways. One led back towards other complexes probably containing more empty parking lots and apartments. The other led her towards I-20/59 and McFarland. She looked towards the apartments.

Trees were missing and the sky was much more visible now. It shocked her to see so much sky looking behind her where it had never been before. She tried not to think about it. If a few trees down was the worst of their problems, she could relax. But that didn't make sense. McFarland was the major road to Tuscaloosa. She couldn't imagine them shutting down parts of it just for some downed trees. She decided to head towards McFarland and see if there was anything there.

The road was what she expected. There were a few office buildings and some apartments along her way, but no cars in the parking lots. People weren't at work. While her small corner wasn't the most thriving part of Tuscaloosa, it was still pretty busy. With it being a college town, many places revolved their schedule around the university and what went on there. But even when the university was shut down during things like Christmas, the town went on. People went to work and did their jobs. Now, though, the only ones she could see were the people trying to escape.

She could see the back of the grocery store. Employees were doing their best to get things out of the store and loaded up onto trucks. Dozens were moving things along like an assembly line into the truck. There was yelling and arguing as things were almost dropped or people moved too slowly.

"Well, we gotta get it all out. No choice."

"It's ain't like we ain't tryin', chief."

"This stuff is startin' to smell bad."

"It ain't smellin' as bad as some of our workers."

"Hey. You called us up here and wanted us here to unload."

"And you need to quit yappin' and get back to loadin' that truck."

"How long they'd say the power'd be out?"

"No clue. Tornadoes hit pretty hard. Could be a day or could be longer."

Hannah did her best to look like she wasn't interested in what was being said. As she began passing them, she moved a little closer to them.

"Can't believe they all hit through here."

"I can't believe down McFarland. I never seen such bad traffic in my life."

"You can't even get here easily like you used to."

"Aw, ain't that the truth? I was thinkin' it couldn't be that bad, but it was. They got you turnin' way before you get to the hit areas and stuff."

"I just don't understand how they couldn't even let us know about this thing before it got here. Why can't they just-"

She was out of earshot then. She looked at the side of the store. It didn't appear to be damaged. She left the street and walked diagonally across the side parking lot. There were no cars there which wasn't unreasonable but a little strange. She could see the corner of the building. She wasn't expecting the store to have power. She just hoped there would be some people there to let her know what happened.

The sky still showed no signs of storms or tornadoes. There was no wind blowing. No sense of disturbance. As she neared the front of the store, she could hear a low hum. She wasn't sure what it was at first. Just a continuing hum that seemed to build as she neared the building. She leaned forward to listen more, but the sound was still foggy.

Did they have generators going? Did they have a little bit of power to keep a few things going until they unloaded stuff from the back? Her pace quickened as the possibilities entered her mind. She thought about what all could be there and what all she needed to take back with her. She could use some cold cuts or something to tie her over for a bit. The sound changed. It wasn't a hum anymore. She could tell it was voices. Many voices. They were all chattering together at once with no distinction between any of them. She walked around the corner.

In front of the store was a large crowd of people trying to get inside. They were talking, arguing, and yelling with each other about conditions of the store, the town, the roads, their homes, and businesses throughout the town. Hannah couldn't keep track of all the places mentioned and did her best to listen, but the voices continued overlapping. Stronger voices over-powered weaker ones and were then overcome by people trying to make their voices stronger. She didn't see enough cars in the parking lot for all the people there. She kept walking. There was no point in joining the crowd by herself and yelling and screaming with them when it obviously was doing no good. She also worried something would happen to her if she joined the massive mob all by herself.

She moved through the parking lot towards the interstate exit for McFarland. I-20/59 ran right through Tuscaloosa on its way into Mississippi. During football season, the westbound side was a mess. Locals took back roads to get into Tuscaloosa to watch the games or get something they needed. People started showing up for football games early in the week and moved on to the next game location as soon as it was time. But now eastbound lane was busy.

She could see the ramp leading to the interstate was backed up. Cars were inching up the ramps as police tried to move people out of the way and keep traffic flowing. Hannah saw the traffic lights were out and people weren't paying attention to the police. She kept going in hopes to get a better look, but the cars began blocking off sections of the road. She saw the police get upset with one driver who almost hit another. She wondered how many tickets had been given out at that intersection alone.

She got closer to them and could see the police had everyone stopped at that moment until the situation cleared up. One police officer stood in the middle of the road stopping all traffic while the other went up to the stopped car and said something to the driver. She couldn't hear any of it, but could tell the officer was unhappy. She reached the intersection and looked both ways. The officers were both busy trying to keep traffic under control and didn't notice her. She walked to the overpass and continued onto McFarland. She listened to the people as she walked.

"I can't believe this. How can traffic get so congested in one day?"

"I told you we shoulda left earlier. Don't wanna say I told ya, but I did."

"There ain't no way we gonna make it back to Birmingham in time now. Too many people not knowin' how to drive ain't helpin'."

"How come they don't just let us through so we can get where we need to? That idiot's done held everyone up 'cause he was in a hurry and didn't wanna just listen to the policeman."

"I like her idea. Maybe we should just walk." Hannah cringed at the last comment and tried not to pay attention anymore. She didn't like people talking about her.

McFarland was the busiest road in Tuscaloosa. It was the primary way to get anywhere in the town. People were angry about the road conditions, yet still driving. She could see drivers blocking intersections and trying to leave. She reached the other side of the overpass and looked for traffic coming down the exit ramp. Nothing. She realized no one had come down the whole time she'd been walking. She turned to look at the cops. They'd moved the car and had traffic on McFarland moving a little. The police still hadn't noticed her or just didn't care. She turned to check the ramp again and continued walking.

The stores were empty and without power. She saw some places empty for the first time. Across the street she saw a gas station with a big sign saying "We have no power so we have no gas." People were probably gonna be stranded on the interstate because they used up all their gas to get somewhere. Maybe places east towards Birmingham were open and could provide gas. That would make the drive even worse considering how bad traffic would be at each exit.

She really wanted to go home, but knew she needed to wait until traffic wasn't horrible anymore. She imagined herself getting all annoyed and freaked out because someone hit their brakes in front of her and scared her. She imagined people behind her not paying attention and hitting her.

The Spencers

Jon stared out the window. The clouds were gone and the sky was clear, but he could see the damage. The tornado touched down at a house in a subdivision behind them. He could see where the roof was missing and maybe cars along the way were gone too. He couldn't take his eyes off the house and its gaping roof. He wondered what happened to the family.

"Hey," Tracy said.

"Hey," he said without looking away.

"The girls are almost packed. How're things in here?"

"Almost done. Just gotta get my shaving kit packed."

"You okay?" He didn't immediately respond. He was still wondering if what he saw the night before was real. He felt her touch him arm.

"Yeah. Sorry, babe. Just a little disoriented, I suppose." Tracy looked out the window at the house.

"Quite a mess, isn't it?"

"Yeah it is. I'm not sure if they're okay or not."

"If they were in their basement or on the first floor, I would think so," she said. "They might be hurt or something, but they might be okay."

"You think?" She shrugged.

"I don't know," she said. "Do you think we should check on them?"

"Huh?" he said. The thought hadn't occurred to him. "I'm not sure. I mean, I don't think it's necessary, right? I mean, their neighbors are already over there and maybe the emergency units."

"I don't see any lights," she said.

"Well, there's a lot between us, including the rubble. Probably just blockin' our view."

"You're right. And surely they're okay," she said. "There's always hope, right?"

"Right. I guess we shouldn't count that out." He turned away. "You think your parents are still good with us staying with them for a while?"

"Yes, Jon. Just like I've told you the last few times."

"I just want to be sure. I mean, I know what they said, but there's nothing wrong with wanting to be sure."

"There is after the 50th time you've asked." He rolled his eyes at her. "I'm gonna get the girls to start loading up their things."

"Sounds good," he said. "I'll finish packing bring them down to the truck." She walked out of the room and down the hall. She looked out the windows at the neighboring houses. There were trees down and the like, but nothing as bad as the house across the way. She got to the end of the hall.

"Okay, girls. Let's get your stuff downstairs and into the truck."

"I can't wait until we have power again," Lisa said.

"Me too," Tracy said. "I miss it already."

"Me too," Laura said from her room. "Did Dad find out when it would be back on?" Tracy shook her head.

"We're just gonna go stay with Pop and Gran until it comes back on."

"They have power?"

"Yup. Dad managed to get ahold of them this morning and asked. They said the storms didn't cause any damage up there."

"That's good," Lisa said. She lifted her suitcase off the bed and set it on its rollers. "This thing is heavy."

"Well, that's good. Means you've got enough stuff in it. We aren't really sure how long we're gonna be gone."

"I need your help, Mom," Laura called from her room. "It's too heavy for me."

"Okay, I'm coming." She turned to Lisa. "You got what you need?"

"Yeah, I think so. I'll check again though just in case."

"Good," Tracy said and walked into Laura's room. Her suitcase was bulging and not wanting to close. Laura pushed down on it as hard as she could but the suitcase refused to give. Tracy smiled.

"Hey Mom," Lisa said. "I'm gonna take my stuff

downstairs now."

"Okay. Be careful."

She walked down the hall to the stairs and carefully pushed the suitcase down the stairs. She held onto the handle and made sure it only went down each individual step and not more than one at a time. The weight of the suitcase pulled her arms and made her feel stretched. She tried to lower it carefully and not move too fast. Each step led out a slight thud and she knew it was time to take another step.

She thought about the night before. She thought about how loud everything had been. She didn't think it was the sound of a tornado, but more likely the sound of the wind beating against their house. Whatever it was, it had been louder and scarier than she wanted. Her dad kept saying they were safe, but the sounds didn't make it seem so. She felt more like they were trapped. They held each other and trying not to think about the bad weather. She'd cried when the sounds got really loud. Then it went away, almost immediately. They all held each other silently. She'd looked around wondering if it was coming back but it never did. The sounds were gone and there was only a hush.

Lisa reached the bottom of the stairs and carefully pulled the suitcase down the last step. She wiped the sweat from her head. With no power, the house was becoming hot and the air a bit stale. They had doors and windows opened where they could, but it wasn't doing a good job in her opinion.

"You all right down there?" Jon called. Lisa looked up at him.

"Yeah. Just trying to catch my breath. That took forever."

"Guess I better see if Laura needs help with hers. She and Mom are probably still trying to get it on the floor or something." They both laughed. "I'll be down in a minute to help you get yours in the truck."

"Okay," she said. He walked away. She continued to pull the suitcase towards the garage. It was scary to think about the storm and what they'd been doing so she tried to put it out of her mind. She carefully walked around the puddle the refrigerator left after being off for so long and opened the door to the garage. She took a moment to recover then pulled the suitcase. In just the few seconds she was in there, she broke out in a sweat. She lowered the tailgate and took a moment to catch her breath. She wrapped her hands around the suitcase handle and counted.

"1, 2, 3!" and lifted the suitcase to the truck. She missed. She let out a sigh and started to get her dad, but changed her mind. She counted again. "1, 2, 3!" This time she made it. The sound of loading the suitcase into the truck resonated. She walked back into the house and Jon stood there.

"You okay?" he asked.

"Yeah. I'm fine. It's really hot out there. Why don't you go open the garage door?"

"That's a good idea."

"Could we move the truck out of the garage? It might be easier for us to get everything loaded up that since we'll have more room and all."

"Sounds good to me," he said. He walked out into the garage and felt the same wave of heat. He rubbed his eyes at the feeling of humidity. He walked to the garage door, flipped the bar, and manually lifted it up. As he did, he felt the cool air from outside rush in under the door. The contrast was startling, but still felt good. Jon lifted the door. The driveways for most of the houses were empty. He looked around him. The colors were vibrant. He wasn't sure if he'd ever seen anything so bright. It seemed so strange to see the beautiful sky so clear after everything that happened just hours ago. How could things change so-

"Dad?" Lisa said.

"Yeah?"

"You okay?"

"Yeah. Sorry. Just a little distracted." She walked out next to him.

"There's no one here."

"I know. Never thought so many people could disappear so fast." He thought about it for a minute. "I'm gonna move

the truck out. Make sure you get out of the way." He walked back to the garage and climbed back into the truck. He maneuvered the truck out of the driveway and backed in so the tailgate was closer to the garage. He pressed the garage door button. He laughed at himself, turned the truck off, and got out.

"What's so funny?" Lisa asked.

"I tried to close the garage door with the button." They laughed.

"I guess habits are hard to break, huh?" she said. They walked inside.

They finished gathering the stuff together and loading it into the truck. Jon and Tracy walked through the house and checked every window, door, and lock.

"Did you get everything up there?" Tracy asked as Jon walked down the stairs.

"Yup," he said. "What about down here?"

"I think so. Want me to check again?"

"Naw. I think we're good."

"I can't believe we're just leaving," Tracy said.

"Yeah. Me either."

"Are you sure we should? I mean, what if someone tries to break in."

"That's why we're locking everything."

"Not funny, Jon. I'm serious. What if something...you know...happens?"

"I don't know, babe. I'm not sure what to tell you."

"Remember all the stories about what happened in New Orleans after Katrina?"

"I do."

"What if that happens here? All our neighbors and friends are leaving the area."

"But think about it. There's only been a few break-ins in this area since we moved in."

"But this is different, Jon."

"Yeah."

"I mean, there's no power anywhere. We have no security

system and nothing to keep people out. Someone could break in and take all our things."

"Tracy. No one is going to break in. Besides, our other car will be here. That'll make it look like we're home and we'll be okay."

"Are you sure it's a good idea to leave it out? I mean, we could move it into the garage where the truck was."

"I don't know," he said. "I think it would be good to leave it because it'll look like someone lives here. That would make the place safer, right?" Tracy looked at their house.

"I still don't like it," she said. "It's like we're abandoning our homes. I don't understand why we can't just stay a little longer. We really should."

"We talked about it already, Tracy. It's better for us to go stay with your parents. They have power and room for us."

"I know." They walked to the door leading to the garage.

"Do we need anything else?"

"I don't think so." He shut the door behind him and they walked out to the truck where the girls waited.

"Everyone got everything?" Jon asked. When he heard "yes", he pulled the garage door down, locked it, and walked out the side door towards the truck.

"Did you lock it?" Tracy asked.

"Yup. And I checked the house door while I was in there to make sure it was shut. The side door is locked too."

"Did you-"

"Checked the garage to make sure we didn't miss anything. It's sealed up nice and tight so don't worry," he said. "I checked everything in there and we both double checked the house."

"Okay. I'm just worried."

"I know you are, but it's okay. We've taken every precaution we can so it's gonna be okay. Everyone ready?" They all nodded. They climbed in the truck. They took another moment to look at the house, and then pulled out of the driveway.

They had trouble getting out of their subdivision.

Branches covered the roads. One side of the road was completely cut off by a tall pine. People driving in that lane were forced to stop and wait for a break or a kind person to let them through. Jon drove past the long line of people in that lane.

"It wouldn't have taken much to let them through," Tracy said. Jon nodded.

"I know. I know. We need to get out of Huntsville before traffic really gets bad."

"Do you think it will?" Laura asked.

"I'm not sure. It probably won't, but there's nothing wrong with being careful."

They reached the University Drive intersection and stopped. Across the street a gas station was now packed with people. Long lines were going in and out of it. People were running up to the convenience store doors and banging on it for someone inside. They watched a fight break out between two men over what seemed to be who was at a pump or needed to be at the pump. Tracy put her hand on Jon's arm as they watched. A police car pulled into the station and two officers got out. One immediately went to break up the fight while the other shouted at people. The sounds were all muffled and none of them knew what was being said.

HONK! HONK! Jon looked in his rearview mirror and waved an apology.

"Honey, you need to pay attention," Tracy said.

"I know, dear. I'm sorry." He looked both ways and pulled on Highway 72 headed west towards Athens.

The satellite radio played Oldies while none of them said anything. Lisa and Laura looked out their windows and Tracy tried to read something on her Kindle. Jon stopped at each intersection and waited an extra moment before going. Witnessing the fight at the gas station had him a little on edge and uncomfortable. He looked in the rearview mirror at the girls. They were now reading and oblivious to anything else. Jon smiled. He didn't want them to worry about what was going on around them. They passed the dead shopping centers in Madison. There were a few cars, but nothing like it was supposed to be. He stopped at each light and continued on.

At Balch Road, they saw an accident. The police ushered cars around the scene. Tracy stared at the mangled vehicles. Paramedics hoisted a woman up into an ambulance and another wrapped a young girl's arm in bandages. Shivers trickled down Tracy's spine.

"Do you think she'll be okay?" Laura asked.

"I don't know, sweetie," Tracy said. "I'm sure they're gonna do their best."

"Where are they taking her if there's no power?"

"Well," Tracy said. "The hospitals have generators and I'm sure they're trying to get those places power first." As the accident faded behind them, they came to a stop at County Line Road, which separated Limestone and Madison County. The girls returned to their Kindles. Tracy turned and saw Jon's face. He seemed to be staring off into space, completely detached. "Jon? Jon, are you okay?" He didn't respond. He inched forward and pointed to their right. Tracy turned.

Along the right side of the road, trees were upended and tangled together. Powerlines were down and spread across the outside lane. Debris from houses were mingled in the trees, but no houses were visible. *The subdivisions are a way back*, he thought.

"Dad, look!" Laura said. As they kept going, they saw more damage on both sides of the highway. What had once been nothing but trees was now an open field of trash and debris. Jon heard Lisa begin to cry. Emergency crews were walking around the area and police officers were motioning people through. Jon carefully drove through and watched for the downed power lines and tried to avoid them. Tracy continued staring at the field.

She'd never seen anything like it. She thought about all the times she'd driven past the trees on her way to Athens or to I-65. As she looked at the people wading through everything, she realized she couldn't remember what it used to look like. She had a vague image that seemed to taunt her. She knew it looked a specific way, but no matter how hard she tried to recall it the details evaded her. She touched her fingers to the window in hopes it would remind her, but it didn't. Instead, all she felt was the slight chill coming from the AC vents blowing on her thin wrists.

They reached Athens. Jon checked the gas gauge. Half full. *Maybe I can stop for gas.*

"Hey," he said. "Will y'all keep an eye out for an open gas station?"

"Jon, you're not thinking of stopping here, are you?" Tracy asked.

"Well, I figured it would be a good idea."

"I don't know," Tracy said. "It might be best if we just keep going and stop somewhere in Tennessee. There's a number of places before 840 we could stop."

"I guess so," he said. "Anyone need to make a pit stop?"

"Not me," Lisa said.

"I'm good," Tracy said. Jon looked in his rearview mirror at Laura, who was immersed in her Kindle.

"You there, Laura?" Jon asked. She jumped.

"Who? What? Yes!"

"You do need a pit stop?"

"Oh. Wait. No. Wait, what?" They all laughed.

"I'm asking if anyone needs to stop before we get on the interstate. It'll be a little bit before we stop again."

"Oh, no. I'm fine," she said and went right back to reading. Tracy laughed and Jon shook his head.

"You don't need anything, do you?"

"I don't think so," Tracy said. "We've got snacks and whatever we need in the back. We can get something when we stop for gas."

"All right," Jon said. "Here we go." He turned onto I-65, set the cruise control, and leaned back.

Hannah Leon

Hannah stopped. McFarland was no longer empty.

In place of traffic, she saw debris scattered across the road and people walking back and forth trying to gather it. Along the sides, she saw people huddled together. They were watching the police as they moved through the debris. Hannah started walking again. She wanted to get a closer look at what was happening.

The crying grew the closer she got. Hannah looked at the group. They were all holding each other and crying. Hannah saw several had dark circles under their eyes and none looked like they slept the night before. They were wrapped in blankets and pajamas and some of the kids were holding their stomachs.

"It's okay, honey," one of the women said. She scooped up her little girl and they walked away. Hannah had to bite her lip to keep from crying. She looked around her to try and take her attention off the sad sight.

More people had left their homes and were now walking through the debris. Hannah had to be careful not to step on any glass or sharp metal that might hurt. People were asked to move away from the street so crews could get into the area and help get things situated and help with the cleanup. This forced Hannah and the others onto the sides, both covered in debris. Hannah did her best to navigate between the people and the metal, glass, and wood scattered beneath her feet.

WHIIIIIIIIIIIIIIIIIIIIIIRH! WHIIIIIIIIIIIIIIIIIIIIIIIIRH! WHIIIIIIIIIIIIIIIIIIIIIIIIIIRH! Hannah quickly looked up as several emergency vehicles went by. She stepped past the people blocking her view to get a better look at where they were heading.

She paused. Milo's, where she'd been before the storms hit, now covered the street in debris. She gasped and ran.

She ran down the side of the road, stepping away from people as best she could or pushing people down who wouldn't move. She fell. She'd been so obsessed with running she hadn't watched where she was going. Her foot had caught on a window frame and left a gash on her shin. People swarmed to her to help. She got back on her feet, thanked them, and continued on despite the sting of the gash. Behind her, people called out and tried to help her with the wound, but she didn't hear them. She was running. She had to keep running. She could almost see it. She stopped. She began to cry. Against the blue sky, Hannah saw the corner of McFarland and 15th Street.

The intersection was covered in debris and emergency vehicles. Police, fire, and medical officials searched through it all. She saw them carefully combing over the piles, talking to each other about what they had or hadn't found. But she still couldn't hear them. She couldn't hear anything. She just stared.

The CVS she'd stopped at was gone. The lot was only debris now. The building materials covered the lot as well as the trees that once surrounded it. The shattered CVS sign was the only clue to show what once stood there. Hannah began walking again. It hurt, but she had to see. She had to see. She pushed herself to get closer and see. As she got closer, she noticed a wide-open area to her left.

Behind the trees and buildings she'd passed so often was a field of missing houses. She could clearly see the pathway cut into the once-hidden subdivision and which way it had gone. *How long have those houses been there? I didn't know there even was a subdivision back there.* Families were moving along the debris crying and yelling. She saw them pushing their way around as if they were forcing themselves to move. Hannah realized she'd never been down that side of 15th Street and never seen any of those houses. She'd driven down McFarland so many times she couldn't count and taken short cuts plenty of times. Still, she couldn't remember those houses.

The thought wouldn't leave her mind. *How could she have missed all that? How could she not see those places until now?* The long line of trees all along McFarland had blocked her view. Now, she could see a row of small townhomes. *Had those been there the whole time? Why didn't she look for those when she needed a place-* She gasped and covered her mouth.

Where had Jillian gone? Didn't she stay with Neil? Didn't Neil live on 15th Street? Her breathing increased. She started sweating. She couldn't remember. *Where did Neil live? Where did he live?* She started crying. She pulled out her phone and looked for the number. She pressed call and put it to her ear.

Riiiiiiiiiiiiiiiiiiiiing. Hannah tried to focus. It wasn't that bad. Jillian was probably fine. Neil may have lived down the other end of 15th. Jillian could be somewhere trying to recover or she may have left. *But why didn't she call me? Why didn't she see if I was okay?* The thoughts knocked each other down in her mind. *Riiiiiiiiiiiiiiiiiing.* The phone wasn't helping. Hannah felt the lump in her throat again and a strong pain in her stomach. She grew light-headed as she fought against the many *What Ifs?* flying through her mind.

"Hi, you've reached Jillian. Sorry I'm not answering the phone. If you'll leave your name, number, and a message, I'll check back soon!" Hannah tried to keep it together when the beep came.

"J-J-Jillian...hey, I'm...I'm outside on McFarland looking and...and I just wanted to...I just wanted to make sure you were okay. I'm not sure where you are or...or what's going on but I just...just wanna be sure. Please call me if...when you get this." She ended the call and stared at the profile picture set for Jillian. It was the two of them, just recently, at a bar two weeks ago. Hannah began to cry again.

"Excuse me?" a man said behind her. She quickly turned around. A medical official looked at her with a bit of worry in his eyes. "Are you okay?" She tried to wipe the tears away.

"I don't know if my friend is okay."

"Well," he said. "I'm sure we can find her. She may have lost her cellphone last night and can't call you right now. Don't worry. Let's get you back up here away from the debris and see if we can find anything out." Hannah looked at the houses. Not all had been completely destroyed, but most were hit by winds or flying debris. The emergency officials moved towards that area to help people.

Jack didn't come home. Why didn't he come home? He wasn't that far. Why didn't he come home? The thoughts swarmed through her head. She tried to put them at bay, but they refused to go. Maybe traffic was too bad for him. Maybe there was an accident and he couldn't get around it so he stayed somewhere. They had several friends in the area so it was plausible. Wasn't it?

She didn't want to leave the apartment in case Jack was just delayed in getting home. If she did, they might miss each other and then would be out searching for longer. It made more sense to wait, but her patience was fading. She found her cellphone and called Jack. It went straight to voicemail without ringing. She figured there had to be some mistake and she tried again. It went straight to voicemail. She hung up. She didn't want to leave a message. She put the phone down and paced the apartment. *What am I going to do? Where is he? Is he going to be here soon? Is he okay?* She couldn't take it anymore.

She needed to find Jack. She made a list of the possible places he could've been, friends he could've stayed with, and possible routes he could've taken to get back instead of the main way. She just needed to go look. He had the truck so she couldn't go far. She left the apartment.

Outside she saw many of the doors of apartments around her open and neighbors out walking. Her apartment was close to McFarland, but she couldn't see anything yet. She went to the security gate which was stuck open. Some men were working on it. She turned and walked towards McFarland. She tried to see if anything had happened that night, but the two small shopping centers on each side of the street blocked her view. No cars were out. She could see people walking along McFarland, but she didn't see any cars. *Where is everyone? It's not that late.*

She reached the parking lot of the shopping center closest to her and found it empty. She walked around and saw none of the stores had power. The parking lots were all empty. She reached McFarland and walked towards the university. Jack's closest coworker lived closer to the interstate off 15th Street.

She saw broken branches and debris scattered across McFarland. A few people walked along the road, but it was more than she expected. She could hear crying.

She reached the bridge and saw the large number of limbs down in the water. The sky was clear and she could see a good ways in both directions. She searched through the waters for a vehicle. She saw nothing. *Where are you, Jack?*

She could see more cars when she got closer to Jack Warner, which led to the university. It might be students or people trying to leave. She hadn't been to the school in all the years she lived in Tuscaloosa.

Although Jack was a big UA fan, Isbel didn't enjoy American football and rarely watched the games unless he had it on. She had some friends she would go visit while Jack had friends over to watch the away games or attend the home games. She wondered how her friends were doing. None of them had tried to call which was probably because of the craziness with the weather.

Isbel realized she'd left her phone in the apartment. What was she going to do if Jack tried to call back? What if he was calling her right now and she couldn't answer because she'd left it? As she walked under the overpasses, she wished she brought it with her.

The sight stopped her in her tracks. Debris covered McFarland. Krispy Kreme and Blue Moon BBQ were both gone. Trees were down and littered among the bricks, metal, and glass. She walked towards them. It looked like 15th, but she wasn't sure. If it was, where would that put Jack? Where was he? She ran up to a woman in a uniform.

"Excuse me?" she said. The uniformed woman turned to her.

"Ma'am, we're asking people to please keep away from the area. There's a lot of damage to the area and we-"

"Where is my husband?"

"Ma'am, I don't know. We're doing the best-"

"Please! Where is my husband?"

"Ma'am, let's go back to the sidewalk for now. We're asking everyone to stay back."

"But where is my husband?! I want to know where my husband is!"

Isbel ran from 15th and continued looking for Jack. The woman was shouting, but Isbel was searching for the truck. She wanted to see it. Some sign of it to show Jack was at least okay. She kept moving down McFarland farther and farther away from the apartment. She hoped he had stopped somewhere. She tried to look at all the cars in all the parking lots but there were too many. A uniformed man came up to her.

"Do you need help, ma'am?" he asked.

"I...I can't find my husband."

"Is he out looking for something?"

"N-no. He didn't come home after the storms. I...I can't...find his truck."

"His car?"

"I...Yes! I'm looking for his truck!"

"What does he and the car look like?" Isbel described everything to the officer. She didn't know what good it would do.

"Thank you, Miss...Banner?"

"Yes, sir."

"And what's your husband's name?"

"Jack," she said. The officer nodded and walked away. Isbel just looked around. She didn't know what the officer was going to do or if it was worth it. She just wanted to find Jack.

"Excuse me?" someone said. Isbel jumped. She turned to face whoever it was talking to her. It was a young woman who looked sad and tired.

"I...I'm sorry," Isbel said. "I was...just...I'm sorry."

"Are you okay?" the young woman asked as she rubbed her eyes. Isbel thought about the question. She thought about Jack being gone and what that meant. She thought about the officer who asked her questions and walked away and the other officer who tried to run her off.

"No," she said. "No. I'm not."

"My name's Hannah," the woman said. Isbel was cautious. She didn't know who this person was and wasn't sure she wanted to confide in her. She considered Hannah for a moment.

"Isbel," she said.

"That's a pretty name," Hannah said.

"Thank you." Isbel could feel herself shaking. She wasn't sure if it was because she was scared or cold. Something wasn't right. She felt lost. Hannah walked away and Isbel looked for the officer who had spoken to her. She couldn't find him. "Te echo de menos, Jack. Me gustaria que estuvieras aqui."

"Who's Jack?" Hannah asked. The question scared Isbel.

"My...my husband. He did not come home after the storms. I waited for him, but he never come home." She tried to hide the pain, but could feel it in her face. She didn't know why she was talking to whoever this was. She couldn't go anywhere. She was waiting for the officer.

"Where was he?" Hannah asked. Isbel closed her eyes and cleared her throat. She fought the urge to cry.

"I don't know," she whispered. The tears streaked down her face.

"I-I'm sure he-" The officer walked up to them.

"Miss Banner?"

"Yes?" Isbel said. He spoke in the same manner as he had when he first approached Isbel with no tell in his voice.

"Please come with me," he said. He held his arm out to usher her towards the way to go. Isbel walked forward a bit, but stopped and turned to Hannah.

"Thank you," she said.

"You-you're welcome," Hannah said. Isbel turned and walked away with the officer.

<u>Ryan Peterson</u>

Ryan sat up in his room. It was unusual how quiet it got when there was no technology. His mind was so used to their presence it wasn't even sure what to do without them.

He thought about how quiet everything had been last night. It was strange going to bed so early and getting up so early this morning. He wondered about what it would be like for the next few days until the power came back on. They would probably go to bed and get up early. It was strange to not use cellphones, iPods, computers, and tablets to make it from one day to the next.

"Knock, knock," Dad said.

"What's up?" Ryan asked.

"You busy?"

"Naw. Just trying to write something but not really getting anything going."

"Ah. I could use your help with grilling the food."

"Oh yeah. Gas."

"Yeah. Can be lethal, but contained we should be fine." They laughed.

"Yeah, sure." Ryan put the pad down and left the room. "So what are we grilling?"

"Just a few vegetables and things from the freezer. Trying to have at least something to eat so we don't starve during this whole thing." They walked downstairs.

"Better to get it now than wait for it to spoil, right?"

"Yeah. We probably have a few days before it really starts to go bad. We have a generator if we can get it hooked up and that'll probably give us an extra day or so."

"That doesn't sound all that healthy. It's not gonna kill us, right?"

"No. No. Like I said, it'll definitely last a few days." Ryan nodded.

"I guess that won't be as bad. I figured we'd be without food the whole time. Or with food but no idea how to cook it."

"Naw. Won't be that difficult." They walked outside, around the house, and to the grill. The food sat next to it on a makeshift table in deli containers. Ken and Brandon were standing next to it as if they were guards.

"Don't want any animals to sneak up and take it," they said almost together.

"You realize sometimes you two are cute, right?" Ryan said.

"No we-" they started, then stopped and looked at each other as if to avoid looking cute again. Ryan and Dad laughed.

"All right, you two," Dad said. "Go see if your mother has anything else for us to cook." They both went into the house. Ryan looked at the grill with some skepticism.

"You sure we're gonna be able to cook anything?"

"Oh yeah. No worries." Ryan watched Dad open several containers and pull out burger patties, portabella mushrooms, and fries. "Open that pack of buns and put them in here," Dad said, motioning towards a metal pan on the grill. Ryan did so.

"Why are we doing this?"

"So we can eat," Dad said with a smile. Ryan rolled his eyes.

"I mean with the buns."

"Just to heat them up. It'll be better than cold ones."

"Makes sense." Dad placed the burgers and mushrooms on the bottom rack. He pulled out a baking sheet, sprayed it, and poured the fries onto it. He then placed the patties and mushrooms on the bottom rack. He closed the lid of the grill.

"So what are the grandparents doing?" Ryan asked.

"They've got a generator they're rationing out as best they can. They're using their Foreman Grill to heat up foods." Ryan thought about how that worked. Dad lifted the grill cover. "Looks like they're cooking right along."

"I'm excited. It'll be nice to have some good food."

"Well, this'll be as good as we can do for now, right?" Ryan laughed.

"Right. But it's better than cold baked bean."

"Hey," Dad said. "Don't knock it until you try it."

"Still sounds disgusting." Dad smiled and let out a sigh.

"Kids today. Don't have respect for what they should."

"Like cold baked beans?"

"Exactly." Ken and Brandon walked up to them.

"Mom said that'sth all."

"Yup. Said we don't have nothing else."

"All right," Dad said. "Here's what you two can do. Go inside and start setting the table for us. Don't get any of the ketchup or mayo out yet. Once you finish, come back outside and we'll see how much we have to bring inside, okay?"

"Okay," they said in unison and left. Dad lifted the grill again and inhaled.

"Mmm. Smells delicious. Bet you never thought we'd be doing this."

"Grilling or grilling because we have no other means of cooking things?"

"I guess the second one."

"Yeah," Ryan said. "Can't say that's ever been something that crossed my mind. I never expected we'd be without power for this long either."

"Well, we don't know how long we're gonna end up being without power. Could be just a few days or could be a while. Haven't heard anything new on the radio. Birmingham is putting itself back together."

"That's good."

"Yup. Maybe it won't be too long until we get things going around here again."

"Sure hope so." Dad put the cooked food in a plastic container and put more food there to cook.

"Is it time to add the fries?"

"Almost. They won't take as long to cook so we'll put them in towards the end. Gotta get some hot dogs cooked for your brothers."

"Oh yeah. They hate burgers right now, don't they?"

"Yup. Give them a few weeks and they'll hate something else and realize they love burgers."

"At least it's easy to order for them."

"True. Just have to get whatever it is plain. Then again, they change what they want so often maybe it's really not that easy." They laughed.

"I guess that's fair," Ryan said. Dad took the hot dogs off the grill, put them into the container, and moved the fries onto the bottom rack. The cover barely shut.

"All right. Let's go ahead and take this stuff inside and come back for the fries."

"Sounds good."

The Spencers

"There's the exit!" Lisa said.

"Yup," Jon said. "We're almost there."

"About five or so more minutes, I think," Tracy said.

"Something like that."

"I'm excited," Laura said. "We haven't seen them since Christmas."

"Yup. And you haven't gotten any less obnoxious." Jon stuck his tongue out at her in the rearview mirror.

"Yeah, yeah, yeah. Still not funny, Dad." They exited and turned east on Old Hickory Blvd. After a little ways, they turned left.

"Not much further," Tracy said.

"Can't remember the last time we were here in April. Looks very nice."

"Yeah, it does!" Lisa said.

"You girls remember to say 'thank you' to Gran and Pop for letting us stay here, okay?"

"Okay," they said together.

They turned into the driveway. There was no sign of any rain or wind damage. Jon noticed on the drive up that once you reached part of Tennessee all signs of the tornadoes were gone. He parked next to the house and they all unloaded. Lisa and Laura ran straight for the house.

"Girls, you forgot-" Tracy rolled her eyes. "Well, they're gone."

"Just let them be, I guess. Later when they realize they need their stuff they'll come out and get it."

"Oh, I know," Tracy said. "They better not think for a second we're going to carry their stuff." Jon laughed.

"I think right now they're mostly interested in Gran and Pop," he said. They unloaded their bags, shut the truck, and carried their bags inside.

"Well, hello!" Gran said when they walked in.

"Hey, Mom," Tracy said. "How're you?"

"Oh fine, fine. How're you doin'?"

"We're making it. Was a pretty pleasant drive, I think."

"Yeah," Jon said. "Didn't have any issues at all." He hugged Gran. "How're you doing?"

"Oh well, you know us. We're always doing just fine. It's good to see Laura and Lisa again. They've grown a bit since we saw them at Christmas."

"Goodness. Don't we know it?" Tracy said. "I think Laura's about evened out, but Lisa has been drinking something. I'm not sure what."

"Jon!" Pop said.

"Hey, Pop," Jon said. "How're you doing?"

"Doing well. Hey, listen, our computer has been popping up with these strange notifications. It looks like something I need to click, but I don't want to chance it."

"Okay, let's go have a look at it." Pop explained what was going on as he guided Jon downstairs to the computer. Tracy laughed.

"So how bad were things?" Gran asked and Tracy told her about what they saw on 72. "Oh my. That does sound awful."

"Yeah. It was."

"We can talk about that later."

"Yeah, of course." Lisa and Laura walked into the living room and came back.

"Hey," Laura said. "Where's our stuff?"

"It's in the truck right where you left it." They rolled their eyes.

"Come on."

"Okay." Tracy and Gran laughed as the girls went to the truck.

Ryan Peterson

It was close to dark. Without power, the sun decided their days and they tried to stick with it as best they could. Ryan noticed he was sleeping better than he had in a long time. Maybe it was because he wasn't staying up late. Maybe it was the lack of stress from driving and going places that made him anxious. He didn't know, but he knew he was going to miss it. Tonight was different though. Instead of going to bed as soon as it got dark, they were at his grandparents getting ready to shower. They hadn't showered since they lost power and Mom had had enough.

"I'm not going to stay in the house much longer with all you filthy, stinky men," she said that day. The twins weren't happy.

"But we like it," Ken said.

"Yeah. It'sth the way God wantsth usth."

"Oh I'm sure it is," Mom said. "We're going to go up to your grandparents tonight and get showers."

"But there'sth no power. How're we sthupposthed to take showersth with no hot water?"

"They have a different kind of water heater, bud," Dad said. "They'll turn on the generator and it'll keep the water hot until we turn the generator off."

"Wow," the twins said.

"Yup," Mom said. "So you guys go get your stuff and we're going to head up there, okay?"

"Okay," they said together. Everyone got what they needed and met outside.

They walked down the driveway and up the hill. Dad had a flashlight, but decided they didn't need it just yet. The twins stuck close to him and Mom.

With all of them (Mom, Dad, Ken, Brandon, both grandparents, and himself), it took a while for Ryan to get the chance to shower. They'd started to draw straws to decide who was going, but he was fine with going last. With a tankless water heater, it didn't matter. It would keep the water hot. He enjoyed spending time with his grandparents and talking to them all. Flashlights lit the house as the sun set. They were all gathered around in a circle that changed with each new person showering. They talked about the lack of power, not having hot water, food, heat, and the calmness of the weather.

"Your turn, Ryan," Brandon said as he walked out. Ryan stood up to go in the bathroom when everything went dark. Ryan chuckled.

"That would happen to me," he said.

"Hold on," his grandfather said. "Let me go have a look." He and Dad got up and walked outside to the garage. There was a funny moment of silence among the five in the room.

"Well," Ryan said. "Now what?"

"Guess you'll just stay dirty, won't you?" Ken said. They laughed.

"No, no," his grandmother said. "I'm sure they're out there trying to get it fixed right now. Probably just needed to be taken care of since so many people were using it. Won't be too much trouble, I'm sure."

The lights came back on.

"Guessth no getting out of a bath now," Brandon said. His Dad and grandfather walked back in.

"Just needed gas," his grandfather said. "You're good to go now." Ryan took his stuff and went into the bathroom.

He had the bathroom light on, which felt strange. He realized he really missed having lights in the house. Using flashlights wasn't the same. He missed having the bright lights there to illuminate the corners of a room. He turned the water on in the shower, shut the glass door, and gave it a moment to heat up.

The glass door began steaming up. He felt the water to make sure it was the right temperature. After adjusting it, he got in. The warmth flooded his body as the water covered him. As he cleaned himself, he enjoyed every moment of the hot water.

It's strange, he thought. *Here I am, taking a shower and I can't believe how much I missed it. Something I do every morning before I go to work and now I'm surprised I made it so long without it.* He finished the shower and fought to turn the water off. It felt so good. After a moment of struggle, he did and immediately missed it. He dried himself and got dressed. He stared at the light switch for a moment then flipped it down and left the bathroom.

"All clean?" his Mom asked.

"Yup, yup. Can't believe I missed it so much."

"We were just talking about that," his grandfather said. "I was telling them it's funny to watch you boys all get your showers and how much y'all enjoy it. I don't know if y'all'd be able to survive growing up like we did."

"Oh, I'm certain I couldn't have," Ryan said. "I'm thinking I might need another shower now." They laughed.

"Ha, I don't know if that's such a good idea," his grandmother said. "Have you all been making do?"

"Oh yeah," Mom said. "We've had to do a few things in a different way, like cooking. But I think the experience has been...entertaining. I didn't think we would enjoy it as much."

"I don't know how y'all did it!" Ken said.

"Kenneth!" Mom said. "Don't just yell that out there."

"But they usthed to live like thisth all the time!" Brandon said. Ryan and his Dad tried to suppress their laughter.

"Well," his grandfather said. "It wasn't easy. Lotta times we didn't get to bathe. Sometimes we had to go several days without a bath and even then it wasn't like that shower in there." Ken and Brandon sat in front of him and curled up listening to the story. Their eyes were wide with anticipation. "We'd get up early in the morning, long before the sunrise. We did that every day."

"Every day?" Ken asked.

"Every day. You gotta get up and take care of those animals. They wanna eat just like you do."

"But why did they want to eat stho early?" Brandon asked.

"Well," his grandfather said. "Animals can be funny. They like to eat and get up at weird times."

"But they're animals," Ken said. "Why didn't they just

sleep in and get up later? They don't have to do anything but eat. That's what I'd do if I was an animal."

"Some animals have their ways and that's just how they are."

"Sthoundsth like Ryan," Brandon said. They laughed. Ryan rolled his eyes.

"Har, har, har."

"Did you always get up that early?" Ken asked. He was more interested in the story.

"Oh yes," his grandfather said. "We had to make sure those animals were taken care of. See, when you have a lot of animals, you have to get a head start on them so when they all wake up they have food. Sometimes they woke up before you got to them and they'd start chattering and causing racket. Then they'd wake up all the other animals and it was just a mess."

"Did they happen a lot?" Ken asked.

"Naw. Not too often, but sometimes. After breakfast we had to milk the cows." Ken and Brandon seemed drawn into the story at this point. They leaned forward. Ryan could see the looks on their face that seemed to express excitement at taking care of farm animals and disgust at the thought of getting milk from a cow.

"Milk...the cowsth?" Brandon asked.

"Yup. That's what you had to do on a farm. You gotta take care of the animals."

"Wasth it grossth?"

"Well, it could be, but it wasn't always. You get used to it as just another chore like the dishes or washing laundry."

The story went on for a while longer. The family all sat around and listened as their grandfather continued talking about growing up on a farm and living with no indoor plumbing and having to bathe with soap and pond water, brushing teeth with sweet gum sap and baking soda, and teaching himself to read. Ken and Brandon continued to ask questions. After some time, Dad began looking around.

"Well," Dad said. "I think it's about time to turn in."

"Yeah," Mom said. "It's already gotten dark. Can't believe we let the time get away from us."

"How late is it?" Ken asked.

"Later than it should be," Mom said. She ruffled his hair and they all stood up.

"Thanks for the showers and the stories," Dad said. "I'm sure these two will sleep well tonight."

"Sure thing, sure thing," his grandfather said. "Hopefully we don't have to do this much more." They said their goodbyes and left.

With no lights coming from anyone and the moon in its last sliver before being new, the road was dark. Stars were numerous, but didn't provide anywhere near enough light to help them see. In the woods to their right, they heard yips. Ken and Brandon grabbed their Mom, who moved closer to their Dad. Ryan moved closer to them, but kept looking around.

"Wh-wh-what'sth that?" Brandon asked.

"Coyotes," Dad said.

"Do you see them?" Ryan asked.

"No," his Dad said. He was waving the flashlight in the woods trying to see any sign of their eyes or movement. They all pulled closer together and moved away from the woods. The yipping seemed to fade. "I think we're good to go."

"Are you sure?" Mom asked.

"Yeah. If they're getting quieter, they must be moving off elsewhere."

"Could they be getting quieter to try and sneak up on us?" Ken asked. Mom smiled and patted him on the head.

"No, no," she said. "That's not how they work. They'll get louder as they get closer 'cause they're talking to each other."

They kept walking. The twins moved faster in hopes of getting home. They took off running when they saw the house.

"Wait up!" Mom called. They twins slowed down to a fast walk.

"I get the feeling they don't like the dark," Dad said.

"Yeah, really," Ryan said. "Can't imagine how they're

sleeping at night."

"They're doing pretty well, actually," Mom said. "I was pretty surprised, but they only got up the first night. Other than that, they've pretty much stayed asleep. Right, honey?"

"Yeah," Dad said. "As far as I know. They haven't woken me up if not."

"That's good. I have to say this is the best sleep I've gotten in a long time."

"Me too," Dad said.

"I could use more circulation in the air," Mom said, "but overall it's not bad. Just leaves me a bit stuffy. I really want my CPAP back." They laughed.

The Spencers

"Security system is still out," Jon said. He was on the bed with his laptop trying to connect to the cameras outside his home. He let out a sigh of annoyance and set his laptop down on the bed and got up. He was ready to go home and be back in his house. He didn't mind staying with his in-laws, but it always felt better to be where you belonged. Tracy looked up from her book.

"Any chance they would be off even with the power on?" she asked.

"Nope. They don't have the battery extension, but they are setup to be back on as soon as possible when power goes in case someone tries to rob a house during a brief outage. That's the best we can do."

"You're sure?" He gave her a funny look. "Okay, okay," she said. "I'm just...worried."

"Honey," he said. "I want to get home as much as you do."

"I know."

"I love being here with your family, but I like being home too."

"I know, dear," she said. "I'm just worried is all. I don't like being this far away from the house with no way of knowing what happens. I mean..." She stopped. "Do you really think nothing will happen?" Jon shrugged.

"I don't know. It's possible, don't get me wrong, but not something we need to worry about right now."

"You think so?"

"I do. We can head back home when the cameras come back."

"I just wish I knew how long that would take," she said. "I don't like all this uncertainty." Jon patted her leg and got off the bed.

"I have an idea," he said. "What if I get ahold of someone from work or church and asked them to go by the house? That way they can see it, let us know how it looks, and do something if anyone has been there messing with it." Tracy didn't response. She was worried about what was going on back home. "Tracy?"

"What? I'm sorry, Jon," she said. "I'm just worried about what's going on. We can't be there but we need to be there, you know?"

"I understand, honey, but we can have someone stop by and make sure everything is okay. That'll also make it look like someone is living there or staying nearby and keep anyone from trying to stop and rob the place."

"Please don't say things like that."

"I'm sorry," Jon said. "I just meant it would be better if someone went over and checked it out."

"Do you really think it'll do us any good? I mean, I don't meant to sound...well, you know...but I'm just worried, okay? Someone could just wait for whoever to leave and then rob it or could be there robbing it when they show up. What good does that do?"

"We can't go back yet because it won't do us any good with no power and no food, right?" She nodded. "With the whole area shut down, it likely won't be easy for us to get anything within a good distance of the house. There might be a few places open, sure, but it'll be a mad dash to get to things. We need to stay up here where we have power and have someone to stop by the house and check on it for us."

"I'm sorry, Jon. I just don't like this. I don't like being so far from home and having to stay here with my parents."

"Hey," Jon said. "They aren't that bad." Tracy laughed.

"You know what I mean. Just them and the girls and everything...it's just a lot."

"I know, dear, but hey." She looked at him. "We're okay, aren't we? We made it through safely and the house looked like it was just fine when we left. Our yard still looked fine. We were lucky." He pointed at his laptop. "There's news reports everywhere about how bad this whole thing was and the number of people dead. They're saying there could be more than 100 dead in just Alabama. And there's no telling if that number is going to go up. We're fortunate we weren't hurt during this thing or while trying to get out of there. Lisa and Laura were scared just like us, but we all came together and managed to make it safely. And you saw everything along 72. All of that was right there next to us and we still managed to make it. We're okay now and that's what matters, okay?" She nodded, went to him, and hugged him tightly.

"Thank you," she said.

"I understand," he said. "You're scared. I'm scared." He held her.

"I love you," she said.

"I love you too." They kissed. "Let's go see what everyone else is up to, okay?" They left the room and walked down the hall into the living room. They didn't see anyone, but heard voices coming from the dining room. They walked into the dining room to see the girls and grandparents playing cards.

"Come on!" Lisa said. "You two need to join!"

"What's the game?" Jon asked.

"Rummy."

"Oh, of course," Tracy said.

"I'm surprised you girls are playing instead of watching TV. Figured you two would be glued to it like you usually are."

"Nothing good on," Laura said. "Might as well do something fun."

"You guys far into the game?" Jon asked.

"Nope," Pop said. "We're still in the first phase. How about we just shuffle and deal again?"

"But I've got a good hand!" Gran said.

"Oh we don't want to come in the way of that," Jon said.

"Don't believe her," Pop said with a smile. "She always says she has a good hand but if we kept playing she still wouldn't win."

"Well, that's because my hand changes as I draw cards."

"Come on, Gran," Laura said. "Let's be nice and let the old people play." Tracy and Jon shared a look.

"I think someone is asking for trouble" Tracy said.

"That's what it sounded like to me," Jon said. "I think we

need to get in here and show these kids how you play this game."

"Now you best be careful talking that cocky talk," Pop said. "I don't want to have to make an example out of you in front of your own kids."

"Well, well," Jon said. "Looks like the trash talk is starting early. I thought we usually waited a round or two before we did that." They sat down. Going clockwise, it was Pop, Jon, Lisa, Gran, Tracy, and Laura. "Okay then. Deal us in." Pop dealt the cards.

"Everyone have 11?" he asked. They all nodded. "All right. You two know the game. You grew up on it after all. First round is two groups of three. Doesn't matter the suit. Just the cards. Everyone ready?" They nodded. He flipped the top card over to start the game.

Ace of hearts. Jon looked at his hand. Three 8s, two 4s, two 5s, King, 10, 6, and a Jack. He raised an eyebrow.

"How many decks are we playing with?"

"Three," Pop said. "Just like always."

"Ah," Jon said. "Now this makes more sense." Lisa and Gran exchanged looks.

"He has a wild card," Lisa whispered.

"Don't kid yourself," Jon said. "But if you have one I'd be happy to take it off your hands." Lisa shook her head and smiled at her cards. Jon drew from the deck. *Ten.* He wasn't happy. He had the 8s and that was helpful, but he needed those other cards so he could lay down. He discarded the King.

"I'll take that if no one else wants it," Gran chimed in almost immediately. Everyone looked at Lisa. Even if someone else wanted it, Gran had first call after Lisa. Mostly it was done out of politeness. Lisa shook her head. Gran picked it up.

"Don't forget your penalty card," Tracy said. Gran looked up. "You know, for taking out of order."

"Oh I know," Gran said. She smiled. "Just hoped no one noticed." She took her penalty card. Lisa spent a moment looking at her hands.

"Some of us can't wait too long, little lady," Pop said. Lisa laughed.

"I'm working on it. Don't rush me." Lisa smiled, put down three Jacks, three 2s, and discarded a King. Everyone sighed.

"Maybe she could've waited a little longer," Jon muttered. Pop just smiled and shook his head. Gran drew from the deck and looked at her hand suspiciously before discarding an Ace.

"Anybody want it?" Tracy asked. Everyone shook their heads and Tracy drew from the deck. She chuckled.

"Uh-oh," Laura said.

"She's just being mean," Gran said. Tracy laid down three 3s, three Queens, and played a Jack on Lisa's group before discarding a 6.

"I get the feeling this isn't going to end well for us," Jon said to Pop.

"Speak for yourself," he said. "I'm planning a comeback."

"Anyone want that?" Laura asked, pointing to the discarded 6. They shook their heads. Laura drew from the deck. She laid down three 7s, three Aces, and played her Queen on Tracy's group before discarding a 9.

"Ha!" Pop said as he snatched the 9. Jon shook his head.

"Oh no," he said. Pop put down a 6 with two wild cards and three 9s. He then put two 3s on Tracy's groups and two Jacks on Lisa's group before discarding a 4. He smiled as he waved his last card in front of him.

"Better get your head in the game, boy, or it won't end well for you."

Jon smiled and took the 4. He laid down three 8s, three 4s, a Jack on Lisa's group, and a 6 on Pop's before discarding a 10. He had three cards in his hands. He wasn't sure how he was going to be able to do this, but figured it would play in his favor.

Lisa drew from the deck.

"Be nice to your Dad," Jon said. Lisa just smiled and didn't look at him. She laid down two 4s and an 8 on Jon's group then discarded an Ace. "Bah. You're out of the will."

Gran was already moving. She drew from the deck and

smiled. She laid down four Kings, two 9s with a wild card, one Queen and two 3s on Tracy's group, one Jack on Lisa's.

"Oh no," Laura said. Gran put a 7 on Laura's group before discarding a 10 to win. Everyone groaned.

"I was so close," Pop said. "So close." Laura had pen and paper.

"What were the scores?" she asked. Everyone counted up the damage and told her.

Jon – 20; Lisa – 10; Gran – 0; Tracy – 20; Laura – 35; Pop – 5.

"It's still anyone's game," Lisa said.

"Say that for yourself," Laura said.

"Hey now," Jon said as he gathered up the cards. "If you can't be a good sport, don't play."

"I'm sorry. I didn't mean to be mean. Was just...shaking my head." They laughed. Jon shuffled the large deck then split it in half and gave part to Lisa to shuffle.

"Anyone want something to drink?" Tracy asked.

"I think I'll take some water," Laura said.

"Me too," Gran said.

"I'll take a coke, please," Jon said. Lisa and Pop didn't answer. Tracy and Gran went into the kitchen and came back with drinks for people. Gran brought Pop water.

"But he didn't ask for anything," Lisa said.

"But I know when he wants water," Gran said. Pop took the glass, kissed his wife, and thanked her.

"Aww," Jon said to Lisa. She rolled her eyes. They finished shuffling and Jon dealt.

They continued playing through the rest of the rounds. There were some close calls and funny moments. Lisa and Laura picked at each other several times, but never ventured beyond a look from Jon or Tracy. With Gran ultimately victorious, Jon went back upstairs. Lisa and Laura put the cards away and offered to help get dinner ready. Jon walked over to the bed, pulled up the laptop, and checked the cameras again. Tracy walked in.

"Any update?" she asked.

"Doesn't look like it. I think things are still down." Tracy rubbed Jon's back.

"The game was a good distraction," Tracy said.

"Yes, it was. Glad the girls got it."

"I think we needed it too." Jon just nodded as he looked at the screen. *No changes. No changes are bad.*

"Let's go eat," Tracy said.

"Okay."

Hannah Leon

She really wanted to go home. She was in bed, staring at the ceiling. It wouldn't do any good to go home now, though. She would be just be traveling farther to get to the same circumstances. If she did go home, she would be near Ryan. Her mind wandered to all the possibilities.

She could just stay there until power came back on at the house and at least she wouldn't worry about driving. If she went back, her family and friends would be there and she wouldn't be alone like she was here. But she wouldn't be able to contact anyone down here and know if they made it safely or not because no one was answering their phones. She sat up and swung her feet off the side of the bed. *Maybe if I just get up and walk around it'll help me decide.* She wasn't sure what gave her those thoughts. Sometimes they worked and sometimes they didn't, but she listened to this one.

She stood up and paced around her room. She looked at the off-white carpet and her thoughts went back to Wednesday. She thought about being there, being scared, and wishing she could leave. She thought about the moment when she had to get out of there and not be alone anymore and ran downstairs to her neighbors.

She remembered the noise. The loud, distinct noise that seemed to follow her throughout the apartment. She remembered the constant hum she thought she could still hear in the quiet rooms of her apartment. She looked in the mirror. She remembered the feeling of sheer terror that shrieked through her body when she didn't know what was going to happen.

She noticed the mirror was crooked. She reached up and tried to reset it. It took several attempts before it was back the same as before the storms. She figured the rumbling from the tornadoes had caused it. She remembered it feeling more like a slight vibration than something that could shake the walls. It seemed to her to be more like a cellphone on vibrate going off in the same room as you. She couldn't believe the storm was strong enough to shake her mirror. She looked at her reflection.

She saw the same look on her face Wednesday night. It was a look of exhaustion, but instead of coming from school, this exhaustion came from stress. Stress from the storms and the things it made. Stress from the things she'd seen when she walked.

Mrs. Banner. She thought about the woman she'd seen standing in the streets. She was so lost and confused. Hannah couldn't begin to imagine how she must've felt not knowing if her husband was dead or alive. Hannah couldn't fathom that. She took some deep breaths and walked into the living room.

She sat on the couch and looked around the messy room. With no power, she couldn't clean properly. She'd done the best she could, but now her clothes were all piled up in a corner. Her entertainment center sat there like a very expensive nightstand that does nothing but add to the room.

She listened for some signs of life outside but there was nothing. More neighbors had left. When she finished her walk that day, she came back to find more cars missing.

Maybe it's for the best, she thought. The silence was driving her mad. She almost spoke to make sure she wasn't going deaf, but she couldn't bear the thoughts of hearing just her voice. There was nothing left in Tuscaloosa for her now. She figured most of her friends were gone by now. She hadn't heard anything from Jillian and was still waiting. Jillian was probably back home in Montgomery with her family. She would hear from her soon and they would cry over how wonderful it was to hear their voices.

Hannah got off the couch and went outside.

While the food had been as good as expected the first time, Ryan was surprised the reheated ones was just as good. He was impressed by how much cooking they'd been able to do. Their meal plan was to eat some breakfast in the mornings with a big lunch in the afternoon. This made it so they didn't need to eat anything when night came around since they went to bed so early. It gave the days a sense of routine and normalcy.

Everyone was gathering their dirty clothes together. They would turn the generator on and wash as many loads of clothes as they could before it gave out.

"How long do you think we'll have?" Ryan asked Dad.

"Probably not long. Here's what we'll do. We'll divide up the clothes into lights, darks, whites, etc. But then we'll all look at clothes we have to have for the next few days and wash those as loads first. We'll try to get through those as best we can. I'd like us to get them all washed today, but that probably won't happen."

"Why not?" Ken asked.

"Yeah," said Brandon. "Why not?"

"Because we won't have enough power to get them all clean. We have to save the gas from the generator as best we can. We don't know how much longer we'll be without power or how cheap gas will stay."

"Oh," Brandon said.

"That makes sense," Ken said. They threw their clothes to the large pile and stared at it as if it would come alive. Ryan added his to the pile and began sorting.

"What sort of things are we gonna say are definites to clean?"

"Well," Dad said. "Underwear is a definite. As much as I'm loving this hippy lifestyle, I'd rather we stay as clothed as possible until we get the power back." Ryan let out a sarcastic sigh.

"If we gotta," Ryan said. Dad looked at him.

"Believe me, you gotta." They sorted through the rest of

the clothes, picking out two outfits a piece for everyone.

"How long will that take?"

"A little over two hours."

"We gonna have enough power for that?"

"Well, my plan is to have you start the washer as soon as we start the generator."

"But what about the dryer?" Ken asked

"We're not using the dryer."

"What?" Brandon asked. "How will our clothesth get dry then?"

"We're gonna use that thing out there in the yard you've been asking about for years," Ryan said. The twins looked at him confusion.

"He means the clothesline," Dad said.

"Yeah, that thing," Ryan said.

"Oh," the twins said. Mom walked up.

"Here you go," she said. She had a white basket in her hand full of clothes.

"Where'd those come from?" Ryan asked.

"From two little boys who only brought a few things so it looked like their room was clean." She gave the twins a look, who immediately looked away. She looked at Ryan. "You gonna drive back and try to talk to Hannah again?"

"I don't know. I mean, I don't know if she'll have her phone on her or anything so it might not be a good idea to waste the gas to drive all the way there and back."

"Nothing wrong with trying," Dad said.

"Yeah. I suppose. Just thinking if it's safe to drive and all."

"I say go anyway," Mom said. "She might need to hear you." He looked at the pile of clothes.

"I'll head down after we get the washer started."

"Okay," she said. Ryan continued sorting the laundry. He wiped the sweat from his brow with his sleeve. The house was hot even with the windows open. There was a slight breeze moving through, but not all that strong. It was enough to keep the place from being unbearable.

"Okay," Dad said. "They're sorted. I'm gonna go outside

while you put this load here in. When you hear the power come back on, give it a few seconds then start the washer. Then you can go call Hannah."

"Sounds like a plan." Dad, Ken, and Brandon left the room and Ryan loaded the first pile into the washer. The load wasn't ideal. There were jeans, darks, and some lights in it. Whites and lights were next. He knew they weren't supposed to mix the clothes up but it didn't matter. They only had two shots at washing the clothes and couldn't really afford to be picky.

The microwave beeped and he heard the fan in the kitchen start up. He'd almost forgotten what it was like for the power to start up. The sounds all creating this chorus that seemed strange to his ears. He selected the setting on the washer and walked through the house.

"I'm going to call Hannah," he said.

"All right," Mom said. "Be safe."

"I will." He walked out and saw Dad checking the generator.

"Is it holding up?" Ryan asked.

"Yup. You headed out?"

"Yeah. The washer seems to be doing fine. Didn't see any flickering or anything in the house, if that helps."

"Good, good. I just wanted to go over this thing again. Be safe."

"Okie dokie," Ryan said as he got in his car. "I'll be back." He waved at Dad as he started the car and backed out of the driveway. He plugged his phone into the charger.

There were no accidents this time. It seemed like either people hadn't been driving or were getting better at it. He turned onto the state highway and drove towards the interstate. He rolled down his window and let the wind hit him in the face. It felt good and was better than inside the house.

As he drove through the small town, he saw more signs of life than expected. As he neared the interstate, he saw more people out and driving. The parking lot to the local grocery store was packed with a large crowd standing outside the doors. He came to a stop at the first intersection and waited his turn. He passed two packed gas stations with lines going into the street.

BZZZ! BZZZ! BZZZ! He grabbed his pocket. His phone kept buzzing. He looked for some sign of power. The intersection light where he'd almost been hit was still out. He came to a stop and checked both ways multiple times before going through.

The restaurant where he'd called Hannah showed some signs of life. There were a few employees inside, but it didn't appear people were there to work but instead getting things cleaned up. He pulled into a parking space away from the restaurant. He turned the car off and pulled out his phone. He had more than 30 text messages from people making sure he was okay or sending updates about the storm. The vibrating had stopped, but he wasn't sure how to respond to everyone. He called Hannah.

"Hello?" she said. Ryan hesitated. Something didn't sound right.

"Hey," he said. "Are you okay?"

"No," she said. It sounded like she was crying or had been crying. "I think I'm going crazy."

"What do you mean?"

"I mean that there's no one down here and no reason to come back to Madison yet. It's just crazy. They've opened a few of the roads down here, but things are still mostly in bad shape.

"Where are you?"

"I'm walking back to my apartment."

"What?" he asked. "Where'd you go?"

"I went for a walk. I needed to get out of the house."

"Is that safe?"

"Yeah. There's no one around. Or if there is I don't see them."

"I'm sure it's okay. Have you heard from your family?" Silence. "Hannah?"

"I-I'm sorry."

"It's okay. Have you heard from your family?"

"I don't think they have power yet."

"You might wanna give them a call. Places are starting to get power now."

"Really?" She sounded excited. "Do you have power?"

"Not yet, but I'm betting it's gonna be there soon. How's your walk?"

"It's okay. It's crazy down here right now."

"Really?"

"Yeah." Neither said anything. "Hello?" she asked.

"Sorry," he said. "Just trying to think about it all. Hey, why don't you get back to your place and pack so you can come back?"

"Really?"

"Sure."

"But there's no power."

"Yeah, but you're alone there. Wouldn't it be better to have you here?" Ryan could hear sirens in the background of her phone, but didn't anything. He looked around. The traffic light nearest him wasn't on yet, but more cars were moving through and were treating it as a four-way stop.

"You might be right. I'll try to call my folks and talk to them and see if they have power yet."

"And you're gonna come home anyway if they don't, right?" She didn't respond. "Right?" he asked again.

"Right."

"Thank you."

"You're welcome."

"Are you almost back home?"

"Yeah. I didn't go very far like I did last time."

"'Last time'?" he asked. "What happened then?"

"Oh yeah," she said. She explained everything she saw on her walk down McFarland. Ryan sat there dumbfounded. He didn't know what to think of everything she described. It was said to be hit bad, but Tuscaloosa was sounding worse than he expected.

"That's just crazy."

"It is. But that's why I didn't go very far today. Just down towards Walmart and back. Don't wanna have to see all that again."

"I understand," he said. "I'm gonna head back to the house before these restaurant people get annoyed with me being here." She laughed.

"That's probably a good idea."

"Hey," he said. "Send me a text when you get home. I probably won't get it but do it anyway, okay?"

"But if you're not gonna get it why should I send it?"

"Because I'm crazy?" He heard her laugh.

"Okay."

Ryan put the phone back down, cranked the car, and left the restaurant. He got back on the road and made his way home. There was a utility crew now at the traffic lights making sure they were working properly. He was careful to watch each intersection. He didn't want to end up in an accident on his way home.

The gas stations were still full and the grocery store was packed as well. It was open but seemed to only be letting a few people in at a time. He figured they probably still couldn't let people buy frozen things.

Ryan continued towards his house. Based on the number of cars out now, news of the power had made its way outside town. He didn't know if his family knew about it yet. He turned off the main road. He looked at the houses around him. People were cleaning up their yards and doing other things. Some kids were in small kiddy pools while others played in water hoses to avoid the heat.

He turned into the driveway. He hoped to hear from Hannah again soon.

Sharon Rogers

Sharon didn't sleep well that night. No power made all the little sounds jump out at her. The creaking house, the bugs outside, and the dogs barking in the distance all seemed right next to her. She couldn't keep her eyes shut for long without something catching her attention. Sharon gave up on sleep and thought about that day.

Colleen hadn't mentioned her Sunday School group coming. Closer to 11, Sharon braced herself for whatever excuse she needed to give about why the ladies hadn't shown up yet, but Colleen said nothing. 11 came and Sharon gave Colleen her sandwiches. She waited for the comment, but nothing came.

"Everything okay?" she asked.

"Just fine," Colleen said. "Just fine." Sharon waited.

"How're your sandwiches?"

"Just fine. Just fine."

"Do you want some water? I could get you some."

"Just fine. Just fine." Sharon returned to the kitchen, poured the water into a cup with a straw for Colleen, and grabbed herself a bottle. *I could use a quick break.* She took the water to Colleen. The sandwiches hadn't been touched. Colleen stared at them, but made no attempt to pick them up. Sharon set the water next to the plate. Colleen looked over at it, but did not move.

"Are you hungry, Miss Colleen?"

"I...I think so. I could use something to eat, yes. Would you mind fixing me something?"

"No," Sharon said. "Not at all. How about some sandwiches?"

"That sounds nice."

"With the crust cut off?"

"Just fine. Just fine."

"How about peanut butter and jelly?"

"Sounds mighty good." Sharon didn't know what to do. Should she take the plate from Colleen and bring it back as though she just fixed it? Or should she go fix two more sandwiches and bring them back? She lifted the plate. Colleen grabbed it and looked at Sharon.

"What are you doing?" Colleen asked.

"I...just...wanted to make sure I got all the crust off is all."

"Well how am I supposed to eat if you take it?"

"Oh, I'm sorry, Miss Colleen. I wasn't going to take it. Just wanted to make sure I got all the crust." Colleen looked the sandwiches over.

"That would be nice, actually." She let go of the plate and smiled. "I just couldn't figure out why you would take my food while I was eating it."

"Oh," Sharon said. "I...guess I thought I told you in my head but forgot to say it."

"Yes, yes. I do that sometimes. Then someone looks at you with such a strange look because you're talking about something and they have no idea what it is." Sharon laughed.

"Yup. I guess that's what happened." Sharon took the sandwiches into the kitchen and set them on the counter. She waited.

"I remember doing that while growing up. My brothers would all be talking about something and I would be listening and then I'd just say something and they'd all look at me so confused. I would ask what's wrong and they'd just look at me and look at each other and start laughing. They knew how to give a sister a hard time, that's for sure. Never thought any of them would get married. Never once in a million years did I..."

Sharon entered with the sandwiches and saw Colleen was staring at her water. It was the same stare she had with the plate. She didn't try to lift it. Sharon watched her for any signs of twitching. She brought the sandwiches back in and placed them before Colleen.

"Oh!" Colleen said. "You made me lunch. Well that's wonderful." She put her hand on Sharon's face. "You really are a treat. Thank you for taking such good care of me."

"Miss Colleen, you know I enjoy doing that. You don't ever have to thank me."

"Why sure I do! You are just a treasure to have around the place and I'm glad you're here with me." Sharon sat down in the chair and watched as Colleen began eating.

"You know," Colleen said as she chewed. "My favorite food growing up was peanut butter and jelly. I couldn't get enough of it. We didn't always have it, you know. We couldn't always get to the store and pick some up. We always had some sort of preserves, you know, with the trees and such, but peanut butter was such a treat. I enjoyed it so much I once asked just for that for my birthday. My mother thought I was so silly, but I just couldn't help it. Those brothers of mine, though. They were so thoughtful. They went out and spent their money on getting me some peanut butter. Mother told me years later they pooled all their money together and got me a nice big jar. It lasted me a long time."

"That was nice of them."

"Yes, it was. I guess they weren't always that bad. Most of the time, but not always. They had some other good moments too. Anytime I was scared of something they helped me. Guess they would rather be the ones doing the scaring than have something else scare me." She drank some water. "When do you think Reggie is going to visit?"

"Who?" Sharon asked.

"Reggie. You know. My brother from Florida. He said he was going to visit me while he was up here to see Mama. She's been really sick lately, but the doctors think she's going to pull through. They said the clots dissolved and it doesn't look like she's in any danger anymore. Reggie was gonna come up and see how she was doing. I told him it wasn't necessary to come see me, but he insisted."

"I'm not sure, Miss Colleen."

"Oh well, I'm sure he'll turn up at some point. Man never could keep track of time all that well. I remember Mama getting so mad at him for being really late or really early. He never could be consistent and it always made her so mad. She always said he would be late to his own funeral." She took a sip of water. "I can't remember if he was, though. I don't think so. I think he was right on time. Of course, that was several years ago. I was so upset about it I don't even remember what I wore. He was the last one."

"Your last brother?"

"Yup. He was the last one. All the others went for different reasons, but he managed to hang around a little longer."

"What happened?" No response. "Miss Colleen?" Sharon looked to see she was staring in space again. She was looking right at Sharon. She didn't know if she should get up or give her a minute. "Miss Colleen?" She blinked.

"Oh," Colleen said. "That was such a nice sandwich. Thank you for making it for me. I believe I'm done now."

"Okay. What about your water?"

"Would you mind leaving it?"

"Not at all. Let me know when it starts getting low, okay?"

"I will." Sharon took the plate into the kitchen.

And that's how the whole day went, she thought as she rolled over in bed. *Another story with more spacing out.* Sharon hoped the low-grade fever would break. She got out of bed and went to Colleen's room.

She was hooked up to her oxygen tank now. She hadn't put up a fight against using it, which surprised Sharon. She didn't know what to make of that. Did that mean she had accepted what was happening or was she getting worse? The sound of the oxygen covered Colleen's raspy breathing. It was like a whisper Sharon could barely hear standing in the doorway. She moved closer to the bed until she could hear that faint sound of Colleen's tired breath. She nodded and returned to try and sleep.

Ryan Peterson

Breakfast, he thought. Ryan was looking forward to it today. The pasty taste of the cereal and oatmeal had been too much for him. He finished getting ready and walked down the stairs. It was early, but he already knew it was time.

Ryan left the addition and walked around to the house. It was still good weather. He could see a few clouds, but nothing that concerned him. As he came around the corner, his Dad and twin brothers were already setting stuff up at the grill.

"Good morning," he called. They all turned to him.

"Morning," Dad said.

"'Bout time, sleepyhead," Ken called.

"Yeah," Brandon said. "Sthleepyhead."

"That's what I said," Ken said.

"Well I sthaid it too."

"But I said it first."

"All right, you two," Dad said. "Calm down, calm down." He looked at Ryan. "You wanna help?"

"Oh yeah. I'm starving!"

"Good. We've got some good things out here."

"Oh yeah? Like what?"

"Well," Dad said. "We've got bacon, sausage, biscuits, potatoes, and eggs."

"Eggs?" Ken asked

"Yup. Eggs."

"How're we gonna fixth eggsth?" Brandon asked.

"What do you mean?"

"I think they're asking because we all like them scrambled," Ryan said.

"Ah," Dad said. "We're going to use the griddle. I'm gonna mix up the eggs, pour them onto the griddle, and scramble them that way." The twins thought about this for a moment.

"Wait..." Ken said.

"What?" Brandon asked. Dad laughed.

"All right," he said. "Just watch."

Ryan was skeptical, too. He pictured a pile of sloppy eggs

swirling around the griddle too loose to cook into anything and running down into the grill and putting the fire out. He chuckled at the vision of Dad trying to keep the fire going and accidentally making things worse.

"What's so funny?" Dad asked, snapping Ryan back.

"Oh," he said. "Nothing."

"Uh huh." Dad cracked some eggs into a bowl. He added some milk and used a fork to stir it all together.

"Still looks like the regular way so that's good," Ryan said.

"Yup. Now what I've done is heated this griddle up to a really high temperature. Instead of putting them in a pan and stirring them up that way, we're going to pour them onto the griddle, give them a moment to cook, and then start breaking them up into bits."

"You mean like making an omelet?"

"Yup. Same idea, anyway." Dad poured the eggs on the griddle as he'd described. The twins watched as it bubbled at first.

"It'sth sthtopping," Brandon said.

"Shh. Watch," Ken said. Dad began stirring the eggs. The twins were sucked in. Ryan smiled at their enthusiasm.

"I'm gonna go help Mom," he said.

"Okay," Dad said. "It'll still be a few minutes before we get everything cooked. Tell her I'm working on the eggs right now, but the biscuits are baking in this foil over here, and the bacon is on this cookie sheet with the sausage. Don't think it'll take us too long."

"Sounds good. I'll tell her." Ryan walked inside. He walked up the three steps to the dining room and found Mom there getting things together. "Good morning."

"Good morning," she said. "You sleep well?"

"Can't complain. I think I might miss how quiet it is out there."

"Oh I'm sure we all will. That quiet has been very nice at night."

"I know. I'm not sure I'll ever sleep that well again."

"Probably not," she said. "Or rather I hope we don't get in

a position where we have to." They laughed.

"Yeah. Sleeping is nice, but I don't know about going to all these lengths to get it."

"How're things going out there?" she asked. He told her. "What about the potatoes?" Ryan shrugged.

"I don't know," he said. "Didn't say." She nodded.

"I'm sure he's got them. And if not, it's not the end of the world. We survived that."

"That we did," he said. "Do you need any help?"

"Actually, you could help me wash some of these dishes from the last few meals. We have enough to set the table, but I think we should get these cleaned and put away for when we get all these others in."

"That sounds like a plan. You wash and I dry?"

"Might as well," she said. They moved the dishes to the counter as she began filling the sink with water.

"Do you think we'll get power soon?" Ryan asked.

"I'm not sure. I hope so, though."

"Yeah. Me too. This has been an interesting experience and all, but I'm ready to be back at work and school."

"You? You're ready for school?"

"I know, I know. Pretty shocking."

"I'm rethinking this whole 'end-of-the-world' thing," she said with a smile. "How is Hannah?"

"She's okay. She's waiting until her parents get power."

"Does she have it down there?"

"No. Not yet. She's been going outside and charging her phone in her car or just leaving it off. Doesn't want to burn up the battery in case something happens."

"How is she holding up?"

"Okay, I guess. I'm really worried about her being down there by herself."

"I can imagine."

He told her about Hannah walking up and down the road.

"Wow," she said.

"Yeah. When Max told me about Tuscaloosa, I thought it was just a bunch of rumors, but I guess not."

"You were right to wonder. Most people around here seem to just be making stuff up and not caring whether it's true or not. As long as they sound like they know what they're talking about."

"What makes you say that?"

"Several of the neighbors talked to me and your Dad when we went to the grandparents and told us all sorts of stuff. Rosetta Falls was wiped off the map. Dawson City had a big path torn through it by a Category 5 that went all the way through Cullman, Morgan, Limestone, and Madison County then disappeared into thin air. Thousands were dead and some were just lying in the middle of I-65 and people weren't even stopping to do anything."

"Wow. That's a pretty active imagination."

"Exactly," she said. "Your Dad never saw any of that when he went for gas."

"Yeah. That sounds like something he would mention." They heard the door open.

"It's ready!" Ken called.

"Bring them up," Mom said. The twins came in carrying two plates a piece with Dad right behind them with the biscuits. She and Ryan had everything laid out. There were pot holders already on the table waiting for the food. Ryan put the plates out and Mom went behind him and added the silverware and drinks. Water had become their favorite drink. They had two Brita pitchers they kept refilling.

Ryan thought about the water. Something as simple as water being clean was something that never crossed his mind. There were days he went without even giving it a second thought, but that had all changed.

"Do we have everything?" Dad asked.

"Looks like it," Ryan said. "I think we have everything we need. Food smells really good, too."

"All right," Mom said. "Let's sit down and pray before we eat." They all gathered around the table and said a prayer of thankfulness. "Amen. Okay, let's eat."

They passed everything around. Ryan loved the smell of

potatoes and sausage. Something about it always made his nose tingle with excitement. He passed the plate of potatoes on to his brothers and let them fight as he took some eggs.

HUUUUUUUMMMMMMMM! BEEP! BEEP!

They stopped and looked up from their food. They shared excited glances. Ken and Brandon started cheering.

"It'sth back! It'sth back!"

They heard the AC and the electronics beep. The refrigerator made a loud whirring and the icemaker in the freezer started. Lights all over the house came back. The microwave beeped at them to let them know the time needed to be updated. They stopped listening to the chorus of sounds and returned to eating.

"Oh man," Ryan said. "I can clean my bedding! Sweating in my sleep has made them disgusting."

"We'll have to figure out how to rotate laundry so we can get everything caught up," Dad said. Ken and Brandon both laughed.

"We don't stink that much!" Ken said.

"No, we don't!" Brandon said.

"I'm sure you two have piles of dirty clothes in your rooms that stink to high heavens," Mom said. "We'll have to get everyone's dirty clothes together so we can get them all cleaned."

"We just did, Mom," Ryan said. "They couldn't have gone through that many clothes." Ken and Brandon looked at each other. Ryan always smiled when they did that. It looked like a creepy mirror, especially when they made the same face.

"Good grief," Mom said, rolling her eyes. They laughed.

"I'm going to my room," he said when he finished eating. "Wanna see if the cell towers are back up."

"We still have to do dishes," Ken said.

"I know, I know. Just want to go see if cellphones are working so I can try and talk to Hannah. I know if we have power here they can't be too far from having them up in Huntsville, right? Maybe her parents will have it soon." They all sort of nodded and agreed. The food was too good to be ignored. Ryan put his plate and silverware in the sink then left to go to his room.

Outside was beautiful but getting warm. He entered the addition and walked up to his room. He could already hear the fan next to his bed blowing. It probably hadn't cooled off yet, but at least it had started.

He walked in and went straight for his phone. As it turned on, he opened his windows to let the hot air out and try to cool the place off. He looked at the top right of his phone and waited for the signal to show up. He wasn't sure if it would, but he hoped.

Isbel Banner

What am I going to do? Isbel stared at the ceiling while lying on her back. She was still in shock from the events days before.

After talking to Hannah, the officer led her back to 15th Street and behind where Krispy Kreme used to be. The officer didn't say anything to her for the most part. He responded to calls on his radio. He guided Isbel through the rubble.

She didn't know where they were going. The houses they passed were flattened. Isbel could see volunteers and people searching through the rubble. People in uniforms were trying to move others away from the houses to help them with their search. Some cried and protested. They had things they wanted or needed to find people. She tried to not listen to them, but so many voices made it hard. Volunteers yelled things to each other about needing help or finding things.

Her chest tightened and she began running. She cried as the officer called out behind her. At one of the flattened houses was Jack's overturned truck. She turned to the officer.

"Where is he?!"

"Ma'am, I don't-"

"Where is Jack?! This is his truck! Why isn't he here?!" She fell down and continued crying. The officer tried to help her up, but Isbel refused. She felt faint. Everything went black.

Isbel thought about coming to. She opened her eyes and saw she was under a red tent. She recognized the symbol as the Red Cross. She heard the volunteers talking to each other and to her. She looked around her. One of the volunteers stood over her.

"Habla inglés?" the lady volunteer asked. Isbel nodded. "How are you feeling?" She nodded again.

"W...where am...where-"

"You passed out from exhaustion and stress. An officer and volunteer brought you here. You've been out for a few minutes." The lady talked to her for a little longer, but Isbel wasn't listening. She missed her husband. She knew Jack was gone.

She got out of the bed in her apartment and tried to figure

out what to do. They still had the truck as her name wasn't on anything. They told her they would hold it and give it to her as long as she brought her marriage certificate, but she didn't want to do that right now. She didn't know where to go. She didn't know what to do. She went to the closet and got her suitcase. She decided it would be best to go ahead and pack. Maybe she could call some friends and see if she could stay with them. She took the safe down from the top of the closet and opened it. She sifted through the many important documents until she found the marriage certificate. She looked at Jack's name and began to cry.

"Colleen...Colleen...Colleen, it's time to wake up...Come on, Colleen." Sharon watched her stir. She patted Colleen's head with a damp paper towel. Her fever had dropped and she seemed to be okay. "Colleen...Colleen." Colleen opened her eyes.

"Is it morning already?" she asked. Sharon smiled.

"No, Miss Colleen. You took a nap remember?"

"Oh, yes."

"Did you sleep well?"

"Yes, yes. Was a good nap." She tried to lift herself.

"No, no, no," Sharon said. "You need to lay down. Tell me what you need and I'll get it for you."

"I just need to get up. People are gonna be here soon and I need to get things ready."

"It's okay, Miss Colleen. I can take care of things. You just stay here, okay?" Colleen looked around.

"Why is the power off? How am I supposed to take care of people when the power's off? I told those people to take care of the power but they didn't do it. Why do I pay them if they don't do like they're supposed to?"

"It's okay, Miss Colleen. They're working to get it back on."

"Well, I hope they hurry. I know people are gonna be worried if there's no power. They won't be happy. How am I supposed to entertain my guests if there's no power? Ain't no one gonna be happy if there's no power. No one."

"I'm going to check your blood sugar, okay?" she asked. Colleen nodded. She didn't move as Sharon checked the numbers. "Oh. Okay. I'll be right back with your medicine, okay?" Colleen nodded. Sharon left the room and measured out insulin. It was almost empty. Sharon knew she'd need to leave for some soon. She returned to the bedroom. She gave Colleen the shot, but noticed she barely winced at the needle. "Do you need some water?"

"Hmm?"

"Do you need some water?"

"Oh. Yes, I think that would be nice. Water's always good for the body. That's what my mother used to always say. She'd say 'Now Colleen you need to get you some water or you ain't gonna get very far 'cause you need it.' And she was right. I'd get me some water and I'd be just fine. My brothers never did like they should, but that's how brothers can be."

"Okay," Sharon said. "I'll get the water for you. You just stay here, okay?"

"Course, sometimes those brothers of mine weren't good. They would work hard sometimes, but then they'd go off and do whatever they wanted. They'd disappear for hours fishing or whatever it is they were doing. Mother would not be happy, but Father would always tell her that's just how boys are. They just gotta go do what boys gotta do. She never did like hearing that." As she continued on, Sharon left the room and went to the kitchen. She could hear Colleen still talking to herself about her brothers and her family. Sharon looked out the kitchen window.

It was eerily still. The sun was much lower in the sky now and Sharon figured night would be here soon. Colleen probably wouldn't want to sleep then because of her nap. Sharon took a pot out of the cabinet and filled it with water. The water was ice cold and she knew that, but there was nothing she could do. She filled the pot three-fourths full and set it on the stove top. She turned the knob and the gas burner lit beneath the pot. She covered the pot and went to the cabinet. She filled two glasses with water and set them down on the table. She opened the cooler with the insulin to make sure it was still cold. She closed the cooler, picked up the glasses, and walked to the bedroom. She could hear Colleen still talking as she entered.

"...and of course, with things like poke salad and the like, as you get older it gets harder to eat it 'cause it stops agreeing with you. I remember when Father wasn't able to eat it anymore he was so upset about it. He'd given Mother so much grief because his favorite food in the world, poke salad, was just too much for his old body to handle."

"The poor thing," Sharon said, without missing a beat.

"Oh yes. He was unhappy when she stopped fixing it. Of course, he died not long after that. My brothers used to say it was because he realized he had nothing to live for if he couldn't eat his poke salad. I didn't really think that that was the case, but you never know. Men can be such strange creatures." Sharon handed her the glass of water and made sure she was able to hold it. "Thank you, dearie." She drank from it, her hands shaking as she put it to her mouth and slowly set it back down.

"Is that better?" Sharon asked. "Do you need some more?"

"I think that's just fine," Colleen said. I don't want to seem greedy over just a little water. Some people in this world don't have any water so I shouldn't be getting worked up over this little bit here."

"It's okay, Miss Colleen. You can have more if you need it. It's different if you need it."

"Yes, yes." Colleen's eyes widened. "Oh dear. My guests! Sharon, I gotta get up and go get things ready for my guests. They're gonna be here any minute and I'm not even dressed. I know those church ladies. They won't be pleased at all if I greet them still in my nightwear. Then I'll never hear the end of it. They'll just go on and on and I won't even get a little bit of peace or satisfaction. They'll just come right in and-"

"Actually," Sharon said, cutting Colleen off. "The ladies called during your nap. They said they don't think they should be going out in this dreadful weather without power." Sharon bit her lip. Colleen seemed to look right through her in awe and shock of the lies. Sharon tried to think of a cover up. *I told you that, remember? They cancelled weeks ago. They came yesterday.*

"Well," Colleen said. "I hope they're all okay. I guess it's a good thing they don't come out and try to be here in this weather. Driving on those roads can be very dangerous." Sharon sighed with relief.

"You're right, Colleen. I think it's good they chose not to do that."

"I do hope they don't think of this as a reflection on me. I enjoy having those ladies come over and see me every now and then. It would be a shame if they didn't keep coming over because they thought something bad would happen."

"I'm sure that's not the case, Miss Colleen." Colleen drank her water again. Sharon wanted to help, but knew the woman needed to feel she had strength left. When she finished, Sharon asked, "Do you want me to take that for you?" Colleen nodded and handed the glass back to Sharon. "I'll be right back, okay?"

"That's fine. Need to get those cleaned so we don't have dishes piling up everywhere. I don't like having a filled sink. Always makes a house look so dirty and unkempt. I don't understand why people can't just take good care of their kitchens and keep their dishes clean." Sharon took the two glasses to the sink. She rinsed, dried, and placed them back in the cabinets. She returned to the bedroom.

"Do you want to take a bath, Miss Colleen?" Colleen felt of her nightgown and realized it was wet.

"I think I should. I don't know what happened but I'm just as wet as can be."

"It was probably the heat, Miss Colleen. It got pretty hot in here. I'm surprised you stayed asleep."

"Dearie, I grew up long before air conditioning and heating were in a house. Used to if you wanted to cool off you had to go down by the little crick where we lived and had to go swimming in it. Sometimes those brothers of mine would take each other's clothes and go hide 'em while they were out there. I tell you what. Boys can be such troublemakers. They did all they could just to cause trouble with each other and would make such a mess at times. I also kept my clothes on when I went swimming. Mother didn't approve but I told her those brothers of mine would take and hide my clothes if I didn't." Sharon pulled a fresh gown out of the dresser along with fresh underwear.

"I'm gonna get the bath ready and I'll come back, okay?"

"Okay. I can come in there whenever you're ready."

"Oh I know, but since you just woke up I'll come back and make sure you don't fall."

"That's good. I don't want to fall and get hurt. I don't need to get myself hurt and in a wheelchair. It's hard enough getting around as it is." Sharon took the clothes across the hall. She knew they couldn't do a full bath, but she could get Colleen in there and get her cleaned up and the dirty clothes off her. She set up the bathroom chair in case Colleen decided to go. She pulled towels from the cabinet and placed them around the bathtub.

From the bathroom closet, she pulled a seat made for the bathtub. This made it where Colleen could sit down in the bathtub and keep water from flooding the bathroom floor and reduced it only to splashes. Sharon couldn't remember where she'd found it. It may have been online on one of the countless websites she'd visited about caring for loved ones. Or she may have just seen it on the TV and thought it would be helpful. She pulled a small, plastic bucket out of the cabinet and set it next to the toilet. She would keep the sponges in there. She left the bathroom and checked on Colleen. She was in bed lightly snoring. Sharon went to the kitchen.

She felt the water in the pot with her fingers. It was pretty warm, but she didn't know if it would be too hot for Colleen. She used potholders to carry the water to the bathroom and pour it into the bathtub. It looked like it would take quite a few more to fill it, so she knew it would take a few more minutes to get it ready. She took the pot back to the kitchen and filled it again for heating.

She checked her watch for the time to keep track of the water and went back into the bedroom with Colleen to keep her company. She didn't want to leave Colleen alone for too long in case she started feeling ill and needed attention.

Colleen wasn't snoring anymore. She stirred when Sharon entered and smiled at her.

"How're you doing?" Sharon asked.

"Oh, fine. Fine. Just having a nice dream."

"Yeah? What was it about?"

"You know, I don't really remember. Just know it was a nice one."

"As long as you know it's good that's what matters, right?"

"Mhmm. I would have to agree with that."

"I'm heating some water up for your bath."

"Thank you, dear. You are a jewel."

"Oh no, Miss Colleen. Just trying to help you."

"I remember the first time you came over to take care of me. You were...so nice. I remembered you from church but didn't know why you were at my house."

"Well I missed you and wanted to see you again."

"Yes. I hated I couldn't go back. I always enjoyed church."

"I know you did and we enjoyed having you there. You were always such a joy to work with and all the children loved you."

"Oh and I loved them. They were so wonderful and always made my day to work with them. It was like having my own children." She paused. Sharon didn't say anything. "I always wanted children."

"I know, Miss Colleen."

"Would have been so nice to have them around. Playing and growing up. Would have been nice." Sharon looked at her watch.

"I'll be right back okay?"

"Where are you going?"

"I'm going to check the water."

"The water?"

"For your bath."

"Oh right. Almost forgot. Guess I was just tired."

"Guess so," Sharon said with a smile. "I'll be right back."

"Okay, dear."

Sharon went into the kitchen and felt the water. It was a little cooler than the first pot, but that was fine. She carried it into the shower and emptied it. The water wasn't very deep. She didn't know if that would be enough to take care of Colleen or if she would need more.

It took a few more trips to get the water where Sharon thought it should be. After about an hour, the bathtub was the right temperature and was about the right amount of water. She put some water, soap, and the sponges in the bucket next to the tub so she could wash Colleen. With everything in place, she went back into the bedroom.

"You ready, Miss Colleen?" she asked. Colleen seemed confused.

"Ready for what?"

"For your bath," Sharon said. Colleen paused.

"Oh yes. As ready as I'll ever be I suppose. It'll be good to get out of these sticky clothes. They're starting to smell funny."

"I have you some nice ones in there waiting for you."

"Well good. I don't mind being a little sweaty, but this is too much for me. I think my bedding is wet too."

"That's okay. I'll change those before you go to bed tonight, okay?"

"Thank you, dearie. That'll be good." They moved slowly into the bathroom. Sharon again did her best to make Colleen feel like she was doing it on her own. She didn't feel as sick as she did earlier. Now she seemed a bit stronger. They got into the bathroom and Sharon stopped.

"Okay," she said. "Let's get you out of this nightgown. I've got the bathtub all set up for you so you don't have to worry too much, okay?"

"That's good. Don't wanna make a mess just getting clean. Doesn't make much sense to me."

"Me either." Sharon unbuttoned the back of the gown and helped Colleen lift it over her head. She helped her remove her underwear and get on the chair in the shower.

"My, my. This water is a little warm, isn't it? I mean, with it being April and all I don't usually take such warm baths. Seems like an awful waste of hot water to do a thing like that." Sharon's heart lifted. It had been so long since Colleen was so close to knowing what month it was. It was such a good sign.

"Me either," she said trying to suppress the excitement.

Colleen rarely mentioned what month it was and hadn't known the day for some time. Sharon was on the edge of tears, but regained control. "How warm was it usually in April when you were growing up?"

"Oh we never knew. We didn't have 'thermo-meters' like there are now and I never looked at the paper to see what those weathermen had to say about it. We just knew it was hot when it was hot and cold when it was cold."

"I guess that's all you really need to know, isn't it?" Sharon asked.

"I suppose so." Sharon used a washcloth to run water over Colleen.

"Is that too warm?" she asked.

"Oh no," Colleen said. "Well, not too bad that is. It could be a lot warmer."

"So it's too cold?"

"Oh, no. No. Just fine. Just fine."

"What're you thinking about?"

"Oh nothing much really. Just wondering what the church ladies are all up to since they can't be here. I hope they've got power. I know they're probably just like me, waiting for the power to get back on. But then once it does come on, they'll get right on to cleaning their places and getting things done. Yup. I bet they're all probably taking a shower at the same time too. That would really make all the water cold for the rest of us. How are we supposed to shower with no hot water if people are all using it at the same time?"

"You mean when the power comes back?" Colleen didn't say anything for a moment. Sharon saw the look on her face showing she was trying to piece everything together. The clarity lit in her eyes.

"Yup. When the power comes back on."

"I understand." Sharon dipped the sponge into the bucket and washed Colleen's back, who shuddered at the first touch. "What's wrong?"

"Oh...It's just a little hot is all." Sharon nodded at the response.

"I'm sorry, Miss Colleen." *Good sign.*

"Oh no, it's fine. Just wasn't expecting it to be so warm."

"Well, you let me know if you need it cooler." Sharon rinsed Colleen with the water in the tub. She put the sponge in the bucket and continued washing Colleen.

Colleen didn't say much at first while Sharon washed her. She looked straight ahead towards the mirror and went through the motions as Sharon dipped the sponge in the warm water to keep it soapy. When it came time for her hair, Sharon leaned Colleen's head back and made sure it was wet. She leaned her back up and gently washed Colleen's hair. She did her best to not hurt Colleen. After a moment, she rinsed the hair.

"Close your eyes," Sharon said. Colleen did. She rinsed Colleen off. "Okay. How does that feel?"

"Much better than before. Don't feel as sticky as I did in the bed."

"Good. After we finish in here, I'll take you to your chair and I'll make your bed for you, okay?"

"Thank you, dearie. I hope this isn't too much trouble for you."

"Not at all, Miss Colleen. You're never any trouble." Sharon handed her a towel. "Do you wanna dry yourself off while I put some of this stuff away?"

"I can do that." Colleen took the towel away and attempted to dry herself. She wasn't making any progress because of her weak rubbing, but Sharon said nothing. She cleaned out the bucket and rinse the sponge before putting them away. She made sure things were back in their place, then took the other end of the towel.

"Let me help some." Colleen gave no objection and Sharon dried her off. "Okay, stand up so we can get the rest of you." She held Colleen's weight as best she could without her noticing. She helped her lift each leg and set it on the bathmat. Sharon then dried the rest of her. She took the underwear from the counter.

"Okay," she said. "Lean on me and put the right leg

through first. Good, now do the left leg. All right. Now let's get the gown." Colleen was able to help with the gown. She put her head through the hole and put her arms in it while Sharon buttoned the back and made sure it was in place. "How's that?"

"I guess that's as good as I'm gonna get, right?" Colleen said with a smile.

"Okay, let's go sit in your chair."

"You know, Sharon. Sometimes I don't think I thank you enough."

"You do, Miss Colleen. I promise you do."

"But you're just so nice to me. I don't know what I'd do without you."

"I'm just happy to be here to help. Anything I can do to make it easier for you is what I'm happy to do."

"And I can't thank you enough for that." Sharon sat her down in the chair.

"Do you need anything before I go clean up?"

"No. I think I'll be fine right here. I'll just look out the window at the weather."

"Want me to open the door so you can see out better?"

"I guess that would be nice." Sharon opened the door and felt the nice breeze come in.

"You let me know if you need anything, okay? I'll be right in the bathroom."

"I will. You just get right on with what you need to do. I know the ladies from church are gonna be on their way soon and we're gonna hafta get things going. I'm pretty sure they're not gonna bring any food like they usually do since it's gonna be so late. But I wanna make sure we have something ready for them in case they decide they are hungry or something." Sharon went into the bathroom as Colleen made plans for her church ladies.

<u>Hannah Leon</u>

She stood at the window. The sun was almost gone. The light shining through the blinds was barely enough to let her see her bed and the other furniture in her bedroom. She turned back to look around the slight darkness. She could see the outlines of her nightstand, bed frame, chest of drawers, and dresser, but night was coming. She pulled the curtains shut and turned to get the LED lantern and immediately regretted it. She couldn't see. There were faint outlines of lines shining through the sides of her window, but not enough to guide her to the lantern. With a sigh of frustration, she opened the curtains again and searched for the light. It wasn't on her bed like she expected.

"Hmm. Where is it?" she said to the darkness. "It's gotta be in here somewhere..." She moved her hands along her unmade bed to the foot of it. *Dang it.* She moved towards the head in hopes she put it there instead. Nothing. She squinted her eyes to see in what was rapidly becoming darkness. She couldn't see well enough to make out any of the items on top of her furniture. She'd put it on the bed. She knew it. Why wasn't it there? Had it fallen off? No. She would've heard it. It was a pretty big lantern. She couldn't remember why she got it.

She ran her hands on the nightstand. She felt her pictures, wrappers from food, and the useless lamp, but no lantern. She followed the bed to the foot of it and felt ahead of her for the dresser.

"Ouch!" she said when she found it. It had been closer than she expected and threw her off. She felt her nails to see if anything had happened. The paint she'd put on weeks before was now peeled and needed fixing. *Maybe I'll do that tomorrow,* she thought. *Would definitely take my mind off of things, right?* She felt the top of the dresser. She found her stereo, some books, unfolded clothes, jewelry, and her necklace holder, but no lantern. She kept moving counterclockwise in the room until she found the chest of drawers. She felt along top of it. Her school books were up there and her laptop. She'd tried tethering her phone to get some internet but it didn't work as well as she needed. It took a long time for pages to load and it sucked the life out of her phone.

Her phone! If she could find it she could use it as a flashlight to find her lantern. Her phone could at least help her find it, and then she could just turn her phone off and not worry about running down the battery. She just needed to find her phone. But where was it? Where did she leave it? She thought it was in her bedroom, but she'd already felt all the furniture. Had it fallen on the floor too? Had she placed it somewhere and couldn't find it?

She stood in the middle of her bedroom. Her eyes were shut. She'd been so focused on looking for light, she hadn't even noticed they were closed. She opened them to see the difference in light. The sun was now set and no light came into the room. There was almost no difference between having her eyes open and shut. She tried to think back. Where had she put them? Where were the lantern and phone? They had to be somewhere in the living room. Unless she left them in the car.

"Yo!" someone outside yelled. She jumped.

"Hey," another voice yelled. "What're you doing?"

"I'm trying to get my stuff together so I can go."

"Well you ain't goin' nowhere you keep messin' with my car!"

"Man, I ain't messin' with your car. I'm just trying to get my stuff together."

"Yo, I heard you. You think I can't hear you?"

As the fighting continued, Hannah ran into the living room towards the front door. She bumped into her backpack, a pillow, and some boxes as she slammed into the door and locked it. The fighting grew and she bolted and chained the door. She backed away from the door as the yelling turned into cursing and threatening. The voices were loud and mean. More were joining in too. She heard women yelling in defense of their boyfriends and men insulting the women. She felt the couch behind her and she sat down on something hard. She gasped.

The lantern! She stood up and felt for the lump again. *The lantern!* She picked it up and searched for the knob. She pressed it and the living room was flooded with light. She took the light into her bathroom to get ready for bed. It felt so good to see again. She took her contacts out, brushed her teeth, took her medicine, and walked back into the bedroom. The blinds and curtain were still open. She turned the lantern off but kept it in her hand so she wouldn't lose it. She moved to the window to look out and see what was going on.

She saw two groups of people now yelling obscenities at and pushing against each other. If they had noticed the floating light in her apartment, they didn't seem to care. They were more interested in their own fight. Hannah shut the blinds and curtains. She turned the light back on and went to the front door to make sure it was locked. She felt the bolt in her hands and twisted it again just to be certain. She tugged on the chain just in case. She walked slowly back to the bedroom, set the lantern on her nightstand and got in bed. She turned off the light just in case. She didn't want them to somehow see something through the cracks of the blinds and decide to unite and find out who was up there. She slid under the covers more and cuddled her body pillow. The yelling hadn't stopped. It didn't sound like they were fighting yet, but she worried it would soon come to blows.

Maybe I'll check the door one more time.

Sharon Rogers

Colleen was sick. Sharon had the last of the insulin on some ice in the freezer, but neither were lasting much longer. Colleen would need more soon. Sharon couldn't say anything to Colleen. It would upset her. But how was she going to get out of the house without her knowing? There was too much of a chance she would know. What if she called? What if she needed help? Sharon had no idea how long it would take. She looked in Colleen's room.

Colleen was asleep. Sharon figured it just happened since they were talking a few minutes ago. Sharon didn't know how safe this would be. Did she need to go now or wait until later? She didn't even know if they would have insulin. *But if they don't,* she thought, *they could point me in the right direction.* She needed to go now.

She grabbed the prescription from the doctor and the power of attorney. *This should be what they need.* She carefully shut and locked the door before getting in her car. She took her cigarettes out of her purse but stopped. It probably wasn't a good time. She could do it later, though. Maybe on her way back. She put the pack back and pulled out of the driveway.

The drive there wasn't what she expected. There were more cars out today and most were obeying the four-way stop law. She didn't see any accidents this time either. She turned onto University towards Memorial Parkway. She needed to go south. The hospital wasn't far. Only two or three exits down Memorial. She would get on Governors Drive and pass the church with the mural.

Colleen loved that mural. She told Sharon it was one of the reasons she started going there. Something about it seemed to call to her and make her feel more secure. More at home. Sharon thought it gawky when she started going there. She preferred the large bell tower and the music it made. When she worked at Huntsville Hospital, she would hear it on Sundays if she worked that day. She could see it from Memorial now. She was thankful the tornadoes didn't knock it down.

She reached Governors Drive and waited. There were more cars here and they weren't all following the law. She wanted a police officer to show up and put an end to it, but one didn't. After a moment, she turned onto Governors. As she passed the church, she saw the mural and nothing looked to be damaged. There were people at the church. She was too focused to see who they were. She passed the other buildings and turned in front of Huntsville Hospital to park in the garage.

People were crowded outside the entrance. She had no idea if she was going to get what she needed. She continued past them and pulled into the garage. It wasn't the closest spot, but it was the best she could do for now. She hoped they could help her. She didn't want to have to go elsewhere, especially with the possibility of Colleen waking up and realizing she was gone. She tried to get through the crowd.

"Excuse me," she said. "Excuse me. I need to get through."

"Whoa, lady," someone said. "You gonna hafta wait just like the rest of us."

"But I need to get through."

"We all need to get through," someone else said, "but that don't mean yer special enough to get through first."

"But a woman is dying!"

"Lots of people are dying," another said. "We're all here for the same reason. You gotta wait like we gotta wait." Sharon tried to maintain her composure. *This is no time to lose it, Sharon. This is no time to lose it.* She bit her tongue and stood among the large group.

They moved slowly. The nurses let only a few people in at a time and asked them what it was they needed. Sharon knew this was for the best, but it bothered her. She checked her watch. It was taking so long. She really needed to get back to Colleen. She figured it would be okay. *Colleen's asleep,* she thought. *She's not going to wake up. She's going to stay asleep. Everything will be fine.*

The doors opened and the crowd moved again. She was getting closer to the door and felt like it wouldn't be long now, but it closed and took a bit of her hope. She wanted to take her mind off of what was going on. She couldn't stand there and think about Colleen and not getting back in time.

"So why are you here?" she said to the lady next to her.

"My husband needs a refill on his oxygen tank." She tapped the metal canister next to her leg.

"They do that here?"

"I don't know," the lady said. "But I hope so. The ER is pretty bad."

"Really?"

"Yup. I walked in and immediately regretted it. The whole place is covered with people for all sorts of different reasons. Lots of homeless people, I think."

"I'm surprised they're even allowed there," Sharon said. The lady gave her a surprised look. "I'm sorry. I meant I'm surprised they let them stay there if they don't have anything wrong with them."

"They probably have lots wrong with them, but what are you going to do?" the lady said. "Can't really turn people away just to turn them away."

"Guess we should all be thankful for that, right?"

"I guess so. That keeps them from just turning one of us away, right?" The door opened and more people entered. Sharon and the lady were closer now.

"Very much so," the lady said. "Why are you here?"

"I'm a caregiver for a woman and she needs insulin."

"Oh my. Are you sure they have that?"

"I have no idea. I'm going to the pharmacy in hopes of getting at least a short-term supply. I only need some until the power comes back."

"Who knows when that's going to be?"

"I really hope it's soon. I don't know how much longer I can take this."

"You aren't the only one," the lady said. "My husband has had trouble breathing without our air unit so we've been using the oxygen tanks. I don't know how much longer we can do this. Especially if the power stays off." The doors opened again and they were able to make it inside this time.

"Best of luck," Sharon said.

"You too!" Sharon walked down a hallway to a map and found the pharmacy. She hoped she had everything she needed. The prescription wasn't at the pharmacy, but she had a copy of it for their records. She reached the pharmacy and, as with the entrance, there was a long line. She looked at her watch. It was taking longer than she wanted. She stood at the back of the line and waited. Some people tried to cut, but security guards were there to keep order.

There was a wide variety of people around her. Some were homeless. Their clothes were ragged and stained. The smells were strong and Sharon winced several times as she tried to get used to it. The pharmacy line moved faster than the one outside. When it moved, Sharon would turn her head away from the smells behind her and do her best to breathe. She then turned around and waited patiently for the line to move again so she could clear her nostrils of the putrid smell. She watched as each person was called and presented their prescriptions and other forms. Some were turned away and some were informed they were out of the items. Sharon was nervous. With each step in the line, she didn't know if she was going to be leaving with what she needed. She looked at her watch.

It's okay, she thought. *The line is moving faster so you're doing okay. She's not awake yet. She's not awake yet.* The line moved. The two people in front of her were called and she stood there. It was a strange moment coated in victory and horror. She was happy to finally be here and be able to get what she needed, but she didn't know what she was going to do if they didn't have it. They could at least give her some, right? They could at least help out a little.

"Next." Sharon almost ran to the man behind the counter.

"Hi," Sharon said.

"Hello, ma'am. How can I help you?"

"Okay. I'm a caretaker for an older lady. I have her prescription here for insulin as well as the power of attorney to show I can get this and my ID to verify who I am. I need just enough insulin to get her through until the power comes back."

"Let me see your paperwork." Sharon handed it over. She waited.

"I promise I have everything there. I'm sorry...I'm just...she's still at home alone right now and as you know there's no power and I didn't want to leave her and don't want her to be alone for long so please, please help me."

"Does she get this through hospice?"

"No, the pharmacy listed. I'm her caretaker. I've known her for years and started helping her when she got really ill."

"Have you contacted this pharmacy?"

"Yes," she lied. "There was no response. I guess it's because of the power. I don't know if they have power now. I tried them yesterday." The man nodded.

"I'll be right back." The man got up and went through a door behind him. Sharon was nervous. She didn't know what this meant. What she getting the medicine? Was everything going to be okay? Did she have to pay any money? She had her card and a check. She could pay it if necessary, but why didn't he just ask for it?

"Ma'am," he said as he came through. "We have a very limited supply of insulin, but we can give you some to get you through a few days, but can't do much more than that. I'm going to need a few things from you." He gave her a list of things. Copies of this and copies of that, but Sharon was so overjoyed she didn't care. She waited for copies to be made of her documents and she signed the form they put in front of her. She paid the money and thank them for their time.

Sharon ran to the garage as best she could. It wasn't a lot of insulin, but it was better than nothing. They just had to make it until she could get more, which she hoped wouldn't be long. She got in her car and left. She did her best not to speed, but she wanted to get home.

Colleen's not awake yet, she thought. *Don't stress over it. She's not awake yet. You know she sleeps for hours and it hasn't been hours. Only feels like it.* Her pep talk didn't make things better. She passed the church and merged onto Memorial Parkway. She watched for cars and changed lanes. *Not that much further,* she thought. *Not that much further.* She changed lanes to allow the cars entering to merge safely. She got back over and merged when she reached University Drive. Under the overpass was an accident involving a motorcycle and a pickup. Police were guiding people around the accident. Sharon didn't look. She knew she needed to get home and didn't want to rubberneck. Not now. She made it onto University and kept driving. She didn't glance in the rearview mirror at the accident.

She reached Colleen's road and turned. It was so close she could taste it. She glanced at the cooler with insulin to make sure it hadn't moved. She pulled into the driveway and turned off the car. She really needed a cigarette.

Hannah Leon

Hannah was tired of going to her car so much to charge her phone. She worried it would drain her battery and cause a new world of problems. If her car died, she would have to talk to a stranger to jump it off and there was no telling what kind of person that would be. She needed to go somewhere and charge her phone without bothering her car. Maybe more driving would help keep the battery going. She also needed something to do.

During the day when there was nothing else going on, she read. She read the books in her apartment that interested her and now she needed to read something else. She'd thought about the difference places she could go. None of the bookstores she'd passed were open. The University was closed, which was a shame because they had such a nice library.

The library! That's where I should go! She didn't know why she hadn't thought of it before. She didn't know if they were open, though. She pulled out her phone and searched online for the local library. She couldn't remember how far away it was or when it was open. Maybe it wasn't open. Maybe she couldn't go charge her phone and get books because the library, like so many other places, had no power. What good would it do to drive all the way there and it be closed? None. The data for her phone was slow and took longer than she wanted to pull up the site for the library. She wasn't used to this kind of wait. Usually her phone had good service and the speeds were fast, but since the tornadoes everything was out of whack. She felt like she was back with dial-up internet waiting with hope for a connection of any kind, let alone one of high speed.

The library's main page came up and she saw the word she needed. *Open.* She let out a sigh of relief and selected directions. While she waited, she thought about what she wanted to read. The Hunger Games had been out a while and she'd been meaning to pick those up. Her friends were all talking about it and how good it was. There was another author she wanted to read. Something Green? She couldn't remember.

Maybe something classic, she thought. *That might be a good idea.* What were some good books? What were some that would grab her and suck her into a world she'd visited so many times and couldn't wait to revisit? Or maybe take her to a new world unexplored and waiting for her. The list wasn't materializing like she wanted it to. She would think of excerpts or plot lines (*...the one with the guy and girl who don't like each other...*) but the titles would evade her (*...the man who wants redemption...*). She decided the best thing to do was to go and see what they have.

"Wait," she said. She looked at the main library's website and selected the phone number. *The website might be wrong*, she thought. The phone rang a few times and made her worry.

"Tuscaloosa Public Library," a woman with a thick southern accent said. "How may I help you?"

"Yes, I just wanted to make sure y'all were open today and had power."

"We are and we do, but we are only opening for a short period of time."

"Oh great," Hannah said. "Thank you!" She hung up and grabbed her car keys, purse, and phone charger. It would do her some good to get out of the house and go somewhere other than her car or on walks. She locked the door behind her as she went to her car. Her neighbors were home, but quiet. No yelling or threatening today. *Staying inside until night, I guess*, Hannah thought.

She drove down her small road and turned left onto Skyland Blvd. She passed McFarland and looked down the road towards the path of the tornadoes. She could go down McFarland, but that didn't seem like the best option as the road was cleaned, but not in the best driving condition. At least, not in her mind. She also didn't want to drive by 15th again. *Maybe that's the real reason*, she thought.

Skyland was empty compared to how it usually was during this time of year. Students could be seen going up and down it getting ready to move out or maybe move in. There was still time until school started in the summer, but Hannah knew from experience some off-campus students liked to get there early and meet up with friends.

Students weren't the only thing on Skyland, though. Lots of homes were down this way belonging to people who lived and/or worked in the area. Some people lived in Tuscaloosa but drove to Birmingham to work. The almost hour and a half drive was crazy, but the traffic wasn't always that bad from Tuscaloosa to Birmingham and the cost-of-living in Tuscaloosa was much lower.

She reached AL-7/US-11 and waited to turn. Traffic here was busier than other places she'd seen and seemed a bit more normal. The traffic brought some relief to her as it reminded her of how things were supposed to be. A break in the traffic came and she turned right.

The local radio station was back and provided background noise that amounted to no more than a hum with how low Hannah had it. She didn't know why, but hearing about how things around her were would put a damper on how she was feeling. Being alone without power was difficult enough, but listening to the details of how bad things really are didn't appeal to her.

She passed 15th and looked down it. The damage looked as bad here as it did at the corner of McFarland. Maybe it was a little better, but she could still see where they'd touched down and lifted. Houses were crushed and trees were scattered across the roads as people continued trying to clean up. She saw families trying to put their lives back together as they moved through the rubble that remained of their lives. Even now, days later, they were still there.

Three more turns and she was on Jack Warner with the Library in sight. The parking lot was three-fourths full.

"Wow..." she said as she pulled into the parking lot and took the first spot she saw. She wasn't interested in searching a long time for a place closer to the door when this worked just as well as any of those. She figured most people were there for the same reason she was: power. She took her things out of the car and walked towards the entrance. As she did, she kept looking over the parking lot in hopes of seeing some friends or classmates, maybe even Jillian, but no such luck.

When she walked inside, the immediate sensation of air conditioning hit her nose. She'd been so used to the stale air in her apartment it seemed like AC was something she'd forgotten. She took a deep breath and took another. It felt alien to her, but good. She walked passed the front desk and looked around the different sections. People lined the walls with several things plugged into each outlet. Some outlets were used by two or more people sitting next to each other coldly without exchanging any words or glances as they waited on their things to charge. Hannah wasn't sure she could find a place for her phone just yet. Might take a few minutes to get a spot. She went to the fiction section and walked through the books looking for something to read.

Walking through the aisles of books, she thought about how normally she would love to have this kind of free time. Her life had been so fast-paced she barely had time to read the emails she got from classmates, let alone 400-page novels. Now she had all the time she needed to read whatever she wanted and she wasn't happy. She didn't want to read. She wanted that rush. She wanted that fast-paced life back. She wanted to juggle a dozen things at once while looking for one more to give her the baker's dozen.

Jane Austin. *Pride and Prejudice.* What about that? She kept going and picked her way through all the titles.

Suzanne Collins. *The Hunger Games.* She picked it up. Many of her friends were talking about it and how much they loved it. Something about kids having to fight for their lives or something. It sounded interesting. She picked it up and kept looking.

Alexandre Dumas. *The Count of Monte Cristo.* Ryan's favorite book. He said he read it almost every year and it was one of the few he could go back to over and over again and love just as much as the first time. She hadn't read it before, which made her feel bad as she was a big fan of French literature. She almost majored in it, but chose to go the business route. She picked it up and flipped through some of it. She knew the story. Ryan enjoyed talking about it. Maybe she should give it a try. She kept it and continued looking through the other books.

John Green. *An Abundance of Katherines.* One of classmates was an Education major and talked about all sorts of young adult novels. Her favorite was Judy Blume, but she often talked about John Green and his stories. Hannah hadn't heard of him until they talked, but she liked everything her classmate said.

She continued walking through the aisles and picking up different books. She went back for *Hunger Games*, grabbed another classic, and considered Green for a moment before she noticed an open space near an outlet. She quickly moved to it with her load of books and plopped down before anyone else could claim the spot. Her phone battery was low and she didn't want to wait much longer. She had all the extra features turned off to keep it alive as long as possible. She figured if it was fully charged, she might be good until she went home.

She thought about home. She hadn't spoken to her family in a while and wasn't sure how they were doing. Maybe they had power back? *No,* she thought, *they would've told me.* She missed her family. She wanted to see them. It was one thing for it to be at school, but this was different. Her friends were gone. School was over. Things just weren't the same.

She sat down and plugged her phone into the wall. The light came on and she smiled. It had been on the whole time, but no one had sent her anything. She opened *The Hunger Games* and began reading.

She disappeared into the story, completely unaware of anything happening around her.

<u>Ryan Peterson</u>

"We need groceries," Dad said. Ryan was surprised they had made it on what they had so far.

"Where are we gonna go?" Ryan asked.

"Probably just to that grocery store towards the interstate. I figured if we've got power then they've got power. Maybe they'd be open enough for us to get a few things. They're probably controlling how many come in at a time and how much they can buy, but we should at least try."

"Maybe you could go in first, shop, then I'll come in and shop. Then we could get twice as much stuff."

"No."

"Why not?"

"Because other people need things too. If we're only allowed so much per family, we need to make sure we follow that."

"But we have more than most families."

"True," Dad said, "but that's no excuse. We need to think about other people first before we go off trying to grab everything we can find."

Ryan thought about that. It really didn't seem right to him, but he knew it would be fruitless to try and pursue that with Dad.

"So what all are we gonna get?" Ryan asked.

"Mom gave us a list of things."

"Any surprised?"

"Not really." He handed Ryan the list. It was simple, handwritten, and covered about what Ryan expected it would.

Grocery Items Needed

1. Bottled Water
2. Bread
3. Milk
4. Eggs
5. Propane
6. Sandwich Meat
7. Cheese
8. Batteries

    9.   Breakfast Foods
   10. Allergy Medicine
   11. Pain Reliever

"Why the allergy meds and pain reliever?" Ryan asked.

"Your grandmother asked for those," Dad said. "Said they could come in handy if power goes out again."

"Do you think it will?" Ryan asked. Dad shrugged.

"Hard to say. The 1993 blizzard kept most of this place shut down for a week."

The storm his Dad referred to was something Ryan couldn't remember. He was three when it came through and only had blurry images he wasn't even sure were real. The storm, like this one, had brought everything in the South, a place unaccustomed to more than a few inches of snow, to a standstill. They walked out to the car.

"Have you heard anything from UAH?" he asked.

"Nothing yet," Dad said. "They've been pretty quiet. My guess is there's no power back yet so they can't send anything."

"Man," he said as they got in the car. "I would've thought they would have them open by now. Figured Huntsville would be on the priority list or something."

"You might think that, but they're still trying to get things up and running right now. Last I heard they'd only restored some power and things were taking longer than they expected."

"Really?"

"Yup. Seems like it could be a few days."

"Wonder why it's taking so long."

"If you think about it, it's not all that surprising."

"Oh?"

"Remember," Dad said. "The tornadoes went right through the main power lines running from Browns Ferry Nuclear Plant. There's no telling what kind of effect that's having on it right now. Since our local radio stations are all out, we haven't picked up any news on what's going on there and probably won't hear anything for a while. There might be a few people down at the store that might be able to tell us something about what's going on around us, but we can only trust that so far."

"Because we don't know the sources of anything being said and how much it's been exaggerated."

"Exactly." They were driving towards the town now, looking at everything around them. The fallen limbs and trees were gone. You could still see marks on the roads where they had been, but that only remained because of the weather since the storms.

"It's strange, isn't it?" Ryan asked.

"What is?"

"How everything looks."

"You mean the sky and all or the tree limbs and things?"

"Yeah," Ryan said. Dad paused for a moment.

"Well, which is it?"

"Oh. Sorry. The weather and all. How much it changed."

"Oh yeah. Can't really tell there was even any sort of bad weather ever, let alone recently."

"I know. It's like it showed all its strength then disappeared."

"Yup. My guess is it'll be a while before we have rain again. Seems to be that way with major storms and all. Remember when the hurricanes came through back in 2005? We had a whole bunch here, then all the rain stopped for a while. Seemed like it was never going to come back and it all came back in a wallop."

"Think it'll do the same with this?"

"No telling. My guess is no. The last time we had tornadoes this bad was over 30 years ago. This is probably a once-in-a-lifetime kind of event. If not, it's definitely a once-in-a-decade thing."

"I was gonna say. You saw the last one and this one so it wouldn't make sense for it to be once in a lifetime." His Dad rolled his eyes.

"Right, right. I guess what I'm saying is it's unlikely to happen again for some time. We don't even know how many people have been killed total."

"How are we supposed to find out what's going on in other places?"

"Like I said. Ask people. They may not be the most reliable, but we'll get a better idea of what's going on than we will just making assumptions." Ryan understood the logic behind this. He didn't think it was such a good idea to just go ask people and not try to find the news for themselves, but it was at least worth a shot. He turned the radio on and searched for anything but found only static. There were some hints of stations there, but nothing came through clear enough for them to make out what was being said. He focused on one station and tried to listen. He could tell it was a man and a woman. He thought he heard "Alabama" and "Tornadoes", but nothing else came through clearly. Dad turned it off.

"Sorry," he said. "The static was giving me a headache."

"Fair enough," Ryan said. "I guess I was just hopeful we could at least pick out some news or events going on. I figured there would be a small station somewhere out there broadcasting right where we could pick it up."

"You tried. Nothing wrong with that."

"It just doesn't make sense."

"What doesn't?"

"There being no stations around here with any power. What about their generators?"

"They probably used those immediately to get as much news out as possible and they might be out now."

"But wouldn't they have some sort of back up or something?"

"You mean a back-up generator for their generator?" He gave Ryan a sly smile. Ryan chuckled. They pulled into the store parking lot.

The entrance was blocked off by a group of people. There were ropes a few feet in front of the doors with employees standing there with hand radios and clipboards. People were trying to push their way through and get inside, but the employees seemed able to keep them at bay.

"That's a lot of people," Ryan said. "How are we supposed to get everything we need?"

"We'll just have to stand there until it's our turn to go in and hope what we need is in there."

"But that's crazy. Why don't we do like I said and just go in separately for stuff?"

"No, Ryan," Dad said. "I told you we're not going to do that. We are going to follow by the rules. I'm not going to take advantage of anyone or cause any trouble."

"But it won't cause any trouble…"

"Ryan. I said 'no'." Ryan sighed and got out of the car. It seemed like a moot point to argue about this, but they needed this stuff and they could get it. He wrestled with it in his head for another moment or two and gave up.

They stood behind several men in plaid and jeans. They smelled of tobacco and body odor as if they hadn't bathed since before the storms. With so many people only having access to cold water and nothing else, he could imagine them sticking it out until they could get hot water. He didn't think he would've showered if it hadn't been for that tank-less water heater.

Ryan wasn't sure what bothered him more: the odor or the tobacco. It smelled strong and old, as if they'd been chewing it since they last showered. He tried to cover his nose and breathe through his mouth as much as possible without being noticed. His Dad was more interested in the conversations going on than the smells. Ryan could tell Dad was eavesdropping on every word he could catch without being rude. Ryan leaned towards the smelly men and listened to their thick accents as they spoke.

"Heard Tuscaloosa was wiped out."

"I heard the whole stadium was destroyed."

"Naw. That ain't what happened. They just had some rough weather's all. The real storms were up here. No way it was all the way down there."

"Oh no. Heard it myself. Said the whole place was flat."

"Can't be. No way'd the whole place be like that. Weren't

that many tornadoes in the first place."

"I heard there were. Heard there were lots of 'em. So many tornadoes people thought there was a war goin' on or something."

"I don't know about that."

"Why not? Sounds exactly like something that'd happen. Imagine so many tornadoes around you you can't even tell if they're coming or going. It'd be just like war. Not knowing where any of the sounds are coming from or if they're ever gonna end."

"I ain't sure it's quite like that."

"'Course it is. You been in a tornado before. Just like that except they just keep coming and coming. Thing about how loud those sounds would be."

"I don't think so."

"Now listen here-" They continued bickering as Ryan moved his attention to others. He wasn't interested in listening to what seemed nothing more than a contest to see who had the best source or knew something the others didn't when the tales just seemed to escalate higher and higher into the unimaginable. Some people were allowed inside as he and Dad moved closer to the door. He leaned towards a couple and their daughter as best he could without being noticed.

"We've got a lot to get."

"We do?"

"Oh yes. And you know your Dad will be wanting his cigarettes."

"What about milk?"

"We'll get that too."

"Is Aunt Jackie gonna make it like you said?"

"I don't know." The husband leaned closer to his wife and whispered so the little girl could not hear.

"You know they said Phil Campbell was hit pretty hard."

"I know."

"There's no telling for sure if Jackie made it out or not."

"Gracious, Langley. I know. Don't you think I've been thinking about that? But I can't just tell her anything if we don't know."

"We haven't heard anything from over there since the storms hit. People are saying...you know...that half of Hackleburg is gone."

"But that's almost 15 minutes away from where she lives."

"You know that don't mean nothin' when talkin' about tornadoes. They'll go straight as can be and won't even change directions. That ain't all, neither. They hit a wide area."

"But we don't know how big that tornado was."

"You're right. Could be it wasn't that big anyway, but it's still something to be concerned about. We don't know nothing so we can't say nothing yet. But we do need to be careful about encouraging her to think Jackie's okay."

"So you think we should just let her think her aunt is dead and leave it at that? How can we do that, Langley? How can we do that to her?"

"Shh. Shh. She's gonna catch on. We just need to keep an ear out for any news from over there and see what comes up."

"You're right." Some people exited and the family was allowed in. Ryan and his Dad were now at the front of the line.

"Okay," the employee behind the ropes said. "As I'm sure you've figured out, I'm in charge of letting people in. Before I can do that, here's how this works. We're only allowing a few people in at a time and there are rules. Please limit your family to 10 items. That's not 10 items a person. That's 10 items a family. We're trying to help people out and make sure everyone can get at least some of what they need."

"But I've got a big family," one man said.

"Yeah," another said. "How're we supposed to survive on just 10 items?"

"You've made it this far," the employee said. Ryan could tell she'd been here for a while. She was unflinching in her delivery and answered the remarks and questions as though she'd heard them all day long. "Now it's not just 10 items. You are also only allowed one of each item." There were groans and complaints, but she didn't falter. "Bread, milk, eggs, bottled water, diapers, propane, ice, and batteries are strictly one per family. If you have one loaf of white and one loaf of wheat, you will have to put one back."

"That's crazy!"

"You can't make us do that!"

"How're we supposed to make it on that?!"

"This is exploitation!"

"You should be ashamed!" But the woman stood firm.

"If you don't like it, you don't have to come in." This made everyone quiet. "We have guards in place to prevent stealing and any fights that break out will result in you being removed from the store and banned from returning for some time." Everyone remained quiet. The hair stood up on his neck as Ryan felt the tension. He worried what it was going to look like inside. Would there be fights? Would people be angry? Would there be anything even left for them?

"What do we need to get?" he asked Dad.

"Don't worry about the breakfast foods or medicines."

"Any of them?"

"Any of them," Dad said. "We'll just get the things we really need."

"What if we still have enough items left?"

"We'll worry about that if it happens," he said. "Right now we just need to get the necessities. I'm going to get the batteries, bottled water, and propane. Think you can handle the rest?"

"What does that leave?" Dad folded the paper in half and tore a piece off. On it, he scribbled the remaining items.

Bread

Milk

Eggs

Sandwich Meat

Cheese

Ryan nodded.

"Got it?" Dad asked.

"Got it," he said. They watched as people exited the store. The employee waited patiently for the signal. Ryan felt people pushing against his back. The man nodded to the employee at the ropes and she turned around. Ryan felt the pressing grow.

"Now," she said. "There will be no pushing, no crowding, no groaning, no arguing, no yelling, and no cursing. Everyone will get in. *However*, you will only go in when I allow you. If you try to get past and I don't call you, you will be escorted out. Any questions?"

"How many come in?"

"Why can't we all come in?"

"I have family that needs things!"

"Who made up this system?"

The questions and remarks came as a blazing fire, but she stayed strong. After the anger settled, she began allowing people in. Ryan didn't know how many came in with them, but he could hear the complaining behind him. He looked down at the list and up at the aisles. He had the place memorized, but wanted to make sure nothing had been moved in light of the storm. He grabbed a hand basket and moved.

People were running. The shelves were almost empty. Some shelves had little or nothing on them (toiletries). Others had a few things but probably wouldn't last long (canned goods). Still, other shelves looked as though they hadn't been touched (pet care). There were only about 15 people in the store shopping, but Ryan focused. He needed to get the things on his list and get to checkout.

Bread was the closest item to the checkout, which meant it should be last. He should grab the cold stuff first because that was farthest away and it would be easier for him to just come back to the registers by way of the bread aisle. He rushed towards the refrigerating units in the back of the store.

As he rounded the corner, he came to a sudden stop. Most of the milk was gone. Very little meats and cheeses were there, and the eggs were down to two cartons of 12. He shook off the surprise and grabbed what he needed. People were right behind him trying to get the same things. He felt like he was in a competition trying to win the right to survive. Everyone wanted what he wanted or had. He followed the rules and only got one of each. There was only one carton left. As he pushed away from them, he heard two women behind him.

"Give me that! I saw it first!"

"But my hands are on it!"

They fought over the carton of eggs.

"You obviously don't need to eat any of those."

"And your teeth say you'll just trade it for meth."

The guards were there immediately and settled the situation. The two women continued bickering out of earshot. Ryan walked past the meats and cheeses and picked up turkey and provolone. He just needed bread. Fortunately the bread aisle was in better shape than the eggs. He pulled down a loaf of wheat, stuffed it in his basket, and looked for Dad. While he waited, he saw people trying to make decisions over things like medicine and milk, canned food and frozen food, toilet paper and water. As soon as someone put something down, another person grabbed it. There was almost no going back once you decided not to get something. It was unnerving.

"You ready?" Dad said from behind him.

"Yeah. Got what we needed. There were only two cartons of eggs left and some ladies got in a fight over the last one."

"Hope nothing bad happened."

"Yeah. Did you get everything?"

"Almost. They were out of the size batteries we needed so we're just gonna have to make do without them."

"How bad do we need them?"

"Not too bad, I don't think. With the power on, we should be okay though."

"I hope so," Ryan said. He looked in the buggy at their items. He couldn't recall the last time they had gotten so few items on a grocery trip.

They were in line to checkout now. People were hurrying up behind them with their things. The woman hadn't said anything about a time limit, but Ryan got the impression it was an understanding: You come in, get what you need, and leave. That's what they'd done. There were only two registers open and trying to cram these people through was taking longer than expected. Ryan figured with so few people the lines wouldn't last long, but he saw why that was wrong. Employees were checking everyone to make sure no one was stealing anything. A man was asked to remove his jacket and a woman emptied her large purse. Neither had stolen anything and were allowed to leave. Ryan was glad they hadn't worn anything excessive that could get them in trouble. They put their items on the counter. 10 things total.

"Thank you for not going over the limit," the cashier said.

"No problem," Dad said. The man rang up the items and bagged them. Dad paid cash. They gathered the items and left.

"Hope you left some stuff for us!" someone yelled as they exited.

"I never want to do that again," Ryan said.

"Yeah. Not the most fun I've ever had. I could've done without all the fast-paced shopping and the angry shoppers."

"I was thinking about how it reminded me of Black Friday."

"With fondness?"

"Mostly hatred." They laughed.

"Well, we survived. Let's get it all home before someone decides to attack our car and try to take the stuff away." They pulled out of the parking lot and headed home.

The Spencers

The phone rang. Tracy shifted from foot to foot waiting for the pickup. Jon was sitting on the bed with his unopened book. He watched Tracy.

"Hey, Sharon. This is Tracy. Listen, I know you're with Miss Colleen, but I really need a favor. Would you please call me back? It's nothing big, but I can't really get ahold of anyone else. Thanks!" She hung up. "I don't understand why she's not answering."

"She probably doesn't have signal, honey."

"But you had signal."

"Different providers. She might have someone else." Tracy nodded.

"You're right. You're right."

"So who is this woman again?"

"Her name is Sharon Rogers. She works...or worked...in the nursery at church with a bunch of us. There was this sweet little old lady named Colleen that was just...a treasure, really. Anyway, Sharon quit helping when Colleen got really sick and became her full-time caregiver. It's really sweet, actually. Colleen is a shut-in now."

"That's awful."

"I know. But Sharon is really great and I know she'll come through."

"It sounds like it. I don't think you need to get all worked up over it, though."

"I'm not getting worked up over it," she said. Jon smiled. "What? I'm not. I just want her to go check our house. Is that such a bad thing?" Jon shrugged. "Really?"

"I don't see anything wrong with wanting to know what's going on. I'm curious about the house too. I want to know if anything bad is happening or not. But at the same time, I'm just not as worried as you because of where we live and the kind of neighborhood."

"Don't you think that's just a little weird that you're not worried? None of our neighbors are there." Jon shrugged.

"I don't know what you want me to say, honey."

"I don't know. I just-" Her phone rang. "It's Sharon. I'm putting it on speaker."

"Okay."

"Hello?" Tracy said.

"Hey, Tracy."

"Hey. How're you?"

"I'm good. Were you all okay?"

"Oh yeah. We managed to survive. We're up in Nashville with my parents."

"Oh that sounds nice."

"Yeah. How's Colleen?"

"She's been better. She's having a really hard time right now."

"Oh goodness."

"Yeah. So what were the messages about?"

"Well, I need you to do a big favor for me?"

"Um, I'll try. What's up?"

"Listen, it would really mean a lot to me if you could just drive by our house and look at it and make sure everything is okay."

"Oh. Tracy, no. I can't do that."

"Why not?"

"Colleen has taken a real bad turn. She's running a fever and we're doing all we can to make it from one day to the next. I haven't seen her in this bad shape before and it could be dangerous to leave her alone for too long."

"Where are you now?"

"I'm outside her house. I've been staying with her while the power has been out."

"Oh, goodness," Tracy said. There was an awkward moment of silence as she tried to think of something to say. She felt guilty now, but still wanted someone to check on their house.

"Listen," Sharon said. "If I get a chance to be out that way, I'll look, but I can't make any promises. Your house is pretty far away so it's a long shot."

"I understand. Thank you."

"Hope you all are safe," Sharon said.

"Thank you, Sharon. You too." Tracy hung up the phone.

"I feel bad for her having so much going on," Jon said.

"Yeah. She is a wonderful woman and just amazing."

"Yeah?"

"Oh yeah. With how much she takes care of with Colleen and all. It's pretty impressive."

"Does she have a job too?"

"No. She was a nurse and really into her career but when Colleen got sick she quit her job and takes care of her fulltime."

"Oh wow. Imagine making that kind of choice."

"Not sure I want to. She's great with Colleen, though, and I know we're all grateful for her."

"Well, I'm sure she's going to do what she can to be there, honey."

"Yeah. We'll have to see." Pop entered.

"Did you get ahold of your friend?" he asked.

"Yeah," Tracy said. "She's got a lot on her hands, but said she might try to make it."

"That doesn't sound too terrible to me."

"And if she can't make it, I'm sure it'll be fine," Jon said.

"That's good, that's good," Pop said. "So, your mother and I were talking and we think we're gonna have the whole family over for dinner tonight."

"Tonight?" Tracy asked.

"Are you sure?" Jon asked.

"Yeah, Dad. I don't know if that's such a good idea."

"Why not? We thought since you were all up here we would let everyone else know they're welcome to come over and join us. It would be nice to have everyone together when it's not just a holiday."

"I understand that, Dad, but are you sure everyone can get here by tonight?"

"Oh, your mother has already been calling people. Ralph and Elisa are coming. Don't know about their kids yet. They might be in school."

"What about Lillian and Bobby?"

"Yup, they're coming. They're bringing Dwight and Lucy."

"Well, I guess that's good. I mean, if everyone is coming we can't really say no, can we?"

"Heh. Not easily," Jon said. Pop laughed.

"It'll be a real treat to have you all together again. Especially since it's already been so long since Christmas." He left the room. Tracy looked at Jon.

"A party?" she said. "Really? Not even telling us until it's already happening?" Jon shrugged, making Tracy roll her eyes. "Don't even."

"Hey, I'm not all that excited about it either, but it could be worse. At least this will help us take our minds off of everything. I mean, we do want to try and forget about everything that happened, right? Your family might be a good way to do that."

"Hey, now."

"Wait; that came out wrong."

"I really hope so."

"No, wait. I just meant..." Tracy smiled and tapped her foot.

"Well?"

"...I love you?"

"Uh huh."

Hannah Leon

She sat on the floor of her apartment with *The Count of Monte Cristo* in her hands. It hadn't taken her long to finish *The Hunger Games* and the other books in the series were checked out so she couldn't continue them though she wanted to. For now she needed to occupy her mind with something else. She requested to be notified if *Catching Fire* came in so she could keep reading, but she didn't know how long that would take. She looked at the cover of the book.

Why does Ryan like this so much? It's about revenge, isn't it? What good does that do? These questions circled her mind as she tried to figure out why something like this made Ryan excited. It seemed strange. Ryan was so calm and collected. Why would he want to read something as down as this so many times? That's what she hoped to find out now as she sat on the carpet with the book. It was her reading place. Snuggled against the side of her couch with the light from the windows hitting the pages enough for her to see what she was reading but not make her squint. The perfect spot.

She opened the book to the Table of Contents. *117 chapters?! Why would the book have so many chapters?* She shook her head and turned to "Chapter One Marseilles - The Arrival". *Well,* she thought. *Let's see what's so great about this.*

"On the 24th of February, 1815, the look-out at Notre-Dame de la Garde signalled the three-master, the Pharaon from Smyrna, Trieste, and Naples."

And she was hooked. She felt the book pull her through at a fast pace. She wanted to know why Danglars hated Dantes, why he had to go to Paris, and why it mattered to know Dantes' father was so proud. All these thoughts swarmed her head and she moved faster through the book.

What? Why is Edmund's father so stubborn?
Aww. They really love each other!
Why does Ferdinand love his cousin?!
What are they doing with that letter?
NO!

She continued reading. Just from those first few pages, she

knew why Ryan loved the book so much. Right from the start she had a hero and a villain and tried to keep them separate as she did her best to understand the reasons everything was happening.

BZZZZZ! BZZZZZ! BZZZZZ! She reluctantly put the book down and picked up her phone. It was Ryan.

"Hey there!" she said.

"Hello. How're you?"

"I'm doing much better now. How're you?"

"Can't complain," he said. "What are you up to?"

"Just reading."

"Anything good?"

"I'll give you a hint."

"If it's Nicholas Sparks, just tell me so I can roll my eyes."

"Aha. Aha. Aha. No. Do you want a hint or no?"

"Sure."

"It's your favorite book."

"Oh! The Count of Monte Cristo!"

"Yup! I decided I would read it because they didn't have the next Hunger Games book at the library."

"Really? That's why you picked up the greatest novel of all time? Because they didn't have *that*?"

"Hey now. Don't be mean. I'm reading it, aren't I?"

"Okay," he said. "That's a good point. Do you like it so far?"

"Yeah. I just finished the marriage feast."

"Oh man! You're at a good part. Of course, the whole book is good so I guess that doesn't matter, does it?"

"Uh huh. I will agree it's really good so far."

"Told you."

"Hey now. I know, I know. But like I said, at least I'm reading it."

"That's fair," he said. "So guess what?"

"What?"

"We have power!"

"You do?!"

"Yup. Came back on Sunday."

"Wait, then why did you wait to tell me?"

"I needed to wait until we had signal and we had other things we had to do."

"But maybe that means my family has power."

"So does that mean you're going to come home?"

"I don't know," she said.

"Goodness gracious. Why not?"

"Because I don't know if I want to leave yet or not."

"I guess that makes sense," he said. "Wait, no. I don't understand." She laughed.

"Well I'm just trying to decide if I'm comfortable leaving all my things here or not. I mean, I haven't seen anything bad going on since one of the first nights, but that was just a lot of people yelling and I didn't know what to do. I don't think anyone would take my stuff, but I don't know."

"No one will take your stuff."

"How do you know?"

"Umm, because my crystal ball said so?"

"Uh huh," she said. "Nice try, mister."

"Listen, Hannah. I don't really know what to tell you. I just think it would be nice to have you back home and closer so I can visit you."

"I guess that's fair," she said. Neither said anything for a moment. Hannah looked around her apartment at her things. It wasn't like everything was going to be gone as soon as she left. When she thought about it, no one knew she was here anyway. Maybe it was time for her to get ready to go home. Maybe she should work on packing things up and leaving.

"You there?" Ryan asked.

"Yeah, I'm here. Sorry. Was just thinking."

"About what?"

"Just stuff. Plus, I'd really like to get back to the book."

"See? I told you."

"Yeah, yeah. I know, I know. Greatest thing ever. Best story on the planet. Blah, blah, blah."

"Yup, pretty much. I'll let you get back to reading thing. And hey?"

"Yeah?"

"Please think about coming home."

"I will."

"Thank you."

Hannah hung up and looked at the picture of Ryan on her phone. It was time to go home. There was no excuse anymore. Well, maybe one excuse. She smiled and began reading again.

<u>Sharon Rogers</u>

Sharon walked around the neighborhood smoking her last cigarette. She'd told Colleen she wanted to check on some of the neighbors and make sure they were still doing okay. That was her excuse for getting out. The last few days had been so stressful. Colleen was barely getting out of bed and wasn't eating like she should. Sharon was worried about what she was going to do. Things looked like they were going up after she got the insulin, but that didn't last long.

The neighborhood was showing more signs of life. People were returning to check on how things were. The power wasn't back yet, but Sharon figured people were probably getting homesick. Sharon saw people walking around outside and carrying things to and from their car. She took a long pull on the cigarette that was almost gone, dropped it, and stepped on it. She waved her hand and waited a moment for the smell to leave before walking in the house.

She did her best to get sandwiches made, but she knew what was coming. Colleen was tired of the sandwiches and chips and anything else being made that required no heating. She felt it was time they warmed some things up and had hot food, but Sharon told her again and again they couldn't do that. She tried to explain it, but Colleen wasn't interested.

She stood over another turkey and cheese sandwich with the crusts cut off. At least she was making an effort to keep the food like Colleen likes. She could've given up and made it the easiest way possible, but no matter how much Colleen seemed to be ungrateful lately, Sharon knew it wasn't real.

She finished Colleen's sandwich and covered it with a paper towel. Bugs were a bit of a problem because Sharon had opened the windows. She couldn't stand the musty smell anymore and needed something fresh inside. She now made sure all food was covered when left out to keep the bugs from crawling all over their food. She took the rest of the ingredients and made herself a cheese sandwich. Those seemed to hold her over longer than regular sandwiches though she didn't know why. She cleaned up what was left on the counter. She took two bottles of water out of the refrigerator she'd placed in there out of habit.

She managed to find time before the store to go by the Spencer's house. It'd been a while since she'd been there, but she remembered the way. The neighborhood was deserted, but none of the houses had been bothered. She searched carefully to make sure nothing had happened to them. When she was satisfied, she called Tracy and let her know the good news. She left and drove to the store for a few things.

She'd found a 24-pack of water and snatched it up before anyone else. Several people approached her, but she wouldn't budge. She didn't give anyone a sob story, but persisted she needed it more. The first few people didn't seem that convinced, but didn't argue. Others didn't want to give up.

"My wife is dying and needs water now!"

"I have 12 kids and we could all die if we don't get a little bit of water!"

"I'm an alcoholic!"

She didn't understand how any of those could be valid reasons for being in a grocery store trying to get a 24-pack of water. If things like that were going on, what were you doing at the store? She wondered if the alcoholic excuse got him anything he needed. She chuckled at the thoughts of that convincing someone he needed water.

"What's...taking...so...long?" Colleen asked.

"I'm coming. I'm coming." Sharon put the water bottles on the counter and went to the bedroom. Colleen was looking around the room for Sharon. She was disoriented. She was pale and looked so frail. Sharon tried not to dwell on how she looked. "I'm gonna set you up and get the tray to bring your food for you. Is that okay?"

"I...think...so...No...sense...moving...if...I...don't...have...to ..."

"Okay." She took some pillows from the closet and set them on the bed. She lifted Colleen as best she could. She didn't weigh a lot, but could not help. Sharon moved the pillows around and propped them up behind Colleen, who then laid back and was sitting up.

"Okay," Sharon said. "I'll take the tray and get your food and I'll be right back, okay?"

"Okay." Sharon picked the bed tray next to the bed up and returned to the kitchen. She placed their food and water on it and carefully walked back to the bedroom. She focused to make sure she didn't spill anything as she set it down over Colleen's lap.

"Here you are."

"I can't...get...it..."

"I know. I'm going to help you."

"Thank...you..." Colleen's voice was almost a whisper.

Until today, her attitude had turned sour and was negative. She imagined her all better and looking at the food with disgust.

"Yuch," she would say. "No sense calling it food. Might as well be back on the farm living off scraps. The food around here has gotten so bad. Don't know why they don't just use some of that electricity they're so stingy about and make some real food. Instead they leave ours off and give us bread and water like we're criminals. Just wrong. Just wrong."

"That's true," Sharon would say.

"Oh, don't you start," Colleen might say. "I know you think I'm just being crazy. I can't help it. I paid my dues and now I want some real food. Can't even get anything decent anymore. Youngins need to be grateful they can choose to be skin and bones. Some people ain't got no choice in the matter and would die over what it is we throw away just 'cause we ain't hungry."

"Sharon," Colleen whispered. Sharon snapped back from her thoughts.

"Oh. I'm sorry, Miss Colleen. What did you need?"

"I said...thank you..."

"Oh. You're welcome." Sharon smiled. She watched as Colleen took little bites of her food and chewed for what seemed like ages. She could see the difficulty of the task on Colleen's face. It seemed as though each bite took more strength. Sharon wanted to give her some soup or something, but with no heat and no one with power it wasn't possible. "The weather is looking much better now, don't you think?"

"Mm...hmm," Colleen said. She reached for her water bottle but couldn't reach it.

"Oh, I'm sorry. Let me get that for you."

"It's...fine...Don't...rush..." Sharon opened the bottle and handed it to Colleen, keeping her hand on it just in case she dropped it. Colleen took a few smalls sips from it and pushed it away. "Thank...you...dear..."

"No problem." Sharon sat back down and watched as Colleen slowly lifted her sandwich to her mouth again and take a small bite.

The Spencers

Dinner was at seven. Lillian and Bobby showed up that afternoon to bring Dwight and Lucy for some time with their cousins. Lucy, three years old, latched onto Jon and didn't want to let go. He didn't know why she had such a strong fondness for him, but he was fine with it. He figured it wouldn't last too much longer anyway so might as well enjoy it. Later, Lillian went with Tracy to get some groceries and Bobby went with Dwight and the girls downstairs to play board games. Jon and Lucy stayed in the living room.

"How're you?" he said.

Lucy held up three fingers. Jon laughed.

"No," he said. "I mean how are you doing?"

She held up three fingers again.

"Okay, let's try again. How do you feel today, Lucy?"

"Good."

"Are you having a good day?" She nodded. "Are you sleepy?" She shook her head. "Isn't it almost naptime?" She shook her head.

"We can't go to bed yet."

"Oh really?" Jon said. "Why is that?"

"Because we have to save the princess."

"We do, huh?"

"Yup. She's in danger from the troll."

"A troll? Where is it?" Lucy hopped out of Jon's lap and ran behind the couch.

"There!" she said as she pointed to Jon.

"Oh no!" he said and jumped and looked behind him. "I don't see it." Lucy laughed.

"No! You're the troll!"

"I am?" She nodded. "But why am I the troll?"

"'Cause you're big and scary and that's what trolls are."

"Why am I scary?" Lucy shook her head.

"No," Lucy said and ran up to Jon and whispered in his ear. "Not in real life. This is just pretend. You're just big and scary in pretend. I like you in real life."

"You promise?" Jon whispered.

"Uh huh," Lucy whispered and returned to her spot behind the couch. "Oh no! It's a troll!"

"Grrr!" Jon said in a monster voice. "I'm here to get the princess!"

"Oh no!" Lucy said. "Someone save me!"

"I'll save you!" they heard someone say. Bobby came around the corner with a blanket around his neck and a foam "We're #1" finger. "I'll save you, princess!"

"Grr! She's mine!"

"I think not, beast. I shall stop you at all costs!"

"Save me, knight! Save me!" Lucy said. Bobby went around the couch to Jon and poked him with the foam finger.

"Gasp!" Jon said. "I have fallen! Goodbye, cruel world!" He fell down, rolled his head to the side, and stuck his tongue out. Lucy ran up to him.

"You're not really dead," she whispered. "It's just pretend."

"Promise?" Jon whispered. She nodded and ran back to the couch.

"You saved me!" she said. "You saved me!" She jumped into Bobby's arm. He lifted her up and pointed the foam finger in the air.

"We're number one!" they chanted. "We're number one! We're number one!" He tickled Lucy. She laughed and begged for help.

"Uncle Jon, help me!"

"I can't," he said. "I'm dead, remember?"

"No," she said while laughing. "This isn't pretend. It's real life." Jon got to his feet.

"Maybe I should tickle you, too!"

"Noo!" Jon and Bobby both tickled her and she screamed and laughed.

"What is going on here?" Lillian asked. She and Tracy came in with their arms full of groceries.

"They tickled me, Mommy. And Uncle Jon was a troll and Daddy killed him, but only in pretend. He's not really dead."

"Oh yeah?" she asked. "Well, that's good. You, missy,

need to go take a nap."

"Okay," Lucy said. She looked at Jon. "Will you tuck me in?"

"Sure thing, Princess."

"Are you sure?" Lillian asked.

"Yeah," Jon said. "Shouldn't be that much trouble."

"Okay, thanks!" Jon took Lucy down the hall to the guest room.

"It's great you guys could make it," Tracy said.

"Oh, Dwight was so excited it was difficult to contain him," Lillian said. "I told him he was going to have to calm down or we were going home."

"Yeah," Bobby said. "You should've seen poor Dwight's face. He was not happy at that. Lucy didn't really like it either. She looked right at him and in as stern a voice as she could said 'Dwight, stop!'" They laughed. Jon came back in.

"What's so funny?" he asked.

"Just talking about Dwight and Lucy."

"Oh, yeah? They are a couple of great kids, Bobby. You and Lillian are doing a good job."

"Thanks, Jon. We're doing our best. They can be a handful at times though."

"Oh, all kids can," Tracy said. "You wouldn't believe how crazy Laura and Lisa can get. Every once in a while...well, they have their moments." Lillian laughed.

"I'm sure. They were so cute growing up, though. They always seemed to get along. Or they at least knew how to fake it."

"Yeah, that sounds more like it," Jon said.

"Come now," Gran said. "Those two are precious. They were so much fun playing cards."

"You all played cards?" Bobby asked.

"Yeah."

"What game?" Lillian asked.

"Rummy," Jon said.

"Ah, yes," she said. "Don't even know why I asked. You can always guess what's being played around here, that's for sure."

"Ain't that the truth," Bobby said. They heard a knock at the front door as it opened.

"Anybody home?" someone called out.

"Ralph!" Tracy said. "So glad you could make it!"

"Oh wouldn't miss it for the world," he said. "Gotta see what all is going with everyone. Heck, it's only been, what? Four months?"

"Something like that," Tracy said. "Hey, Elisa. So glad you could make it."

"Oh thank you," Elisa said. "Like Ralph said, wouldn't wanna miss it."

"Could the kids make it?" Jon asked.

"No, they couldn't. Still at school. They won't be out for another week or so."

"Poor things," Tracy said

"Yeah, right," Ralph said. "All we've heard from them is how much they wish they could be home."

"Uh huh," Jon said. "Alabama and UAH are both closed."

"Man," Ralph said. "Yeah. Any idea how many?"

"How many what?" Tracy asked.

"People. How many people were killed?"

"Oh gosh," Jon said. "No idea. We've heard estimates, but nothing concrete. It's expected to be in the hundreds but we don't know if that's high hundreds or low hundreds or anything, really."

"That's horrible," Elisa said. "I can't believe it got so bad."

"Yeah," Tracy said. "We were shocked."

"Well, did you guys get a lot of damage?" Ralph asked.

"Actually, we were fortunate," Jon said. "We saw it not far from our house, but no it didn't hit us. I couldn't believe it when we looked around the next morning, but no. Nothing."

"That's incredible," Elisa said.

"Oh yeah," Tracy said. "We're very blessed and we know it." No one said anything for a moment. Tracy felt the tension. She didn't know whether she should direct the subject towards something more.

"So, Elisa," he said, turning to his sister-in-law. "How's your job going?"

"Oh. Well, if you can believe it, it's gotten worse."

"No!"

"Yeah, I know. You'd think two robberies in six days was pretty hard to top, but I'm here to say you would be wrong. It just went all downhill from there. You just wouldn't believe how crazy a gas station can get."

"Didn't they move you off the night watch, though?" Tracy asked.

"No," she said. "Well, they did, but then they just put me right back on it 'cause they said no one else was willing to work as much as I can."

"Which sounds like crap to me," Ralph said.

"Ralph, please," Elisa said. "But yes, it sounded like crap to me too when I heard it. I couldn't believe it."

"So who do they have working the days?"

"Oh, some old guy who's been there forever and then some teenagers who can't work nights because of school come in and work until 9 or so."

"Well," Tracy said. "I guess if they can't work because of school that's not such a bad thing."

"Yeah," Elisa said. "I suppose. Kids gotta work too, right?"

"That's true," Jon said. "Makes college a lot easier on them."

"Oh yeah," Ralph said. "I didn't like paying my way through college one bit. Can't imagine kids doing it today. School has gotten so expensive it's crazy."

"Tell me about it," Elisa said.

"Who is that out there?" Gran called from the kitchen.

"It's just us," Elisa said.

"Oh boy," Pop said. "The trouble has arrived."

"Hey, Dad," Ralph said. "How're you holding up?"

"Well, the belt still seems to be the way to go," he said. They chuckled.

"Glad you're still wearing it," Elisa said. "Wouldn't want

you getting out of your favorite chair without it."

"Oh no," Pop said. "That wouldn't be a good thing. No, sirree." They all went to the kitchen.

"Hey, Lillian. Hey, Gran," Elisa said. She hugged them both. "Mmm, something smells really good."

"That's going to be dinner," Gran said. "We've been working on it for a while now."

"Well, it smells fantastic and I'm starving."

"We all are, I'm sure," Lillian said. "Hey, Jon?"

"Yeah?"

"Do you mind going and getting the kids?"

"Oh no. Not at all."

"Do you need help?" Tracy asked.

"Naw. Shouldn't be that hard, right? I guess send Bobby down to save me if I'm not back in 10 minutes."

"Hey. You're on your own, buddy," Bobby said. Jon went to the door leading downstairs.

"Hello, down there!" he called.

"Yes?"

"Uh huh?"

"What?"

"Who was that?" Jon walked down the stairs.

"It's just me," he told them. "You guys need to get upstairs so we can eat."

"Is it ready?" Dwight asked.

"Yup. Uncle Ralph and Aunt Elisa are here. They're helping set the table and we need you all up there too."

"Aww," Lucy said. "But I'm still playing. I can't leave the settlers without their food. What am I supposed to do?"

"How about we go get their princess some food so she can rule them? A hungry princess can't do her job, can she?"

"Nope," she said after a moment. "I guess not." Jon reached the bottom of the stairs, took a bow, and motioned towards the top of the stairs.

"If you'd be so kind as to follow me to the dining quarters," Jon said in a British accent. Lucy curtsied.

"Thank you, Sir Uncle Jon," she said. Jon laughed.

"You guys come on, too," he said in a normal voice. They all walked up the stairs and went to the table in the kitchen.

"That smells good," Dwight said.

"Uncle Jon, sit next to me!" Lucy said.

"No, he's sitting next to me!" Dwight said.

"Actually, you guys," Lillian said. "He's going to be sitting in here with the adults while you all sit in here."

"Aww," Lucy said.

"That's not fair," Dwight said.

"Yeah," Lucy said. "Not fair."

"Hey, kids," Bobby said. "Now you guys know how this works. The mommies and daddies all eat in the main dining room while you guys eat at this table. Why?"

"Because you'll kiss each other," Dwight said.

"Bleh," Lucy said. They all laughed.

"That's right. And you don't want to see that."

"Not any more than we have to," Laura said.

"Exactly," Bobby said. "Now you all just chill in here and eat." Bobby went into the main dining room.

"Are they okay?" Jon asked.

"They'll survive. If the worse thing in their lives is not sitting next to someone, I think they'll turn out okay."

"Oh, Bobby," Gran said. "You shouldn't be so hard on them. They just want to spend time with their Uncle Jon."

"Ah, that's 'Sir' Uncle Jon, according to Lucy."

"Oh, boy," Tracy said. "There's a name that'll stick for a while." They gave thanks and began eating.

"Oh man," Jon said. "This is really good."

"Old family recipe," Tracy said. "Gram-Gram used to make it."

"Ah," Bobby said. "She always made the best food."

"Yeah," Lillian said. "She knew you were hooked when you dug into half of one of her pies. She said you weren't going anywhere and you sure haven't."

"Hey, it was a good pie."

"What kind was it?" Pop asked.

"Chocolate pecan pie," he said. He closed his eyes in

reverence of mentioning the name. "It was so good. I couldn't stop eating it."

"She made the best pies," Pop said. "Blueberry was my favorite."

"What about her apple pie?" Gran said. Everyone sighed in agreement.

"Oh, those were the best," Ralph said

"With that homemade ice cream?" Tracy asked.

"I remember that," Jon said. "That stuff was so stinkin' good it should've been illegal."

"With schools how they are today, it probably would be," Pop said. They laughed.

"I just feel so sorry for kids, you know?" Elisa said. "Not getting to have all that good stuff we grew up with."

"Yeah, but with all the gadgets and gizmos out there now, can you imagine how they would be?" Ralph said. "We all had those wide open fields to run out in or could do something outside. Kids wouldn't know what to do." They all laughed.

"Mmm," Jon said. "This is so good."

"Why thank you," Tracy said. "We worked hard on it."

"We sure did," Lillian said.

"And it shows," Pop said.

"Yes," Gran said. "These are some old recipes, but they still hold up."

"The best recipes do, don't they?" Pop said.

"I'm gonna need some more," Jon said as he stood up.

"You finished that already?" Tracy asked.

"Goodness gracious," Ralph said. "You weren't hungry, were you?"

"Oh yeah," Jon said. "Princesses really zap the energy out of you."

"So I've heard," Bobby said. They laughed as Jon walked into the kitchen.

"How're you guys doing?" Jon asked the kids.

"We're good," Laura said.

"Uncle Jon, are you coming to eat with us now?" Dwight asked.

"Not yet."

"But why not?" Lucy asked.

"Because we're all talking about you guys."

"Nu-huh," Lucy said.

"Uh huh. We're talking about what a lovely princess you are. What are you guys talking about?"

"Nothing," Laura said

"Nothing?"

"Nope," Laura said. "Well, we're just talking about school and stuff."

"Oh really? I thought you said you weren't talking about anything."

"Well," Laura said. She blushed.

"Uh huh," Jon said. He continued adding food to his plate. "How is school going?"

"Who are you talking to?" Lisa asked.

"Sorry. I was talking to Dwight."

"It's okay. School is boring."

"School is boring?"

"Uh huh."

"No, it's not," Jon said. "School can be fun."

"Not my school," Dwight said.

"Why is that?"

"'Cause the teacher is real old and it's hard to understand her. Sometimes I can't concentrate."

"Why is it hard to understand her?"

"'Cause she's old, I guess." Jon tried to hide his smile.

"Well," he said. "Maybe you should try sitting in another desk or something. I'm sure the teacher wouldn't mind you moving."

"We have to sit alphabetically."

"Eww," Jon said. "That's never any fun. Well, hang in there. I'm sure it'll get better."

"I hope so."

"How is your school, little princess?" Jon asked.

"It's good," Lucy said. "I get to draw a lot."

"You do?"

"Yup. I drew a 'pitcher' of a pony yesterday."

"Oh yeah?"

"Uh-huh. The teacher said it was pretty. I like my teacher. But, it's not really school. It's just preschool. I don't go to real school until after preschool."

"Yeah?"

"Uh-huh."

"Well, I'm sure you'll be good at it, right?" Jon said. Lucy nodded and continued eating. Jon smiled at Lisa and Laura. "And I don't need to ask about you two."

"Nope," Lisa said.

"Not at all," Laura said. Jon laughed and returned to the dining room.

"No, no, no," Bobby said. "The Titans aren't gonna do any better under Munchak than they did under Fisher. I mean, really. Fisher was the Titans. You can't imagine a Titan football game without at least a few shots of that mustache out there. I mean, he *is* the Titans."

"Well, hold on, hold on," Pop said. "We don't know how good Munchak is. He did play football for the Oilers back in the 80s and he's been with the team a long time. He might be a pretty good coach."

"Yeah, right," Ralph said. "I'm gonna have to side with Bobby on this one. I just don't know about it. I'd rather see him first, don't get me wrong, but I don't think it's as good a decision as everyone is making it out to be."

"How're the kids doing?" Elisa asked.

"Oh fine," Jon said. "Just talking about school."

"They thinkin' of quittin'?" Pop asked.

"Man, I hope not. We've made it this far. Let's hope they'll keep it going just a little bit longer."

"I think I'm gonna follow Jon's idea and get me some more food," Ralph said. "You want some more?"

"I think I'm good for now," Elisa said.

"I'd like some more," Lillian said. Bobby stood up.

"Here, I'll get you some. I want some more too."

"Not too much," Lillian said.

"Don't worry."

"So how was your house?" Elisa asked.

"Oh, it was fine," Tracy said. "We managed to make it through without any noticeable damage. We looked through every part of the house and couldn't find anything damaged."

"Did any of them hit close?" Gran asked

"Yeah," Jon said. "We think one landed on or next to a subdivision behind us. We were in such a rush to get down to the storm cellar we didn't stay to watch."

"Wow," Elisa said. "That sounds a little scary, to me."

"Oh it was," Tracy said. "We couldn't believe it."

"Weren't there any warnings?" Lillian asked.

"Well," Jon said. "I guess. Don't get me wrong. But in Alabama the weather people are wrong so often, alotta times we don't even bother with it. Their winter storm warnings are so crazy I think they just stick their hands in a bowl and pull out whatever forecast they think is best."

"Jon," Tracy said. "You know that's not true. They did give warnings and they increased throughout the day. But I think the problem is no one took them seriously. Weather is hard to predict there. The schools didn't help either. UAH didn't even let Jon out until right before the power went out. They kept him a long time." Bobby and Ralph came back.

"That sounds dangerous," Elisa said.

"What sounds dangerous?" Ralph asked. Elisa filled him and Bobby in on what they were talking about.

"Oh wow," Bobby said. "Did it look real bad there?"

"It didn't for a while," Jon said. "Honestly, the only annoying thing was the wind. We tried to load and unload things on the truck and it didn't make it easy with the wind blowing the doors shut so much."

"Man," Ralph said. "Did it make, like, a wind tunnel or something?"

"Pretty much. It just made it hard to carry stuff in and out, you know? Nothing that really caused a lot of trouble. Just made it more difficult."

"Mm, mmm," Elisa said. "Well, I don't think it was such a

good idea to keep y'all there so long. Especially with the students."

"Exactly. We had one student who worked with us that lives down in Rosetta Falls which is about 30 minutes from the office."

"That's just crazy," Lillian said.

"Yeah. Well, what are you going to do?"

"Watch the weather and believe them more often," Tracy said.

"That sounds like a good idea," Gran said. "Who wants some dessert?"

"You know I do," Pop said. Everyone laughed.

"Who didn't see that coming?" Ralph asked.

"I'm gonna finish mine up and I'll be ready for some," Lillian said.

"I think I'm about done with this for now," Bobby said. "I'd be good for some dessert."

"You need to eat all your food," Lillian said.

"But I want dessert," Bobby said in a pouty voice. Lillian rolled her eyes.

"You want some?" Jon asked Tracy.

"No thanks," she said. "I'll just eat off yours some."

"Sure you will," he said. He carried their plates into the kitchen. Gran and Pop were already in there.

"Okay. Who wants dessert?" Pop asked the table of kids. They stopped their conversation in mid-sentence and all raised their hands.

"Well, dear, I really hope we have enough for them," he said. "They're liable to eat us out of all our sweets."

"Wonder who taught them that?" Jon asked.

<u>Sharon Rogers</u>

Colleen was no longer fully conscious. She just muttered. She kept making noises and groaning before rolling back away from Sharon.

"Come on, Miss Colleen. You need to get up." No response. Only groans. "Please, Miss Colleen, you need to get up. I need you to talk to me."

"I...don't...feel...good..." The response was bittersweet.

"I know, Miss Colleen, but you need to use the bathroom." She just muttered and tried to get away. Sharon felt her head. It didn't feel unusually hot or cold. Colleen muttered something.

"What?" Sharon asked.

Colleen muttered again. Sharon couldn't figure out the words and had no idea what brought this on. She thought maybe it would go away after a day or so, but it hadn't. *It's getting worse,* she thought.

"I'll be right back," she said. Colleen muttered. Sharon stepped out of the room and mapped a path. She spoke as she walked through the house.

"Okay. If I get her to the hall, I can help her shuffle here into the living room. She can have her walker to help. We'll get through the living room and here to the door." She stopped at the door. There was a small lift from the floor to the frame, then onto the porch. Sharon had a portable ramp in her car and would need it to help with the steps down from the porch.

She walked to the car, pulled out the ramp, and set it up over the stairs. Getting Colleen out of the house was going to be difficult. She was slow moving and might fight most of the way thinking she wasn't supposed to leave. She might think of some reason she has to be at the house and argue with Sharon until one of them gave up. Then again, she may not do anything at all. That would make it even more difficult. She walked over the ramp several times to make sure it was in place and could withstand the two of them. If she was going to move Colleen, the last thing that needed to happen was a fall. She walked back inside.

"Miss Colleen?" she called. No response. She kept walking through the house. "Miss Colleen? We need to get going." *If she asks any questions, just stick to the story.*

No response.

"Miss Colleen," she said with as sweet a voice as she could muster. "We need to get going. We need to go, remember?" No response. Sharon pulled the walker over from the corner so she could hand it to Colleen. She was in a cold sweat. She knew this was going to take a lot of work getting Colleen out of the house as carefully as possible.

"Let's get you up, Colleen." Colleen moved sluggishly and didn't seem to be trying to help. Sharon helped her up in a sitting position and leaned her against the wall. Colleen wasn't moving on her own. Sharon looked in her eyes. It seemed hazy and distant. Her pupils were dilated and didn't seem focused on anything specific. Sharon slowly moved her off the bed and onto her feet.

Colleen folded in Sharon's arms like a toy doll. There seemed to be no strength in her body. Sharon tried to lift her as best she could, but couldn't tell if she was making a difference. There seemed like so little could be done for her. Sharon placed her arms on the walker.

"Okay, Miss Colleen. I need you to try and move, okay? I need you to move your legs so you can walk, okay? We can do this. We can do this." Colleen didn't move and didn't acknowledge her. She shifted her weight to try and compensate. She pushed the walker just a little, but Colleen didn't move. Sharon tried moving them again. Colleen slipped and Sharon rushed to catch her.

"Are you okay? Can you hear me?" Colleen didn't respond. Sharon lifted her back up and laid her back in the bed. It was harder than expected.

"Colleen! Colleen, I need you to listen to me, okay?" Colleen didn't react. "Please, Colleen. I need you to show me some sign you understand what I'm saying." Colleen slightly groaned. Sharon wiped the sweat from her head. "Colleen, you're sick. You're not doing well. I'm gonna try to get help, okay? I don't know how long it will be, but I'm going to try. I need you to understand what's going on. Do you understand?" No response. "Colleen, please. Do you understand?" No response. Sharon felt Colleen's head. It was hot. Sharon held her breath. She was scared.

She walked into the living room and started to leave. She had to get to the hospital. It was her only hope. She didn't want to leave Colleen and wished her cellphone worked. She needed to be there with Colleen in case anything-

PHONE! The thought caught her off guard and made her so happy. *Colleen has a landline! I can use that and not leave her!* Sharon went back inside and went to the landline phone in the living room. In all the hustle and worries, she'd forgotten about it. She grabbed it and prayed for a dial tone. She lifted it to her ears, sighed with joy, and dialed.

"9-1-1. What's your emergency?"

"Yes. I need someone immediately. I have an elderly woman who is unresponsive and running a fever. She's diabetic, but has had steady insulin, and became unresponsive late last night."

"What's the address?" Sharon told them. "Okay, ma'am. EMTs are on their way. What is your name and relation to the person?"

"My name is Sharon Rogers and I'm her caretaker."

"Okay, ma'am. Is there anything else you need?"

"No. Thank you."

Sharon hung up. She rubbed her eyes. The stress was really getting to her. She needed a cigarette. No. She needed to focus on Colleen. She went into the bedroom. Colleen hadn't moved.

"Colleen?" she asked. No response. "Colleen, can you hear me? Listen, I called 9-1-1. They're sending someone to help us. Can you hear me?" No response. "It's okay, Colleen. Everything is gonna be okay. They're gonna get you some antibiotics and get you taken care of. Just...just don't worry. There's nothing to worry about, okay? There's nothing to worry about. I...I know they're going to get here soon and take care of you. They'll take us to the hospital and...and it'll be great. Promise." Colleen grunted.

"I...I remember the first time we met, Colleen. You were there in the nursery with all those little kids. You just loved them. You loved talking to them and holding them and seeing their little faces as you talked to them. I remember coming in for the first time. I'd never been around children but I always wanted to. I always wanted to hold kids and see what it was like to take care of them. You knew I had no experience. You took one look at me and smiled.

"'Never been around little ones, have you?' you said. I was so embarrassed at how much it showed. I always thought I was good and could hide it, but you saw right through me.

"'No,' I told you. 'I haven't. Always wanted to, but just...haven't.' I was so scared what you were gonna say to me. I just knew you were gonna call over one of the other people and have me thrown out for whatever reason. I don't know why I thought something like that. I just...was worried. I wanted to spend time with all those kids and wanted to get to know more about the kids, but...you just smiled. You were so wonderful. You smiled and just invited me in.

"'Well,' you said. 'Why don't you come with me? Let me show you around.'" You took my hand and walked me around the nursery. You showed me the diaper-changing station, the baby books, the napping area. You were so sweet to me. I couldn't understand why, either. I mean, I probably didn't even belong there, but you were...you were great. You didn't even care. You just wanted to make sure I was okay and comfortable with all those kids." Sharon wiped the tears from her eyes. She held Colleen's hand in hers as she spoke. She didn't know what good it was doing, but she wanted to keep talking to Colleen as if everything was normal.

"Remember the first time you helped me change a diaper? I was so terrified. I'd never done anything like that. I mean, I have no brothers or sisters and couldn't begin to know how to change a diaper. You were so kind to me about it. I remember the smell first.

"'What's that smell?' I asked.

"'Oh, that's just a little one wanting some attention.' I was so confused and wasn't sure what you meant. Then it hit me.

"'You mean...' You gave me such a sly smile. I wasn't sure if you were messing with me or just found my ignorance humorous. 'I don't know what to do.'

"'That's okay,' you said. 'I'll help you.' Even though it scared me, which I'm sure was visible, you were there. You didn't hesitate and you helped me get everything taken care of. I was so grateful. I couldn't believe someone could be so wonderful to me. We took care of everything. We got the baby changed and happy. You kept telling me encouraging things and helping me. I was so grateful. I knew then we would be friends. That you were someone important to me." Sharon cried as she dabbed the sweat away from Colleen's head. She could hear some sirens coming from somewhere. She hoped it was the ambulance.

Help is on the way, Colleen. Help is on the way.

Hannah Leon

She went over the list for the fifth or sixth time. She wasn't sure if she'd covered it enough. *What should I do? Should I stay here in hopes the power comes back? Should I just stick it out and not try driving on the road considering they are probably packed with people still?* She remembered how they looked the day after the tornadoes. Would it be like that now? Would she have to hope for everything to be okay as she tried to get passed everyone? She hoped not. She wanted to get home. Besides, it'd been a week since that happened so why would traffic still be crazy?

Hannah looked around her apartment. For a place that still had her furniture and most of her things, it felt bare. Something about it seemed off. She'd only packed her essentials. There was no way she could get everything she owned in her Nissan. She felt like she was abandoning her apartment. *It doesn't matter*, she thought. She needed to be with family and friends.

She had already tried calling her parents, but they didn't answer. She left a message saying she would be on her way and hoped they would get it. She thought about trying again on her way home.

She closed the door and locked her apartment. She hesitated before walking away. All the *What Ifs* flew through her head at breakneck speed.

What if someone breaks in?
What if there are more tornadoes?
What if I come back and my stuff is gone?
What if I die on my way home?
What if I can't get home?

She shook her head. She didn't need these thoughts. It wasn't the time or place. She should wait until she's home and sees how many people were alive and were doing okay.

She walked down the stairs and looked all the dark apartments. Even with it being daytime, the apartments usually showed signs of life. Now there was nothing. She went to her car, got in, and backed out. She told herself not to look at the apartments.

"Just leave," she said. "Just keep going." She pulled out of the parking lot and drove to I-20.

She got on the interstate and began the long drive home. It would take two hours assuming traffic wasn't backed up. She sped up, set the cruise, and let out a sigh. She watched in the rearview mirror as Tuscaloosa disappeared behind her. She took in a deep breath and focused on what was ahead.

The drive was uneventful for a long time. I-20/59 was a relatively straight shot to I-65 in Birmingham. There was a part that connected to I-459 which went to the southwest part of Birmingham. Hannah rarely went that way.

Hannah looked at her speedometer. 85 mph. *Better slow down*, she thought. *Don't need any trouble today.* She took her foot off the gas and tried to bring the vehicle down to the speed limit. She looked around for cops, then sped back up to 75. She didn't like how slow it felt with the car going that speed and wanted to get home. It felt like she almost was going too slow or maybe even not moving. She just wanted to be home.

Traffic was sparse. She figured it would still be packed with people cutting each other off or maybe accidents spread across the roads, but there wasn't. Many of the trees had been knocked over and were now on the sides of the road. She could see where they'd been pulled off of the interstate and kept away from traffic.

She saw the I-65 junction ahead of her. It stood as a sign she was halfway home. A smile crossed her face. It was relief. She couldn't believe she was doing okay. It felt almost-

VRRRRRRRRRRRRRRRRM! *The tornado. Bangs. Loudness. Flash of lightning. The thunder. Stop it! Stop it! STOP!* A loud motorcycle flew past her. She took her foot off the gas in panic.

"Just a motorcycle," she said. She took deep breaths and tried to calm down. "Nothing bad. Just a motorcycle." A man on a Harley wasn't wasting time getting home either. She shook away the nervous feeling and focused on driving again. She realized she was gripping the steering wheel.

She went around the loop and merged onto Northbound I-65. Home seemed much closer now. All she needed to do was stay on the interstate until I-565. She thought about getting off at Rosetta Falls and seeing Ryan. That wouldn't be so bad.

There was more traffic on 65 than on 20. It was nice to see something that looked normal. People were all speeding just like she was used to and helped give that sense of normality she wanted. She saw a sea of red lights. She slowed down. *What's going on? Why are people stopping?* There was always construction in Birmingham, but it shouldn't have been affecting traffic this close to the junction. She switched lanes to avoid hitting anyone.

She was getting annoyed. She wanted to be home. She wanted to be heading home. She'd already spent days sitting around not doing anything. She didn't want to be doing that again. Why wasn't the traffic moving? What could be the hold up? It was almost rush hour, sure, but it wasn't close enough to be causing this much trouble. Maybe there was an accident. Maybe there was some trouble she couldn't see. It was annoying her, whatever it was. She felt the frustration climb. She just wanted the traffic to be gone.

She inched along at a steady speed her speedometer couldn't read. She wasn't even going fast enough where it would matter. She felt like she could just get out of the car and walk faster than this. It wasn't even worth burning up the gas that was probably scarce. She looked at all the cars going around her. Many of them were families, not singles. She imagined they were coming up from the south part of Birmingham and headed towards friends and family elsewhere. She didn't know the extent of the damage in Birmingham. She'd been so out of touch with everything she couldn't imagine, but judging from all the people around her it couldn't have been good.

As they moved along, she saw what the trouble was. Two cars in the southbound lane had collided and were slowing traffic. This made Hannah more annoyed. After all, that was in a different lane headed in a different direction. Why would her traffic be so slow because of that? She knew the answer. People who slowed down to turn and look at the accident even though they had no connection to it at all. Sometimes this inadvertently caused more accidents and more delays for people. Hannah took her mind off of it and focused. She just needed to get a little farther. She could see it ahead. It wasn't that bad. She passed the accident and saw the clearing.

Traffic picked back up and she was back at 75. She turned her iPod on shuffle and tried to take her mind off things. *Just think about home. You're going to be home. You'll get to see your friends and family.* It wasn't helping. She was still frustrated at the traffic. Her iPod blared Aretha Franklin. Singing at the top of her lungs made things so much better. It helped take her mind off what was going on in the real world.

Different songs played and she was able to leave the traffic and frustration behind her. She didn't think about it. She just focused on what was coming. She was going to be home and be able to relax and enjoy being with her family.

She saw the Rosetta Falls exit. She started to call Ryan and let him know she was coming, but she didn't. As she merged onto the exit, she smiled.

Ryan Peterson

Ryan was on his bed. It felt so good to have AC and clean clothes and lights. Air, power, hot water, cleanliness. They were simple, everyday things. Most didn't even flitter for a moment in his mind. They were things that just were and that was that. Now he was grateful for these things he once took for granted. He was there in bed with a book enjoying the comfort of a fan. Maybe that was it.

When a person goes to a remote part of the world, they are ready to put everything aside and see things through different eyes. They make the preparations to ensure they can make the transition. That didn't happen for Ryan. He just woke up one morning with everything gone.

"RYYYYYAAAAN!" he heard the twins call.

"Yeah?" he called back. He was slightly frustrated at the interruption, but did his best not to show it in his voice.

"Someone is here for you!" they called out in sync. He wondered who could be showing up for him. Since getting power back, he'd tried checking in with people to see if their power was back or not. Only a few had come through so he figured the rest were still out there in the dark.

Hannah, he thought. He'd forgotten she was headed this way. Usually when she drove, she sent updates and let Ryan know she was making it safely from place to place. They were usually in the same places too.

"Leaving Tuscaloosa."

"Made it to BHam."

"Cullman exit."

"Waving at you." (Sent whenever she passed the Rosetta Falls exit.) He generally didn't respond unless he received a question. Just wanted to be updated on how safe she was and all.

He went downstairs. The twins stood at the bottom of the stairs grinning at him before they ran off. He heard them slam the door and he rolled his eyes. He could see her car outside as he walked towards the door. She stood next to her car and waved excitedly at him as he left the house.

"HI!" she said as she ran towards him. She jumped into his arms and caused him to stumble. He laughed as he tried to regain his balance.

"Well, hello there," he said. "How're you doing?" She gripped him tighter.

"So much better. I missed you so much."

"I missed you too."

"No," she said as she started crying. "No, no. I missed you so, *so* much."

"It's okay. You're here now."

"I was so scared, Ryan. I was so scared about the sounds. I was scared about the rain. I kept hiding and trying to stay away from everything but it only got louder. I kept imagining it was all a dream and hoping I would wake up, but I didn't. I never did. It just got worse and worse. I could hear everything. Every rattle, slam, thunder. Every flash of lightning seemed to grow and grow in my mind and made it so much harder, Ryan."

"Harder to what?"

"Harder to be strong. Harder to stay focused on getting to see my family again and my friends and be able to go back to school." She stopped as she tried to pull her sobs back together. "I tried, Ryan. I tried so hard."

"I know you did. But hey," he said, lifting her to meet his eyes. "You made it."

"I know...I know, but it-"

"Shh," he said. He pulled her close to him as she started crying again. He just rubbed her back as she cried. "Let's go inside." She laughed and wiped her eyes.

"I can't go in like this. What will your family think?"

"They'll probably just think you've had a really bad week with the storms and weather. I mean, that would be my assumption." They went into the main part of the house. Ryan's Mom ran and hugged her.

"I'm so glad you made it!" she said. "We were so worried about you!"

"I know," Hannah said. "I promise I'm okay though."

"Aww."

"I'm glad y'all got power back," Hannah said.

"Oh yes," Mom said. "We've really missed it but it's good to have it back. Have to decide what to fix for dinner since we can finally cook and have a real meal."

"What have you been eating?"

"Oh, we've been eating food," Ryan said. "We've just had to use the grill to cook things, which was an adventure in itself."

"Where's your Dad?" Hannah asked.

"He's at my grandparents. They got power back and he's helping put the generator and other things up."

"That's too bad," she said. "I hoped to see him."

"I'll let him know you stopped by," he said.

"I guess I have to get home," she said. They went to her car.

"Did you have a safe trip?" he asked. He saw a change in her. "Hannah?"

"What?"

"Are you okay?"

"Yeah. Of course. Sorry. Yeah, it was good." He wasn't convinced.

"Hannah." She looked at him. "Are you okay?"

"I don't know. I...it was...I don't know what's going on with Jillian. I haven't heard anything and no one has been responding to my messages. I just...I just don't know what's going on..." She stopped. Ryan didn't know what to do or what to ask. She seemed to be somewhere else. He rubbed her arm in an attempt to both comfort her and bring her back. "I think I'm just still shaken by the whole thing."

"The tornadoes?" he asked. She nodded. "I know, but it'll be okay. We made it through this and that's what matters." She hugged him. "Let me know when you make it home, okay?"

"I will."

<u>Sharon Rogers</u>

She stood in the hospital room watching Colleen's heartrate monitor beep slowly. Colleen had been unconscious for days now and showed no signs of returning. She was pale and gaunt. She hadn't responded to any of the nurses, doctors, or Sharon.

Sharon had held her hand for most of it. She stayed next to Colleen and sang to her, called her name, and just talked to her in hopes it would cause some sort of reaction, but it never did. Colleen remained still and silent and the only response Sharon got was the continuous beeping of the machines. It had already been so long she didn't know what to do.

"Colleen," she said. Her voice wavered and made her uncomfortable. "Colleen, I...I'm sorry. I know...this isn't what you wanted. No one wanted this. I guess...things just happen and there's nothing we can do about it." Her voice cracked. "Colleen, you need to come back. You need to wake up. I don't know how long we can keep this going. Your savings is almost gone and I don't have enough to help you. I'm worried. I'm worried about you. You just...I just want to help you, but I don't know what to do." Sharon stopped as the nurse entered.

"Am I interrupting?" she asked. Sharon shook her head. All the nurses knew her and most figured she was Colleen's daughter. She'd corrected them several times, but finally gave up. *Let them believe what they want.*

"Any updates today?" Sharon asked, though she already knew the answer. She mostly asked out of politeness. At this point, it didn't matter.

"No, ma'am. I'm sorry." Sharon wasn't surprised. "Can I get you anything?"

"No thanks," Sharon said. "I'm just going to stay up here a little while longer."

"It might do some good to get out a bit," the nurse said. "Or maybe go down to the cafeteria for a while and get some food." Sharon knew the woman was just being polite, but didn't like being told what might be good for her. She'd been here for days and wanted to stay with Colleen. *What if she wakes up? What if she calls for me and I'm not here?*

"I said I'll stay here," she said with a snip in her voice. It slipped out by accident. She didn't mean to show signs of being upset and hoped the nurse didn't notice.

"I understand. The nurses will be in here in a minute to move her," the nurse said and she turned to leave.

"Wait," Sharon said. The nurse turned to her. "I...I'm sorry. I didn't mean...it's just been so scary, you know? I mean, she's been going downhill for so long that it seemed to be a gradual thing, but this all happened so fast. It's been just in the last week. Since the tornadoes."

"It's okay, ma'am. We've had a lot of people come in since the 27th who had bad reactions with the sudden changes. It could've been the weather, air filters, or a number of other things."

"Wow. How busy has it been?"

"Very. Lots of elderly people too. It's okay, though. We're doing everything we can." Sharon didn't feel much better.

"Thank you," Sharon said.

"No problem. Let me know if you need anything." The nurse left.

You don't understand, Sharon thought. *You just don't understand.* Sharon rubbed Colleen's face. Her skin was oily and she needed a bath. The nurses came in and moved her to help prevent pressure sores and she was given a light washing, but she really needed Sharon to bathe her. Sharon pulled a chair and held Colleen's hand.

"I'm...I'm gonna go get something to eat. Okay, Colleen? If you need anything just let me know." She stood and looked at the nurses. "Please page me if you need me."

"We will, Miss Rogers. Do you need directions to the cafeteria?"

"No, thank you. I know where it is." She squeezed Colleen's hand again before leaving the room.

She got in the elevator and pressed the floor number of the cafeteria. She'd been down there a few times since Colleen got here. She mostly went during the afternoons when the nurses were checking her status. It made her more comfortable when everyone was around her so she knew if something happened, people were ready to respond. The doors opened and she went to the cafeteria. She picked out what she wanted to eat, paid for it, and sat down at a table in the corner away from people.

When the ambulance had gotten there, she had been so happy. It faded when she remembered why they were there in the first place. They checked Colleen's vitals, put her on the stretcher, and loaded her into the ambulance. They took her medication and the documentation Sharon kept.

"How long has she been this way?"

"A few days. I thought maybe it was just something small at first, but it's only gotten worse." She told them about her diabetes and how it was monitored.

"Has her blood sugar spiked or shown any other issues?"

"No. She's been stable."

She followed them to the hospital. She had never followed an ambulance before and found it scarier than expected. Traffic was fairly sparse and made the trip easier, but they were going fast.

Arriving and checking into the hospital was a blur to Sharon. The next thing she knew, they were upstairs in the ICU. Tubes and machines ran from Colleen's frail body and kept track of numerous things. There she remained for days. Sharon couldn't believe the lack of change in Colleen.

The nights were the most difficult. Colleen's labored breathing became more prominent and made it hard for Sharon to sleep. She would look over at Colleen and see her struggling and it hurt her. Thinking about it made it hard for Sharon to eat.

"Sharon Rogers to ICU, please. Sharon Rogers to ICU." She ran to the elevator, almost knocking down several people in her way. The elevator was open and she jumped in quickly. She pressed the floor for ICU many times and felt her heart pulse as the elevator slowly moved. Every time the doors opened, she would tell them she was heading up. No one joined her. She reached the ICU and ran to Colleen's room. The nurses and doctor were there. They looked at Sharon.

"Miss Rogers," the nurse said. "I'm...I'm sorry." Sharon started crying.

"W-w-what happened?"

"She crashed," the doctor said. "Heart monitor went to nothing almost immediately. I'm sorry." He left the room. Sharon moved to the side of the bed and held Colleen's hand.

Hannah Leon

Hannah pulled into the driveway. She was home. She got out of the car and walked to the house. She had too many things to go ahead and empty herself. She'd called her family once after she left Ryan's to make sure they were home. They didn't answer either cellphone. She opened the front door.

"Hello?" she called. With the power out, she felt kind of like she was breaking and entering instead of coming home.

"Hey!" her Mom called.

"Where are you?"

"Coming!" her Dad said. The two of them walked around the corner to the parlor and went straight to her and hugged her.

"Hannah!"

"We're so glad you're home!"

"We were so worried!"

"What took you so long?"

"Sorry," Hannah said. "I tried to call you earlier but no one answered."

"We heard the messages, but didn't want to distract your driving in case traffic was bad," her Dad said.

"I see. I stopped at Ryan's on my way and made sure he was doing okay."

"I guess that makes sense," Mom said.

"Yeah. He's okay. His family are all doing different things to eat and what not."

"Oh we're all having to figure out what to do," Dad said. "We've been eating mostly cereal for breakfast and grilling for dinner. Good thing we got gas before the weather all happened or we would've been out of luck."

"Yup, yup," Hannah said. "We wanna get the stuff unloaded from the car? I need to call Jillian's house."

"Did you ever hear anything from her?" her Dad asked.

"No. Not yet."

"Well, maybe things are okay," her Mom said. "She's probably just so swamped with things going on she hasn't been able to keep things straight." They stood there for a minute.

"Let's empty the car," her Dad said.

"Sounds good," Hannah said.

It took them some time to empty the car and carry it to Hannah's room. They would stop and talk about the weather or what had happened during the last few days and what they'd expected to happen in the coming days.

No reports from Huntsville Utilities on how long it would take to get everyone's power restored. They'd heard some people in Limestone County across County Line Road had received some power, but it was spotty and inconsistent. Hannah had already endured a lot of powerless nights and felt better being with family through them than alone in her one-bedroom apartment. She looked through her car once more to make sure they didn't leave anything. Her car needed cleaning out, but that could wait a while. Maybe if she had time over the next few days she would get to that. She locked her car and went inside.

"I'm gonna call Jillian," she said.

"Okay," her Mom said.

"Hope everything's okay," her Dad said.

"Me too," she said before going to her room. She shut the door and sat down on her bed. She sat there for a moment, taking deep breaths and trying to keep calm before calling. She was scared what they would say. There was also the chance Jillian could answer. She wanted that to be the case. She wanted to have Jillian answer and everything to be fine.

"Oh. I couldn't answer because I was too busy."

"My phone was lost in the storm."

"I was just so worried I couldn't get ahold of anyone."

The possibilities were endless and the excuses limitless, but somehow Hannah knew that wasn't the case. She looked at her phone and the number of Jillian's parents. After all the calls she'd made to Jillian's phone that brought nothing back, she wasn't sure if this would be any better. As the phone rang, she played through the scenarios.

RING.

She could answer.
Mom could answer.
Dad could answer.
RING.
Sister could answer.
She could be sick.
She could not be home.
She could-
"Hello?" she heard. It was Jillian's younger sister, Ashley.

"Hey, Ashley. This is Hannah." There was a pause at first. Hannah was worried.

"Hi, Hannah," she said abruptly.

"How're you?" Hannah asked. She didn't know what to say or do since she was calling about a difficult topic. She heard a thud followed by Ashley's voice in the background.

"Dad, it's for you." Silence. She didn't know where or what was going on and wanted an answer. What was she supposed to say or do? There was some sort of sound on the other end, followed by throat clearing.

"Hello?"

"Hi, Mr. Clarkson. It's me, Hannah."

"Oh. Hi, Hannah. I'm glad to know you're okay." Hannah could hear something uncomfortable in his voice. She could feel the scratching in the back of her throat. She didn't want to ask. She just wanted everything to be okay. "Hannah?"

"Oh," she said. "I'm sorry."

"It's okay. Listen. Are you at home?"

"Yes, sir?"

"Good. Good. Glad you...glad you made it. I've been...meaning to call you."

"Oh?"

"Yes." There was tension. "Hannah...I'm sorry."

"What?"

"Hannah...Jillian passed away." Hannah went numb. "I'm sorry, Hannah."

"No. No, I'm sorry. I'm...I'm sorry, Mr. Clarkson."

"Thank you," he said.

"I...thank you for telling me."

"You're welcome. Glad you made it safely."

"Thank you…Goodbye."

"Goodbye."

Hannah stared in disbelief. She couldn't see anything, she couldn't hear anything. She set the phone down and felt distant and detached.

The Spencers

It was early that Friday. 5:30am? Jon couldn't sleep. He stared at the same spot on the ceiling as he had for the last hour or so. He wasn't sure how long he'd been doing that as he hadn't checked the clock when he first woke up. He decided he needed to go for a run. He wanted to clear his head. Tracy was lightly snoring and he wasn't worried about bothering her. He got out of bed and went to the bathroom. He knew the grandparents had their hearing aids out and couldn't hear him. He used the bathroom, washed his hands and face, and returned to the bedroom. He found some shorts and a reflective t-shirt and changed.

It was dark outside. He was glad he had his reflective shirt or he might be in trouble. He stretched before walking towards the road. He increased his speed until he reached the road. He stopped, looked both ways, and began running.

It felt good. He hadn't run since they arrived in Nashville a week ago and he missed it. The air was crisp and clean. Even in a bustling place like this, there were no cars out on the road. The grandparents lived in a somewhat backwoods area, but they still received a lot of traffic during rush hour. Jon went to the get the mail one afternoon and was surprised at how many cars he saw.

He reached the end of the road and turned left. He didn't want to stop yet. He thought about being in the house for the last week. It had been a pretty long week, too. He wasn't sure why, either.

It hadn't been a bad visit. He enjoyed getting to spend time with everyone. It'd been a long time since they were all able to come together and get all caught up on what was going on.

Jon reached a small church and entered the parking lot. He stopped and stretched his legs and back. Even a few days of not running had thrown him off. He wasn't sure how he'd managed to get messed up in such a short timeframe, but that didn't matter. He tried to control his breathing. *Short breath-Short breath-Long exhale. Short-Short-Long. Short-Short-Long.* He continued this for a moment. He started running and got back on the road. He decided to run to the interstate exit. It wasn't far away. Maybe two miles. He wanted that. It would take him a while to get back, that's for sure. He knew Tracy would worry at first, but would see his shorts and shirt missing and know what happened.

They'd tried running together once, but it didn't work. He wanted to keep going the whole time and she wanted to alternate running and walking. While hers was the recommended method, it didn't suit him. She'd taken to biking and Zoomba now, which was fine with him. As long as she enjoyed it, he didn't care. Lisa wanted to join him for running, but didn't want to get up that early. He chuckled and interrupted his breathing. Lisa was like her mother. Hated mornings. Laura wasn't keen on them, but she got up when she had to. As Jon neared the interstate exit, he could hear more traffic. There were a few subdivisions ahead of him and several cars pulled out of them as he got closer. The number of cars had him questioning if it was a good idea to keep running. He decided against it and turned around.

Tracy wouldn't be happy if I got hit, he thought. The sound of the cars faded behind him as he passed the small church. He was going to make it all the way this time. No sense in resting this time. *I can make it back.* More cars were out now. It'd been almost 40 minutes. Pop was definitely up by now and maybe Gran too. They were probably in the dining room eating their oatmeal and talking about how wonderful it was for everyone to be back even if the circumstances weren't the best.

Jon turned onto their road and picked up the pace a little. He wasn't tired now and wanted to take advantage of his energy. If he could make it all the way home, it would be a heck of a victory for him. His prize: A nice hot shower. He didn't like to jump in a cold shower after a run no matter how hot he was. He didn't like the sharp contrast against his body. He didn't know if it was better for him like alternating, but it didn't matter. He knew what he wanted to do and that's what he was going to do. He could see the driveway ahead of him.

So close. So close. He sprinted to the driveway and continued to the house. He reached their truck, touched it, and slowed down. He stopped when he reached the steps of the house. The rush felt good. He struggled to catch his breath, but it was worth it. He stretched as best he could. He could see the dining room lights were on as he expected. He walked inside and went to the kitchen.

"Good morning," he said. Pop and Gran both looked at him.

"Well," Gran said. "Good morning." She was laughing. "You okay?"

"Oh yeah," Jon said. "Woke up pretty early this morning so decided I might as well get up and run. Haven't done it in a while."

"Understand that," Gran said.

"Why don't you sit down and join us?" Pop said.

"I'll do that after a quick shower. I'd hate to stink up your breakfast."

"Well, I greatly appreciate that," Pop said. "I'm sure we can keep each other company and just keep talking about you."

"Oh, he's kidding," Gran said. "You go get cleaned up. We'll still have plenty of food when you finish." Jon walked down the hall and entered the bedroom. Tracy was still asleep. He reached for his pajamas from the night before and entered the bathroom. He looked in the mirror and saw just how sweaty he really was. It was pouring now. He stripped and climbed in the shower. Halfway through, he heard a knock at the door.

"Who is it?"

"It's me," Tracy said.

"Good morning. How're you?"

"I'm good. Why are you up so early?"

"Just got back from running."

"Oh. Okay. Did you sleep okay?"

"Could've been better, I think."

"Did you have a good run at least?"

"Oh yeah. Much needed."

"Well good. I'm gonna go eat some breakfast."

"All right. Pop and Gran are already in there."

"Okay." She left. Jon finished showering, dried off, and got dressed. He went into the bedroom and put on real clothes. He picked up his laptop and checked to see if the cameras were up. He was just another thing he did every morning to make sure he was keeping track. It worked better for him to check in the mornings and afternoons. He didn't make it a habit of watching all the time.

His breath caught in his chest.

Searching for signal…

The words stretched across the screen. It meant one thing. There was power. He almost let out a loud "YES!", but stopped. He didn't want to scare anyone. Instead, he made plans for them to pack. Would they leave that day or later? How long would it take to get ready? He refresh the page.

Searching for signal…

He wanted to see the house. He wanted to know it was there and see how things were before they all took off. He also didn't want to get everyone's hopes up about getting to go home. He had to be absolutely sure. He refreshed the page.

After a long pause, the image of the house appeared. He smiled. It looked intact. Nothing was damaged or missing. It didn't seem to be broken into. He cycled through the different cameras. He set the laptop down and walked towards the kitchen.

Pace yourself, he thought. *Don't try and look over-excited. They'll think something's up.* Gran and Pop were still seated at the kitchen table and having their food. The girls were still downstairs asleep. Tracy was fixing eggs.

"You want some?" she asked.

"Sure. Looks good."

"Thank you." Jon got a glass of water from the cabinet. He went to the fridge and started filling it.

"Power's back on," he said in as casual a tone as he could muster. Everyone turned to look at him.

"Really?" Tracy asked.

"Yup."

"Are you sure?"

"Yes."

"If you're trying to be funny, you're not," Tracy said. He shook his head.

"No, no. Promise. Just checked the cameras and everything looks to be back up. I checked them all and everything looks just as we left it." Tracy looked at him. Jon motioned to the stove. "Eggs, sweetie." She turned.

"Oh, right. Dang it."

"That's fine. I like them a little done." Tracy moved the pan to a different eye and looked back at Jon.

"Show me."

"Show you...that I like them a little done?"

"No, no. I want to see our house."

"Oh sure. Come on." They went to the bedroom and he picked up the laptop. He hit refresh and there it was. Tracy cried as he cycled through all the cameras. He put the laptop on the bed and gave her a big hug.

"I'm so happy," Tracy said. "We'll have to get everything packed up so we can leave!"

"Won't be that much trouble," Jon said. "I'm sure the girls will help each other and we can take care of our stuff. No need to rush out right now, right?"

"Well, yeah. We need to get home and check on our house. We haven't been there for days."

"Really? You sure you don't wanna stay with your folks a few more days? Wouldn't be anything wrong with that. Could spend a little longer with them and let them know we appreciate this so much." Tracy gave him a confused look.

"Uh huh," she said. "You get the points for being polite, but I ain't buying it." He laughed. She nodded. An evil grin crossed her face.

"Let's go scare the girls awake and tell them!"

Hannah Leon

The power came back on while they were out getting groceries. The Wal-Mart in Athens already had power and was flooded by lots of people, but they said they needed food and other things. Hannah was worried they would be surrounded and barely able to find anything they wanted. She was half right.

They walked from aisle to aisle looking, but could only find a few things here and there. They weren't the important things either. They wanted some extra paper towels just in case and some more soap, but both were sold out. They were able to get some more things for sandwiches and toilet paper.

Their first clue they might have power came from the light. When they reached their street on 72, they noticed the light was on. It was flashing, which meant it had recently been out and wasn't reset, but flashing. They got so excited. They kept going towards their house in anticipation. *Maybe it's back? Is it just that one place? Is it gonna be on everywhere?* Hannah was so excited to walk into the house and feel the central air blowing. It was much better than she'd expected. The feeling of air circulating made her so happy she cried.

She laughed at herself through her tears, which made it sound even funnier. She grabbed her phone and called Ryan.

"Hey," he said.

"We have power!"

"Really?"

"Yeah!"

"That's great! When did it come back?"

"We don't know! It just came back while we were getting groceries."

"You went to get groceries?"

"Yeah."

"How was that?"

"Ugh. It was horrible."

"Aww. I'm sorry."

"Thanks. Yeah, it was really bad. It wasn't like we were trampled or anything by people. Actually, there weren't as many people there as we expected."

"Well that's good, right?"

"Not really. They weren't there because there was nothing there to get."

"Wait. It was empty?"

"Well. Not really. It was more like there just wasn't a whole lot there so there wasn't any reason to be there."

"I guess that makes sense."

"Yeah. We weren't able to get a lot of stuff we needed."

"What about Target or Walmart further down 72?"

"In Huntsville?"

"Yeah."

"They don't have power."

"Might as well go check, right?" She didn't answer. She wasn't sure if they would be open and also wasn't sure if it would even be worth the drive. It was still a few minutes away and more towards Huntsville. She had no idea what it was like over there.

"You there?" Ryan asked. She jumped.

"Oh. Yes. Yes, I'm here."

"What's wrong?"

"Nothing. Nothing's wrong." There was silence.

"Is it still Jillian?"

"No...Yes...I don't know."

"What's wrong?"

"I don't know. I'm just...I'm just upset. I mean, she's gone, Ryan. She's gone. I'm not gonna see her anymore. She's...she's gone."

"I know. I'm sorry."

"Yeah," she said. "I miss her, Ryan. I miss her so much. I don't even know what I'm supposed to do. We were such good friends. We've known each other for all of college."

"I know."

There was a moment of silence. She didn't know what to do or say.

"When do you think you'll go back to work?" she asked.

"Probably Monday," he said. "Are you gonna be up here

all summer?"

"No. I have that internship in June, remember?"

"Oh yeah. Excited?"

"Yeah. A little. I think it'll be good."

"It will. It'll be good to take your mind off of things and work, right?"

"That's true."

"When do you start?"

"June 6th. It's a Monday."

"Makes sense," he said. "Does it go through August?"

"Yeah. All summer." They didn't say anything for a moment. "Will you come over tomorrow?"

"Yeah, I can do that. I can't do anything Sunday, though."

"You can't?"

"No. It's Mother's Day, remember?"

"Oh right!" she said. "I forgot! What do I do?"

"What do you mean?"

"I mean I have to get something for Mom. What do I do? I don't know where to go."

"You could try going to Target, remember? See if you could find something there. Maybe they still have a few things you could get."

"I don't know...I don't know."

"I'm sure your Mom would understand. You guys just got power back. Why would you think she would be upset?"

"Yeah. You're right," she said. She was already trying to figure out what to do. "Hey, I need to talk to Dad. I'll talk to you later, okay?"

"Sure thing."

She put the phone down. She and Dad needed to figure something out. What were they going to do? How were they going to surprise her? After all, they usually couldn't get anything over her. She was almost always one step ahead. Maybe there was something else they could do to really pull it over her.

"Hey Dad!" she called out and left the room.

"Yeah?"

"Where are you?"

"Living room." She walked in the living room and saw Dad and Mom there.

"Umm," she said. "I need to talk to you."

"Talk to me?"

"Yup. Talk to you." Mom gave them a funny look. Dad got up and followed her.

"What's up?"

"Mother's Day is Sunday," she whispered.

"Yes," he whispered. "Why are we whispering?"

"Because we have to get something for Mom, don't we?"

"Yes. What are you thinking?"

"I don't know. I mean, all the stores are closed. We need to find something."

"Like what?"

"I don't know. But something."

"We could probably slip away tomorrow."

"If we both go, she'll figure us out."

"Hmm."

"By the way, it's okay if Ryan visits tomorrow, right?"

"Sure. It'd be good to see him."

"Good." Her Dad's face lit up.

"Wait. I think I've got it. How about you go get something and I'll keep her occupied here. You can say you're going to get stuff to fix something desserty for Ryan."

"That's a good idea! I'll do it!"

"Sounds good."

"Now...just gotta figure out what to bake..."

The Spencers

Jon checked the room one more time. He wanted to be sure they had everything they needed. Although the in-laws kept assuring him it was okay, he felt they had overstayed their welcome. Besides, he wanted to get home to his house with his bed and his shower and his things. They'd already been gone so long.

The girls didn't take long to pack. They'd scarfed down their breakfast and hurried to their rooms to throw all their things together in their suitcases and get out. After the first two attempts to shut their suitcases didn't work, they decided to try packing them instead.

He'd already packed everything into the truck. Tracy and the girls were saying goodbye while he checked things. He went downstairs to the girls' room to see if they got everything. He spied a charger still plugged into the wall next to Lisa's bed. He grinned, picked it up, and slipped it into his pocket. Nothing else caught his eye. The beds were unmade and closet standing wide open, but he wasn't going to get onto them this time. It'd been a special circumstance so some things could slip. Jon went back upstairs.

"Thanks again, Gran," Laura said before giving her a hug.

"Yeah," Lisa said. "It was nice to spend time with you."

"Oh, it's always nice to spend time with you two," said Gran. "Even if it isn't the best of situations. Always good to see a grandchild's face." She gave them both a kiss. They hugged Pop.

"Thanks again, Mom," Tracy said. She fought back tears. It wasn't easy for her to have to leave again. She always had this terrible nightmare of leaving and never seeing them again because of some freak of nature and the last week hadn't helped that thought either.

"Anytime, sweetheart."

"Thanks, Dad," she said.

"You know our home is your home," he said, causing the floodgates to open. She didn't try to hold it all back this time.

"I know," she said. "I'm just so glad you guys could take

us in on such short notice. We didn't think we'd have to pack up and move so quickly."

"We know," he said. "We've been through enough over the years to know to always be prepared for the worst." He let out a chuckle.

"Thanks again," Jon said to them both.

"Anytime, anytime. Y'all be safe getting back."

"Oh, we will," Jon said. They all walked to the truck and waved goodbye. Jon whispered in Tracy's ear and she smiled.

They were a good ways down the road when Lisa gasped.

"My charger!" she yelled. "We left my charger!"

"Are you sure?" Tracy said.

"Yes! I can't find it!"

"Oh no," Tracy said nonchalantly. "Well, I don't think we can go back. Do you, Jon?"

"Yeah, I don't think so. I mean, we really need to get home. We have to get back and check on the house and see how things are. We have to get there and see what things look like."

"You're right. We're too far out at this point." They heard the frustrated sigh from behind them.

"You know," Jon said. "Why not use this one for now until we come back later?" He pulled out the charger. Lisa grabbed it.

"Not funny," she said. Everyone laughed.

The drive was uneventful. They sang songs, they played games, but mostly they talked about what to expect at the house.

"How bad does the house look?" Lisa asked.

"It's not that bad," Jon said. "We looked at it on the security cameras."

"Yeah. Looks like it wasn't messed with."

"Really?" Laura said. "Aww."

"What do you mean 'aww'?" Tracy asked.

"I figured people would've gone through and ransacked the whole place looking for things," Laura said.

"Yeah. Or maybe some people got trapped in there and

died," Lisa said.

"How would that have happened?" Jon asked.

"I don't know," Lisa said. "But maybe a gang took up our neighborhood and are using our house as their headquarters."

"Really, Lisa?" Laura said. "They would totally take our house out and use everything they could find. They wouldn't use ours for the headquarters."

"Sure they would!"

"Yeah," Jon said. "Why wouldn't they?"

"Well, Dad. They...just couldn't."

"Oh no," Jon said. "I don't know about that. What's wrong with our house? Are you saying our house isn't good enough to be headquarters to a gang? Because I strongly disagree with you, young lady." They laughed. Tracy's phone rang. She looked at it.

"Oh, it's Sharon," she said before answering. "Hey. No, it's not a bad time. We're headed back now, actually. Hey, thank you again for looking at the house. I know with Miss Colleen that wasn't easy but it meant so much to us for you to go do that. Uh huh. Yeah, how is she doing? What? Oh my. When? Oh, I'm...I'm sorry to hear that. Yes, she...she really was. How...how are you? Okay. So when the funeral? Okay. No, I understand. Thank you for letting me know. Okay, bye." She hung up the phone.

"What's wrong?" Jon asked.

"That was Sharon. Colleen passed away."

"Oh no."

"Yeah."

"Who's Colleen?" Lisa asked.

"The nice lady at the nursery, right?" Laura said.

"That's right."

"Oh, the little old lady?"

"Yeah."

"Aww." They all went quiet. Jon put his hand on Tracy's.

"We'll definitely be at the funeral." Tracy nodded. She looked out the window at the passing trees and interstate.

When they reached their subdivision, everyone was quiet.

The first houses they came across looked fine. They'd been through some wear and tear, but that came from the storm.

"So far so good," Jon said. They turned onto their road and drove towards the house. At last it came into sight.

The collective sigh of an undisturbed house filled the truck. They were so happy to see things were okay. Jon backed into the driveway and they all got out. Because he'd manually opened the door before, it would have to be reset so they could use the automatic door opener. He opened the door as they got the suitcases out of the truck. Jon looked around the undisturbed garage with relief. He opened the door to the house. It had a strange musty smell to it, which wasn't surprising since there hadn't been any sort of airflow in it for a while.

"Everything looks good!" he shouted towards the truck. He smiled and looked around his home. He walked back out to see if they needed help.

Hannah Leon

Hannah was a little ashamed at how fluttery her heart got when she heard the knock at the front door. There was a slight hesitation. *You shouldn't be so excited,* she told herself, but it gave her pause. *Why not? What's wrong with being excited to see my boyfriend?* She opened the door for Ryan.

"Hello," she said.

"Hi," he said. They hugged. "How're you?"

"I'm good. I'm glad you could come over today."

"Me too."

"Are you having a good day?" she asked.

"Yup, yup. Dad found out UAH is opening back up Monday so it'll be good to go back to work."

"Oh yeah?" she said. "That's great!"

"I know. It sounds weird, but I kinda missed working. Wasn't really expecting to, but I have to say I do. Just made me feel really productive, you know?"

"Yeah, I understand. I mean, it's better than just loafing around doing nothing with your life, right?"

"Exactly."

"That's 'cause you work too hard."

"Har har har," he said. "I can't help it. Gotta pay for school somehow, you know?"

"Yeah, I know. I'm just playing."

"I know. So what smells so good?"

"It's a surprise."

"Oh yeah?"

"Yup. You don't find out until dinner."

"Hmm. I don't know if I like that."

"Well that's just too dang bad." She put her pointer finger in his chest. "You stay out of the kitchen, mister. Understand?" Ryan threw up his arms in mock surrender.

"You said it. Not going anywhere near it."

"Thank you," she said. "Go see what Dad's up to while I finish lunch."

"What're we having?"

"It's a surprise."

"Well, you're just full of surprises today, aren't you?"

"Yup. Now go." Ryan went to the living room and she returned to the kitchen. She took the lid off the crockpot and took a deep breath. She stirred it some and tried to break the chicken breasts up so it could even out. Satisfied, she put the lid back on it.

Earlier she prepared a dish she'd found called Cream Cheese Chicken Chili. She knew Ryan liked cream cheese, chicken, and chili and figured he would enjoy something with all of them.

"Did Ryan get here?" her mom asked

"Yeah," she said. "He's with Dad."

"You sure that's safe?"

"Well," Hannah said. "I guess I didn't really think about it?"

"Guess not."

"Yeah...probably should have." Hannah's Mom lifted the lid of the crockpot and smelled the chili.

"Mmm," she said. "That smells good. What all is in it?"

"Not a lot of stuff. It's really easy, actually, and it's not that bad for you. Only 600 calories or so if you follow the recipe, but you could make it less if you wanted."

"That's not too bad. What did Ryan say about it?"

"I didn't tell him. Just sent him to the living room."

"Ah," her mother said. She lowered her voice. "So he doesn't know about the cake?"

"Nope," Hannah said.

"Good. I know it would be better to surprise him. I'm sure he'd like that."

"I hope so. It's got all his favorite stuff."

"Was this the 'Get-Me-A-Man Cake'?"

"Yeah. The chocolate chip pound cake with pudding and sour cream and extra, extra chocolate chips."

"Oh yeah. I'm sure he'll like that. It's so good."

"Yes it is. I know he'll like it."

"I hope so. It should be ready in time. I'll have to start the rice right before we have it."

"How long will that take?"

"Probably 25 minutes? Not sure. Have to check the box."

"That sounds about right to me."

"Good," Hannah said. "Let me see what they're up to."

"It can't be good."

Hannah checked the cake in the fridge. It still looked good. She closed the door and went into the living room. Ryan and her dad were sitting there watching Mystery Science Theater 3000, a show she dreaded. She didn't like people talking during movies and didn't like bad movies so she couldn't understand an entire show based around the combination.

"What film is this?"

"Santa Claus Conquers the Martians," Ryan said.

"What?"

"Yeah," her Dad said. "It's...It's really bad. Way worse than you think."

"I can't believe that."

"Oh yeah," Ryan said. "It's so bad you wouldn't believe it." They paused it. "So, basically, the Martians want Christmas, but Santa doesn't go there."

"Why not?"

"Um..."

"No one knows," her Dad said. "They don't explain it in the movie."

"Yeah," Ryan said. "So anyway, once they kidnap him so they can have Christmas, they decide to kill him. So they try to kill him and the two kids they kidnapped."

"That's awful," Hannah said. The two laughed.

"That's the point. It was made in...what, the 60s?"

"64, I think," her Dad said.

"Just wow," Hannah said.

"Yup," Ryan said. "Did you want to go do anything before dinner?"

"Yeah," she said. "Can we go to the grocery store? I still need a few things."

"Are things open around here?"

"Yeah. They're mostly opened back up, but we have to go

further down University to Target."

"Okay. Sounds good to me."

"We'll be back in a little bit," she said.

"Oh," her Mom said. "Okay then. I may call you if I think I need anything."

"Okay. I'll have my phone on. Oh, will check the recipe for the next step in about an hour?"

"What's that for?" Ryan asked.

"Nothing," Hannah said.

"I can do that," her Mom said.

"Thank you." Hannah and Ryan went outside.

"So what do we need from Target?"

"I need to pick something up for Mother's Day."

"Oh, right. Nice to be a distraction, I suppose."

"Uh huh," she said.

"What are you going to get her?"

"I don't know yet. Dad already got her something a while back before the power went out."

"Good for him."

"Yeah," she said with relief. "So what do you think I should get her?"

"I dunno. Is there something she wants?"

"I was just thinking of doing like a card and some chocolates or something."

"What kind of chocolates do they have at Target she'd like?"

"No. There's a place on the way back we could stop and get some. She really likes their dark chocolate."

"Okay," he said. "Sounds good. It'd be nice to spend some time together."

"Yeah," she said. "That's what I thought." They got into Ryan's car. They pulled out of the driveway and headed towards Highway 72. As they left the subdivision, Ryan put his hand on Hannah's. She smiled and wrapped her fingers in his.

"You know the rules," she said when they got back. "No

going in the kitchen."

"I know I know," he said. "Want me to put the bags in your room?"

"Yes, please. But put them on the side of my bed so she doesn't see them."

"Will do."

Hannah entered the kitchen.

"Did you put the water on?" she asked her Mom.

"Yup. You can check to see if it's ready."

"Thank you."

"No problem." Hannah went to the crockpot first. She stirred it some and switched it to warm. She moved to the stove and checked the water in the pot. It was boiling. She looked at the box of rice on the counter and checked the instructions. She put the rice and some butter in the pot, lowered the heat, and covered it before setting the timer.

"How long will that be?"

"About 25 minutes," she said.

"That's good. I'm getting hungry."

"Me too. I hope it's good."

"Yeah, us too," her Mom said.

"That's just sooo funny."

"I thought so. Did you two have fun?"

"Yeah. We just went out and spent some time together. Just tried to get caught up on some things."

"That's good. How's his family doing?"

"They're doing okay. They got power back before we did."

"Oh yeah?"

"Yeah. On Sunday."

"Huh. I guess it was easier to get power restored where they live. Not sure how that works."

"Yeah, me either. I mean, they live pretty far out in the middle of nowhere. I don't know why they got power so soon. Ryan said most of that area got it though and it worked its way to them."

"That's interesting," her Mom said.

"Yup. They've been going to town more, though, and

getting stuff together. Seems since the power came back things are getting back to normal for them."

The timer went off and Hannah checked the rice.

"Almost done," she said. She stirred it some and put the lid back on. She went into the living room. "You two behaving in here?" Ryan and her Dad quickly turned to her.

"What?" her dad said.

"Yes?" Ryan said.

"Of course."

"Why wouldn't we?"

"What?"

"Yeah."

"Right?"

"Of course." Hannah stared at them.

"Uh huh," she said. "I was gonna say you can come help set the table. It's almost ready."

"Okie dokie," Ryan said.

"Sounds good," her Dad said. The three of them went to the dining room.

"Wow," Ryan said. "That smells really good. What is it?"

"A surprise."

"Really? Still not gonna tell me?"

"Oh, you don't know Hannah," her Dad said. "She can hold a secret forever."

"Well, have to remember that. Might come in handy later."

"Oh you know it." Her Dad got four bowls and handed them to Ryan. He placed them and trivets on the table.

"These in the right spots?" he asked. Hannah looked at the table.

"I don't think we're gonna need those," she said. "We're gonna need glasses though."

"Actually my vision is pretty good," Ryan said.

"Aha. Aha. Aha. You're just so funny."

"Meh, I try." Ryan got glasses down and handed them to Hannah's Dad. He put ice in them and he and Ryan took them to the table.

"What do you want to drink?" her Dad asked Ryan.

"Dr. Pepper would be good."

"I think we have a can or two left."

"I'll have tea," Hannah's Mom said.

"Just water," Hannah said. "It's weird. After drinking it for so many days, I just can't get enough of it."

"Never thought you'd give up cokes," her Mom said.

"Yeah," she said. "Me either. But I guess I just got so used to the water I can't quit drinking it."

"Nothing wrong with that," her Dad said. "Much healthier for you, anyway."

"Yeah, that's true. So should we bring the crockpot to the table or just leave it here?"

"We can just leave it there and refill if we need it," her Dad said. "Here. Ryan, hand me the bowls and we'll just fill them up and set them again."

"Okie dokie." Ryan gathered the bowls and gave them to Hannah's Dad. Hannah put an even amount of rice in each bowl and covered the rice with the chili.

"Here you go," her Dad said as he handed the bowl to Ryan.

"Ooo," Ryan said. "That looks really good. What is it?"

"Cream Cheese Chicken Chili," Hannah said.

"Oh wow. That sounds really good."

"Good," she said. "I hoped you would like it."

"Oh definitely. It sounds really good."

"It's been cooking all day. Just didn't want you to try and find it."

"Well I'm really glad I didn't," he said. "Might've ruined the surprise."

"Oh, this isn't the surprise."

"It's not?"

"Nope," Hannah said. She gave a sly smile.

"Then what's the surprise?" As Ryan set the last of the silverware, Hannah went to the fridge and pulled out the cake. Ryan turned back around.

"TA-DA!" she said. Ryan smiled.

"Oh, is that the famous 'Make-Me-A-Man Cake'?" They all laughed.

"No, it's the 'Get-Me-A-Man Cake'," Hannah said.

"Oooh," Ryan said. "That makes so much more sense."

"Nice to see it finally worked," Hannah's Mom said with a smile. Ryan laughed.

"Have to see how it tastes. I've heard good things about it."

"Well good," Hannah said. "I'll just leave it here on the counter so it's not too cold when we finish eating."

"Sounds good." Ryan gave her a hug.

Sharon Rogers

Sharon sat in her car looking at the house. She tapped the ashes from the cigarette in her hand into the half-full ashtray and took a long pull. She wasn't ready for this. She needed to go inside and get things in order.

The funeral was lovely. Colleen left instructions for it to be something for her friends. Many of the ladies from the nursery and her former class showed up. Most of the family members that had once been close to Colleen were now older or dead. Though she wanted to meet some of Colleen's family, Sharon enjoyed meeting Colleen's friends. Many of them were just like her in mannerisms and speech. They gave their favorite stories and moments with Colleen. Sharon was touched by it all and loved hearing more about her friend.

Tracy and Jon were there. Sharon didn't know if they would be able to make it with them being out of town, but it was so good to see them.

"How're you doing?" Tracy asked.

"I'm...I don't know yet," she said and it was true. It hadn't set in at the time. Sharon hadn't thought about what she was going to do.

"It's going to be okay," Tracy said.

"I know," Sharon said. "I'm just...I don't know."

"It's a lot to take in," Jon said. "But from what Tracy tells me, you were great."

"I appreciate that," Sharon said. "Thank you for coming." Sharon continued thanking people until time for the service.

They sang a few verses of *Amazing Grace* and *It Is Well* and ended in prayer. Nothing major. Colleen was buried next to her late husband earlier that morning before the service. At the end of the service, Sharon thanked everyone for coming. Many gave their condolences and offered words of encouragement to her. She continued to smile until they all left.

She got out of the car now, dropped the remains of the cigarette on the ground and smothered it with her shoe. She walked to the front door. It was a beautiful day and people were outside in their yards mowing or doing other things.

Sharon entered the house.

The smell hit her. The memories of Colleen and everything they'd done together swarmed back to her. She fell to the floor and cried.

MONDAY, MAY 9

Ryan Peterson

Ryan and his Dad were traveling down the interstate. It was time to go to work again. They sat in silence for a few minutes as NPR continued playing. Ryan looked out the window at the clear sky. There were clouds today, but nothing like when he drove down this road days ago. The clouds were white, fluffy, and simple.

"Can't believe it's already been 12 days," he said. "I mean, it feels like this just happened and now we're back."

"Well, we're on our way, but not back yet."

"Har har."

"It's been quiet. I'm not sure I'm gonna remember what it sounds like to have electronics running all the time."

"It'll be crazy. Maybe I'll remember what all I'm supposed to do. It's probably going to be crazy getting things put back together and all up and running." They arrived at UAH and turned into the parking lot. "Looks like it survived. Wonder how everyone was doing. I'm hoping everyone was okay and wasn't hurt-" His Dad reached for the radio and turned it up. "What are you-"

"Shh!"

"-and that's what we've been told. Sources are still releasing details about the operation that killed Bin Laden."

"What?" Ryan asked.

"Shh!"

"As many of you know, on May 1st, President Obama made the announcement from the White House that the operation was successful and Bin Laden had, in fact, been killed."

"What?!"

"Yup."

"How did we miss that?" His Dad looked at him. "Oh," Ryan said. "Right." They were quiet as the story continued playing. Ryan was shocked. "I can't believe it."

"I know. Got him."

"No. I mean that we were so out of touch with everything and didn't even realize that happened."

"Yup. Hard to believe." They pulled into the parking lot at work.

"Man," Ryan said. "How...We were so out of touch with the world, with...everything that we didn't even know the man we've been chasing for years is gone, has been gone for days."

"Yup."

"Wonder what else we've missed." They got out of the car and walked inside.

"Guess it's time for things to get back to what we're supposed to do," his Dad said.

"Certainly hope so," Ryan said. He turned on the lights in the main room, walked to the table, and set his things down. He smiled.

THE END

Author's Note

This novel holds a special place in my heart as it shows the devastation that hit my home state and took the lives of more than 340 people across multiple states.

For those wondering, I was there, as were my wife, family, and friends. The stories of the characters here are based on real people I met and talked to in the years following the outbreak. These individuals were kind enough to open up about what happened to them and how they coped with the events. Their courage and determination provided the basis for what you read here.

In my research for this novel, I found the National Weather Service, Tuscaloosa News, al.com, Birmingham 33/40, and National Public Radio (NPR) to be very helpful in finding out more details regarding the order of events, the details of the outbreak, and any important issues regarding the specific parts of the storm described. I returned to them many times while writing to ensure I captures the events as accurately as possible. Any errors are my own.

I want to thank my wife who encouraged me to write this since it happened. It's hard to believe how long ago this was.

I also want to thank my team of readers who gave this a go-over several times as I worked it and made the changes necessary to keep the story on track. Your help and encouragement continues to drive me even when no one else thought this was a worthy story and I thank you.

www.ingramcontent.com/pod-product-compliance
Lightning Source LLC
Chambersburg PA
CBHW072300130726
47910CB00012B/2178